Lord Ramsey's Red-Headed Ruin

Scarlett Affairs
Book 2

Cerise DeLand

DRAGONBLADE PUBLISHING, INC.

ARE YOU SIGNED UP FOR DRAGONBLADE'S BLOG?

You'll get the latest news and information on exclusive giveaways, exclusive excerpts, coming releases, sales, free books, cover reveals and more.

Check out our complete list of authors, too!

No spam, no junk. That's a promise!

Sign Up Here

www.dragonbladepublishing.com

Dearest Reader;

Thank you for your support of a small press. At Dragonblade Publishing, we strive to bring you the highest quality Historical Romance from some of the best authors in the business. Without your support, there is no 'us', so we sincerely hope you adore these stories and find some new favorite authors along the way.

Happy Reading!

CEO, Dragonblade Publishing

Additional Dragonblade books by Author Cerise Deland

Scarlett Affairs Series
Lord Ashley's Beautiful Alibi (Book 1)
Lord Ramsey's Red-Headed Ruin (Book 2)

Matrimony! Series
If I Loved You (Book 1)
Because of You (Book 2)
You Made Me Love You (Book 3)

Naughty Ladies Series
Lady, Be Wanton (Book 1)
Lady, Behave (Book 2)
Lady, No More (Book 3)
Lady, You're Mine (Book 4, Novella)

The Lyon's Den Series
The Lyon's Share
The Lyon's Perfect Mate

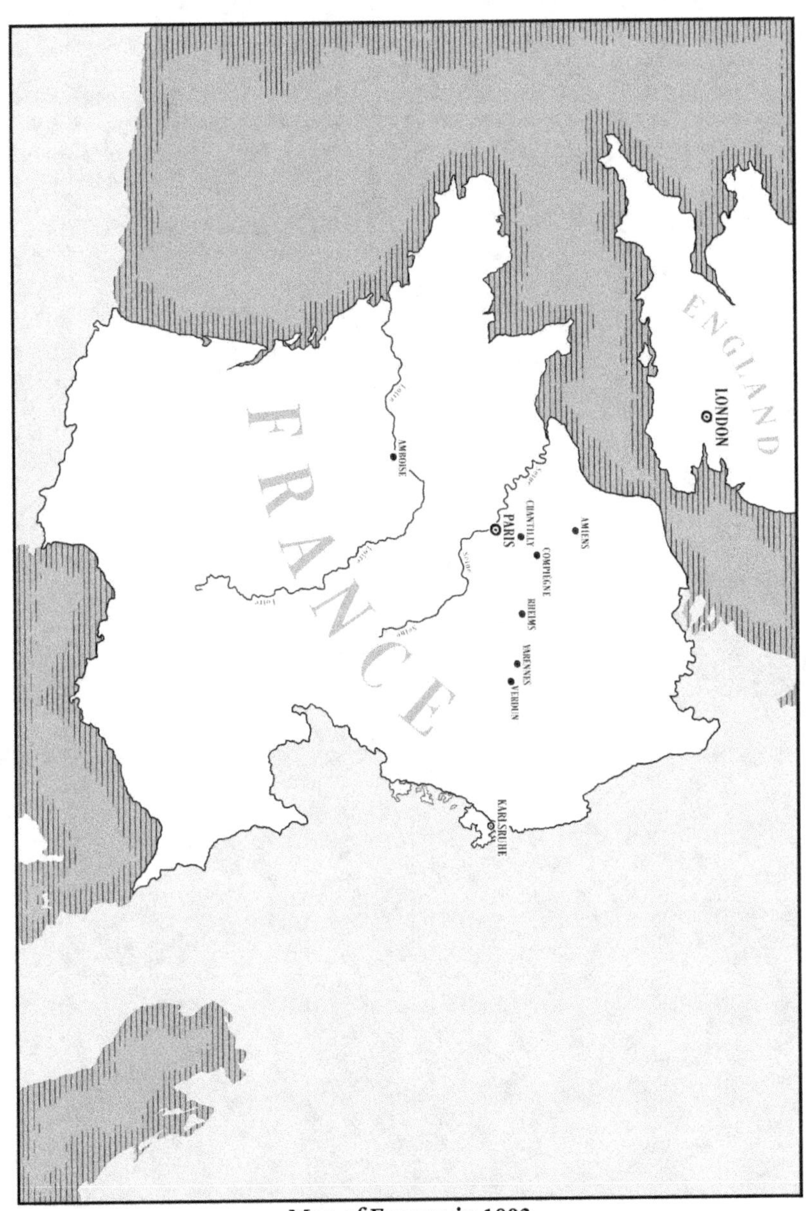

Map of Europe in 1802
Designer, Xenia Sukhareva

Chapter One

April 30, 1802
Reims, France

AMBER PAUSED, HUDDLED in her ragged clothes against the chill of the night, her hand midair ready to knock on her own kitchen door.

"Swallow your reluctance, *ma chérie*." Her husband's baritone filled her senses. Maurice was gone now, dead these many months, but she heard him clearly. So like him to come to her here, where they had lived and loved and where she now had to enter to save herself.

"You are brave, *mon amour*."

And also stupid to have come to this juncture, Maurice!

"*Non!* March on!"

His encouragement, always, was dauntless when she hesitated in her work.

Still, she shivered. Fingers to her trembling lips, she breathed deeply to quell her fright. It was not for herself that she feared, but for those in the house. Never would she wish to bring darkness to their lives and sully the years of devoted service they had rendered to her husband and her.

She rapped on the old wooden door. The sound resonated

along the narrow cobbled *ruelle* behind her townhouse—and she flinched.

But no other sound filled the alley. No one walked here. No one usually did after midnight. Especially not on a cold night at the end of April.

Spurred to action, she knocked on the door once more. The *majordom*, Bonnet, would be in bed. Their kitchen maid had a tendency to stay up far after the other two servants in the house. The housemaid, deaf Nancy, would not hear a thing, though often she compensated for her lack with an uncanny awareness of things gone awry.

Amber cared not who answered the door, only that someone came quickly. She did not want her hired carriage and grooms questioning where she'd disappeared and roam the streets searching for her. They were to circle the ancient cathedral for forty-five minutes, then come to a stop across from the great west door and wait for her. They would return, she knew, because she had to pay them the promised balance of their fare. Then she would dismiss them and vanish into the night to escape the ghouls who pursued her.

A light shone in the kitchen window. Was it the kitchen maid, Mimi, who lit a candle to light her way to the servants' back door? It had to be…unless Amber's butler Bonnet had hired someone new since Amber had been away. She prayed that was not so. She curled her shoulders round her. These days she trusted no one new in her life.

The peephole in the kitchen door slipped aside. One wizened eye peered out at her, and the female's gasp within told her that Mimi recognized her. Even in her men's floppy hat and worn frock coat.

Amber heard Mimi scramble away, the three-hundred-year-old floorboards creaking beneath her feet. She inhaled, at peace as a ray of light appeared above in the butler's rooms atop the old house and spilled out to the alley. The warmth of that light, and the promise of relief that it signaled, had Amber panting in relief.

Sounds of other footsteps down the stairs and around hallways offered her more comfort. Then the kitchen door swung wide.

"*Madame!*" The broad smile of her fierce and fond *majordom*, Monsieur Bonnet, thrilled her and filled her with his warm affection. "Come in! Come in!"

The fragrance of cinnamon floated out from the vast kitchen. That brought her peace as well.

Bonnet gave her a little bow of polite welcome, the smile on his thin face broad and effervescent. "Madame, you are cold. The night air predicts a piercing sleet. Let me light a fire and make you warm."

"No, Bonnet." She swept off her hat and tucked it in her coat pocket. "I am not here long. Do not bother with that."

"But surely a drink? Mulled wine? Tea?"

"*Oui*, that would be quick and good. A drop of good calvados brandy with my tea, *s'il vous plaît*. It is all I have time for."

"You do not stay? *Je regret*, madame."

"*Et moi*, Bonnet." She swept inside and went up the servants' steep stairs to the main floor, then stepped out into the long hall and paused. Ever was she struck by the Rococo beauty of the three-hundred-year-old house, especially the circular stained glass window that sparkled as the moon poured all the colors of the rainbow upon the thick red and blue Turkish carpet runner.

She hurried on before she let her tears fall. This had been her beloved home with Maurice. Now she had none. None! She clutched at her throat and swallowed her despair.

"Forgive me," she said as Bonnet followed her into the salon. She smiled and pointed toward one large Louis Quatorze overstuffed chair. "I must sit in one of my good chairs. I've been riding in a terrible carriage, and the jostling hurts my back."

She had developed tenderness in her spine after she miscarried her baby last year. She had writhed so in the ordeal that she had put her bones in distress. Ever after, she'd had to sit in well-upholstered chairs.

"You have come, madame, in a carriage not your own?"

At Bonnet's question, she realized not only his surprise but also the fact that she'd imparted more information than was good for the man to know. The less he heard from her, the less he could repeat if ever Rene Vaillancourt's men came here to call upon him.

"No." It would not have been wise to ask her Aunt Cecily's grooms to bring her here. She had not because they too could be arrested and interrogated by the deputy chief of police, Vaillancourt. The man wanted too much of her that she could never give.

She changed the subject as she sank into the huge chartreuse silk chair near the fireplace. "I apologize for disturbing the household, Bonnet."

"Madame, we are delighted to have you at any hour of any day or night."

"You are sweet, Bonnet. I've missed you," she said, and absorbed the beauty of the shadowed room where once she had laughed and loved oh so well. The lively pink walls and lime-trimmed paneling was usually sweet. Tonight, it was forbidding in the solemn dark. Bonnet had not lit a fire in this room. Nor had he indicated, in this room at least, that she was gone indefinitely by throwing cloths over the delicate furniture. She appreciated her butler's care of her charming home.

"Rest," he told her, his hands out in the manner of a priest giving benediction. "I will get your tea and brandy. Enjoy the chair." Then, with raw concern in his large brown eyes, he spun on his heel.

She melted into the plush chair cushions and ground her teeth that Vaillancourt had taken this from her, this pleasure, this satisfaction. But then, he had taken much more from so many others. For so little reason. Hatred of him and what he did for the consulate, what he had done over the years to her friends, boiled in her brain.

She wrung her hands, but, noticing, pulled them apart. She

would not fret. Must not. But keep going. Always.

"March on," she whispered to herself, and smiled at the memory of her beloved husband's words.

Maurice had supported her in her quest. Shocked as he was initially at her revelation of her purpose, her solicitous, gentlemanly husband had blinked and rallied to her cause within minutes of her disclosure. That she was not a woman of frivolous thoughts and superficial desires he had always known, he told her.

"Why would I think you would sit home to gossip and crochet when the world burns for justice?" he had said.

"I had enough of inactivity in Carmes," she had replied, laughing though her insides crawled with the memory of her months in the Paris prison. The filth and the gruel were awful, yet bearable. But the jeering, salacious guards, who demanded sexual favors from the female inmates, had made life a living hell. Amber had escaped ruin because her dear aunt and that lady's closest friend had forbidden the men to touch her. She remembered the men's leering faces and their threats to have her.

Bonnet's smile took her from the past as he appeared in the doorway of the salon, carrying a tray. "Your tea will be ready in a few minutes. As you wait, I have brought you bread and cheese, jam, and a small cake, too. You appear thinner, madame. I hope you are well."

Bonnet was the closest any man had ever come to being a father figure for her. She accepted his offerings with the kind regard of the girl she no longer was. "I am most grateful, Bonnet. I will avail myself of this and then adjourn upstairs."

"Would you like me to awaken Nancy? Is there any task she may help you with?" Bonnet arched both thin gray brows. She was dressed like a pauper from the slums of Compiègne, and Bonnet did her the honor of not perusing her body in her rough, mannish clothes.

She shook her head. "*Non*, Bonnet. I will do as I will quickly. Let Nancy rest."

He stood watching over her. "I will leave you, if you wish."

"No, stay, *monsieur*. I will only be a minute." She broke off bits of the almond cake and enjoyed the delicacy of it. "I will do this fine repast what little justice I have time for. My thanks for it. But now you must listen to me, Bonnet."

He stood at attention, his voluminous vermilion banyan swirling around his frail frame. "Whatever I can, madame."

"I will go upstairs in a few minutes to my rooms to change these clothes. When I come down, I will give you these rags. You are to burn them in a good, high fire."

"Madame!" He bolted upright, shocked.

"*Oui*. Do it, Bonnet." She had lived in them in the tunnels beneath her aunt's house Compiègne for the past six weeks. They reeked. *As do I.* "I suggest the kitchen roasting pit. If anyone asks, even Nancy or Mimi, say you were cold this night and could not sleep for the frost in your limbs."

Strained with the horror of her words, he nodded. "I will, madame."

"I was not here. Nancy and Mimi must say that, too. I fear they may notice some little thing about my presence here, but still this is a severe matter, Bonnet. They must not say I was here. Ever."

"Madame, I am very worried about you. Our monsieur would not like this and would argue against it."

She nodded, sad and silent. *Maurice would urge me on. He knew the power of the chief of police, Joseph Fouché, and his acolyte, Rene Vaillancourt.*

"Can you tell me why you are not in Paris with your aunt, Madame la Comtesse, and your friend, *Mademoiselle* Augustine?"

"I had to leave, Bonnet. Suffice it to say, I had good reason. I doubt I will ever return." She finished the last of her cake. She hated to leave. The very thought had her recoiling again like a ninny. She hung her head a second, before she recovered herself and struggled to stand. "I must go now. It is best if you not know where I go."

"Vaillancourt," Bonnet said. "He did not like my Monsieur St. Antoine."

"He hated that I loved and married Monsieur St. Antoine, and he seeks his revenge. I will not allow it, Bonnet."

"No, madame. And rightly so."

She nodded, then turned for the hall and took the stairs. At the top of the landing, she felt the kindly glow of the moonlight through the dome above. No sounds came from the servants' floor above. Nancy had not awakened, and Amber was pleased she hadn't. The girl slept soundly, working hard each day, deaf though she was, and hampered by the club foot that she dragged along with her every step. Amber would miss seeing the girl who always hurried to embrace her each time she came home to Reims.

Frowning, Amber hastened down the hall to the master suites. She opened the sitting room double doors and smiled at the wonderful, yet heartbreaking, familiarity. The last time she'd been here was months ago during a fierce snowstorm. Gus had been with her, her friend, her finest comfort in her grief over the death of her husband, Maurice.

She strode to the window overlooking the cathedral where kings and queens of France had always been crowned and who now must turn in their graves in St. Denis at the catastrophic end to their kingdom.

"For lack of moderation of your arrogance and greed," she murmured in insult for their failures, for which they were now replaced by others with the same foibles.

She sucked in air and marched to her dressing table. As per her instructions to Bonnet when last she was here, this piece of furniture was not covered in a clean white cloth. During her all-too-brief marriage, she would sit and Maurice would stand behind her to comb and brush her long red hair before he took her to their bed and they made exquisite love to each other.

Before her lay her combs and bushes, her hand cream, her perfumes, all five of them. The bottles and jars were in their exact spots. The ivory comb, sleek. The china-handled brushes, without a trace of her hair. That was how it would remain, too. She would leave nothing behind.

Still, she could not resist pulling open the right-hand drawer. Her face cream lay there, untouched. Giving in to temptation, she applied dabs to her dry cheeks and chin. Who would know from their movement in the drawer that she had been here? That she liked using them. That she needed such amenities to soothe her.

Gus would know.

Amber stood a long minute, considering her next move.

Should she leave a note for Gus? The question tormented her so that she crossed her arms and strode about the room, circling, thinking.

Augustine Bolton was the closest person to Amber in this world. Gus would panic when she realized she had left Paris without any indication of where she truly went, or why, or how long she would stay away. Gus, to Amber's dismay, had become involved in the same work she was. For that reason alone, she would most likely come here searching for her. *At her own risk.*

Amber considered opening the last drawer and penning some words of comfort. A directive or a line of consolation could be helpful.

No.

Gus would come.

But she would find nothing.

It would be safest for her to know nothing.

Vaillancourt would snap at the chance to detain Gus and harass her for information. And the man was capable of such atrocities. Especially against women.

So no. I leave nothing.

Instead, Amber made quick work of the wall safe and took a suitable amount of gold Louis pieces and small silver coins. She'd sew them into the hem of her trousers tomorrow.

And when she used all that?

She froze.

Then what? Return here for more?

She ran a hand through her short-cropped curls. *No.*

On to business.

She removed her boots and socks, then laid aside her dagger and dropped her tattered clothes in a pile. Hat, too. But she kept the cotton binding around her breasts. She had little time to fiddle with that. Instead, she donned a fresh set of Maurice's aged vineyard breeches, shirt, and wool coat. Old boots and a floppy, dark-gray wool hat finished off her look. The fine stiletto she carefully inserted into her thick knitted socks, then spun away.

But she caught sight of herself in her grand cheval mirror. She stood, paralyzed as sudden tears stung her eyes. Far from the fashionable wife of the dashing, gray-haired vintner, this woman looked like a thin, sad man.

She swiped her tears away and stood a moment. Rallying, she pondered how to find the priest who was in hiding in the town in some brave soul's cellars. *Pere* Josef, the former canon at Reims Cathedral, was a crafty fellow who for years, at risk to his own life, had still tended to the city's pious Catholics. In addition, he also aided those like Amber who tended to the country's dissident democrats. Far from a religious zealot, Josef was a believer in the rights of men and women.

But at one in the morning, she would not find him. Anyone who hid the priest was tucked into his bed, sleeping the rest of the righteous.

"Christ, too, was hunted," she blurted as she pushed away thoughts of Josef, caught up her pile of dirty clothes, and headed for the stairs down. "I flee Herod's kingdom and I hate that I fear him. More, I hate myself for the coward that I am."

Chapter Two

June 5, 1802
Varennes, France

RAMSEY HAD TRACKED a few unsavory characters in his career with Scarlett Hawthorne. Six years ago, the beautiful director of the British merchant enterprise Hawthorne and Company had recruited him for his sharpshooter skills. Later, she appreciated his talents at sniffing out traces of those who had vanished, voluntarily or not.

Tonight, Ram sat at his table in the tavern room of his *auberge*, unremarkable in his subdued country attire. From this vantage, he had spied his fiery renegade as she slipped past the entrance to the stairs up to the guest rooms. To his room, to be exact. She moved like a sylph, fine boned, exotic, a woman who danced in a man's mind long after she was gone. Yet she was dressed as a boy and resembled no young male he had ever known.

He smiled to himself. She was going to discover who and what he was and why he tracked her. She'd sighted him, just as he'd allowed, this afternoon. He'd even permitted her to follow him back here. So now he'd give his lovely mark three minutes to pick the lock to his door. Two to rummage through his belongings. Then he'd thrust open his door...

And you will be mine.

This particular lovely wraith whom Ram was assigned to find had special skills he'd not observed in most others. For one, she insisted on men's clothing. Odd that, for a female formerly of courtly refinement. But she was a refugee, even though her numerous changes of wardrobe did not hide from him who she was. Tall for a woman, lithe and deliciously buxom despite the boring binding, she had lush lips and a rarely seen but flashing bright smile. Forced though that last was in her current state of flight from Paris and the deputy chief of police who threatened her, she was a refined beauty with shocking red hair and a heart-shaped face. Up to now, Ram had admired her only from afar, but by her beauty and her pluck, she stirred his interest and his loins. Amber, Madame St. Antoine, could indeed launch a thousand ships—and create in a man a million fantasies of bedding her.

If that were not enough to intrigue a man like Ram, the lady had the habit of vanishing for days. It didn't deter him or discourage him. Resourceful, she had availed herself of disappearing into hovels among the desperate poor of the countryside. One night, she'd hidden in tunnels near the riverbank. Alas for his radiant and devious mark, Ram had never feared navigating France's numerous chalk tunnels.

The woman also had friends—or made them easily. A butcher on the edge of a village south of Varennes. The owner of a small barge who plied the waters of the river Aisne. Her diversions didn't dissuade Ram from his efforts to find a means to corner her. He had listened to enough of Paris court gossip at Josephine's Tuileries to know that his bewitching quarry had an adventurous streak as well as the charm of an accomplished leader of the Parisian *beau monde*.

Funds she had in endless amounts—or so it seemed. She spent them sparingly, but bought herself good food, odd places to lay her head at night, and a supply of men's old clothing. Ram had money in ample store too, so he was able to follow her with any disguise of his own choosing. For three days, she had not noticed him.

He concluded that if she discovered him without his knowing, she would have dispensed with him immediately. Would she not send one of her minions to wait for him in a dark alley? Would she not try to slip a dram of arsenic in his soup? Or use her skills with her little knife to rid herself of him?

She had done none of that. Was she not as mercenary as he thought?

He pondered that with a sip of his wine—and smiled to himself.

Yes. He made mistakes. Everyone did in this work one plied in the shadows. He'd had setbacks. It was natural to lose a mark. One could not always predict the nefarious nature and cunning of a spy.

But he'd had extraordinary successes. Tonight was one. A great one. His friend Kane Whittington, the head of their continental espionage operation, would rejoice with him at finding this missing lady. What to do with her, now that Ram had found her, was another matter. One that did not bear great deliberation. Whatever the woman planned, whatever she desired, was his plan, his desire.

He cared naught for the future or for arguments. He had time. He had options. He was to find the woman. Keep her safe. Simple. Having watched her for days and seen her in trousers, Ram could only expect what days and nights with the luscious lady would do to test his good manners. But test them she would not. He was on a mission—and he knew how to keep his hands, and his cock, to himself.

Ram suppressed the grin that bubbled up from his chest—and drained his mug.

She might delude some, but never him. He was too refined a connoisseur of feminine assets—and so what if his mouth watered to savor hers? He gave her credit that she had managed to elude so many for so very long. Was it five or six weeks that she had avoided recognition? A record, it was, that she had been able to deflect the efforts of many who sought her. Especially the attempts by the vainglorious likes of the deputy chief of police, Vaillancourt. Her act was an astonishing victory for her. No one that Ram had seen who sold her bread or apples had hinted in their manner that they surmised she was a woman. That was best for her in this town, where the last king and his family had been arrested by suspicious local *gendarmes* and hauled back to Paris to die.

Ram had taken his accommodations here two days ago and paid for the privilege of renting the largest room with the largest bed. What could he say? He'd not pretend humility when he gladly paid any price for clean sheets and a bed that accommodated his very long length.

Here, however, he was not so interested in the bed, per se, as he was in the knowledge that it was on the top floor of the three-story carriage inn. So then. Once the lady's curiosity was piqued and she had decided that she needed to learn who and what he was, he would trap her.

He paid the proprietor the sum for his satisfying wine and *pot-au-feu* and rose to his feet.

It was time.

Time to stop following. Time to lead. Time to help Madame Amber St. Antoine realize her solo flight had come to an end. If she wished to continue her wandering, he was with her from now on.

Oui, he had her.

And he was not letting her go anywhere alone.

Chapter Three

AMBER BLEW HAIR from her eyes and applied herself to the prickly lock one more time. Her mystery man sat below at his table enjoying his dinner, but if she didn't get his door open, she'd be sitting in the local gaol. She twisted her hairpin and caught the rod on the grate and...*viola!* The door swung wide.

She dropped her tools in her breeches pockets. They were fisherman's trousers, useful for carrying items to pick a lock or poke an eye. She didn't wish to spoil the spellbinding good looks of her ghost, but oh, how she did need to know who he was and why he was so poor at his attempt to stalk her.

She moved into the room and shut the door carefully, wincing at the sound of the lock clicking in its plate. His was the only room on the top floor of the auberge, but she did not like to arouse any undue attention to someone on the stairs who might casually hear mice about on the upstairs floor.

Hmmm. He had kept a hip bath in the room. Empty now, but with a large sponge on the nearby stool. So he liked cleanliness. *Don't we all, sir!* A good quality to add to his dark, compelling aura.

Usually, he sat at his dinner for more than two hours. She applauded his good taste...and his effort to aid his digestion. Vaillancourt's men usually tended toward the erratic, the intense, the quick, so this man's tendency to linger over his repast was odd. So was the deft artistry of his tailor, who had sought in vain to make his client appear a country gentleman. This man who shadowed her these past three days could wear rags and yet would not be able to hide the poetry his profile inspired. Indeed, he needed not a stitch to make her widow's empty arms yearn for so devastatingly handsome a lover.

Foolish, Amber. Put your mind to the job!

She glanced around, hands on her hips. Whatever his predilection to adorn himself so expertly—or even to dine so deliberately, if he were in the employ of the deputy chief of police (because who else wished to examine her closely?)—she did, of course, prefer him gone at least. Dead at best. Although he did focus on her in subtle ways, he was quite interested in her. Many men always had been, but with crude and lascivious motivations. Vaillancourt's men had political designs in addition.

However, she had no desire to aid this particular man in his effort to insert himself into her life. Therefore, she had not gotten closer to him than twenty feet away. Still, she had noted his habits. *Vin rouge.* Beef. Polite regard of ladies. Congeniality toward men. Long walks in the mornings, wherein he learned the streets of the town. But the ones in Varennes were not so large or numerous. His perambulations, therefore, were laudable but necessarily repetitive.

Here in his rooms, she smiled to herself and rubbed her gloved hands together. She glanced about at the large expanse. He was neat. Hanging his nicely tailored waistcoats and frock coats on two different mannequin forms, he showed a tendency to be a dandy. He could never be mistaken for a *poseur.* He walked the earth as if he owned it all. Were he not in employ of Vaillancourt, she would wish to walk beside him, grasp his arm, feel his strength as he held her in a dance. Certainly, his breadth of shoulder and length of leg told the tale of a man who mastered every task with vigor and sturdy good health. A part of her quivered with longing for the touch of such a virile man.

She shook her head. *Foolish! Look around! Who is this creature?*

She pressed a hand to her stomach and quelled the old ache for a true lover. Maurice was gone, and this man…

This man was who?

He had no valet accompanying him here, but his small clothes, clean and folded, were put away in the tall chest of drawers. A hand-drawn map of the Meuse-Argonne area sat in the top drawer. It was folded just so. Upon the map lay small coins, French and old. Had he put them in such precise array to catch anyone who would peruse his personal items? Of course he had. Just as, under his bed, he had tucked his satchel, the thick leather straps smartly secured, to detect if anyone tampered with them.

Where her gaze took her was to the array of his personal items on the far bureau. The fellow carried his own soap, beautifully shaped in an oval. She bent to sniff the bar. Sandalwood and a trace of orange oil inspired her to grin. She liked citrus on the skin of a man. Maurice had always asked that lemon be milled into his soaps. This man, as particular as her dear husband had once been, liked his own razor and strap, too. No rough country barber could shave him with poorly tended implements. She put out a finger to touch the bristles of his hairbrush—a frisson zipped through her at the two stray strands of his rich brown-black hair that lingered there.

The stairs creaked.

She snatched back her hand.

Someone—a man—with a sure stride strode across the hallway planks.

The *proprietaire*? At this hour?

It could not be… She'd seen him behind the bar.

No matter who it was, he was coming here, and she…

Frantic, she flew toward the only hiding place, a narrow closet wherein her man hung his greatcoat on a peg. He could not need it tonight.

Could he?

She slipped open the door, winced as the rusty hinge

squeaked, and shut herself inside.

Just in time.

She heard the door handle jiggle, the portal creak open wide. Through the slats of the closet door, she could see him. Closer than she had ever been to him, she smothered her gasp of appreciation. He was taller than she had imagined. She was no petite woman, but he loomed, large and imposing, as he strolled about the room. Then he wandered closer, his frown arresting her breathing. His face, with its classic arches and shadows, captured her imagination. He was Mars, Thor, no man she'd ever encountered. The curve of his lips as he gazed around the room in some private satisfaction was as alluring as his kisses must be. But then he spun toward her, focused on her hidey-hole—and grinned.

"I know you are in there," he said with a bass voice that could rival the depths of Lucifer's. "Do come out."

To run was impossible. She'd get one step and he'd catch her in those long, muscular arms. But before she complied, she stopped to consider one startling fact. If he wished to kill her, to do away with her in the name of Vaillancourt and the glory of the consulate, he would have simply opened the flimsy door and assaulted her. He could snap her neck and be done with her in ten seconds. So. He was on a different mission.

But what?

"I rather like it here," she told him with a sniff. All bravado it was, too.

He settled before her door and, hands on his hips, scoffed. "I've no idea why, madame."

He knew she was a widow? She wore no ring. She'd sewn that into her coat hem with her gold. Well then. Informed scoundrel, wasn't he?

"I prefer dark, close spaces," she told him. "Especially when I am being intimidated."

"I assure you, madame, I've no wish to do that. In fact, I wish to save you from yourself."

"You cannot. No one can. And you cannot talk me into a quick trip to Paris to demonstrate the error of my ways."

He inhaled. Between the slats of the door of her little closet, she could see how he smiled like a hungry jungle cat. His expression was not sadistic, but benevolent. Few rakishly divine men ever developed the capability of compassion. When had he? "I've no desire to take you anywhere you do not wish to go."

Despite his tenderness, she scoffed. "Who are you, then, if you are not Vaillancourt's man come to haul me back to him?"

"I would never do that man's bidding."

"Whose do you do?"

"Scarlett Hawthorne."

She sat with that revelation for far too long. Her hesitance gave credence to his words, but still, they stunned her. Even more, she realized he spoke cultivated English. She had returned the favor, and never noticed in what language they conversed until he revealed this about Scarlett. Speaking English did not make him an agent of her friend's, but it soothed her feathers a bit. "I know her."

"She definitely knows you. She showed me a watercolor portrait of you. A fine one."

Whose painting could that have been? Only Augustine. For years, her best friend Augustine had refined her art by redoing Amber's portrait in ink or pencil or watercolor over again and again. "I know you best," Gus had often said when Amber complained. "It gives me joy."

However, the gentleman before her was not joyful. He frowned at the door slats. "That portrait is how I have been able to track you in and out of town the past few days. Even in your men's attire, to say nothing of your numerous changes of public carriages, hired coachmen—and haylofts."

"I tracked *you* today," she blurted at him as a ripple of despair shot through her.

"I know. A double play, eh?"

This man trailed her. Were there others? More whom she had

not noticed? Were they from Scarlett or from Vaillancourt? What had she not seen? Who else was out there plotting her capture?

Her bravado was for naught. She clutched her middle. If she had had more space in this cramped closet, she would have doubled over in distress.

"Come out, madame," her captor murmured with sweet appeal. "I long to meet you face to face. I have admired your courage."

"And my stupidity to allow you to corner me?"

He waved a hand. "Curiosity was bound to snare you."

That was true. "You allowed me just enough of you to lead me on."

"Ah, well. Essential to one who wishes to meet you."

"But sir, I have no desire to meet you."

"You will."

Did he toy with her? *Rather carefree, isn't he?* Yet his discovery of her was so dire a challenge to her. "Huh! You think very highly of yourself."

"I think very highly of you, madame. You are quick, nimble, thoughtful in your escapade. Add to that, you are lovely from afar. I can only imagine how stunning you are closer."

She snorted. "I am no *imbécile* who will welcome your compliments or your protection in exchange for my obedience."

His jaw, square and blunt as it was, went rigid with his displeasure. His pale eyes grew eerie. "Madame, you test my good nature. I do not want you servile. I am here on a mission. You are my quest. I have found you, and now you will do me the courtesy of appearing without further ado. This delay grows tiresome. We have much to say, more to plan." He extended one hand toward the closet and waggled his fingers at her. "Come out, I say."

Out, she had to go. With a huff and a shake of her trousers, she emerged into the golden candlelight of his presence.

She stood toe to toe with him. But that was all that matched. Her breasts came to his ribcage. Her chin was level to his throat. Her gaze took in his mouth, generous and strong. His own eyes, in the fuller light now afforded her, could have sent her to her knees. How could a man possess such an erotic gaze of Nordic blue with long brown lashes so sweeping she could envy them herself?

"Yes." He pronounced the word in a long, low drawl that had her sensing his bass voice down through her stomach to her loins. "I see one reason why Vaillancourt pursues you. 'Tis not simply your hair. Though the red does claim the eye, burn the mind. It is your demeanor."

"Far from it!"

The fellow shot up a hand to make her pause. "You are rare."

"Not at all." How unique, she dared not say.

"I disagree. No freckles. No blemishes. No girlish whimsy. No frailty of bone or eye or gumption." He grinned, broad and nigh unto evil in his praise of her.

Praise. She would have no more of this. She spun to one side and strode toward his sideboard. "Have you whisky in that decanter?"

"I'm surprised you did not pour yourself a draught."

She flashed him a withering gaze. "That would have been poor manners. Besides, I was not here long enough to sample it. I do gather you clocked how long I've been here."

"Upstairs?" He fished his watch from his waistcoat pocket and noted the time. "Eight minutes. Perhaps not long enough for your particular taste."

She availed herself of the decanter and one earthen cup. A strong dose of spirits would be just what she needed to endure this inquisition. She downed it, and the warmth sank through her limbs. With her cup empty but still in hand, she sat upon the edge of his firm, wide bed. The sumptuous feel of it had her spine easing. She smiled in relief but killed the expression, for this man would not need to know how she desired the comfort of his bed. "Now that you have me, what do you propose to do with me?"

"I hoped you would readily see the value of my company." He offered her a brilliant sample of his most pleasant bow.

"Fit for the Tuileries, you certainly are." She lifted her cup in fake homage.

"I'm thrilled you see it that way," he said with sarcasm. "But we both know you do not wish to return. Frankly, I don't blame you. I have been there, and I did not find the court's questionable charms amusing."

She snorted. "Touché. So then, regale me with your solution."

"We travel together." He said it with such finality that it left little room for her objections.

"You are presumptuous."

With a theatrical sigh, he turned on his heel and claimed the only good chair in the room. "I am prudent."

Whatever she might think, he would argue against. From his commanding position near the door, he watched her like a king on his throne. At his leisure, so easy in his skin, he ran his large blue eyes over her as if she were a diamond to regard, measure, and seize. She was no man's. But she tipped her head and said, "Do enlighten me."

"You are in a precarious situation. A woman alone. Fleeing not merely one man, albeit one who is the second most capable of detaining anyone in the country, but eluding his entire cadre of underlings. You have limited resources. Money goes only so far for so long, then you must return home to Reims or to Paris to get more. Under disguise and in the dead of night, too. That carries dangers of discovery. Alternately, you could try to leave France and go to the coast, Britain, or south to Spain or one of the Italian states. But they are far and require a long journey, perilous and hot. Going to one of the German duchies on the Rhine is not a good idea, either. They, after all, are beholden to Vienna."

"Not for long, from what I hear."

"Right you are. For once they are officially aligned with France, you cannot find succor there. Plus, one thing more." He lifted a finger. "You do not speak any German."

She sat taller. "You have done quite a bit of research about my background."

He smiled. It was perfunctory. "I have."

"So then you offer me your presence, your protection, and your funds. I am shocked, sir. Do you not offer me, as well, your prayers?"

"If you wish." Humor warmed the cool self-confidence in his gaze.

"I have no need of them."

"Because you are on the right side of your quest?"

She nodded.

He gave her the sharp regard of a predator about to attack prey. "Never in this country, or in any other on this green earth, did being right assure one of victory. Give over, Amber."

At his use of her given name, she stilled and gazed down into her empty glass. He had a point.

"You need me."

Do I? How can I avoid it? "It is safer for you if you simply leave me."

He gave little nod. "But I won't."

She had to get rid of him. "As much as I would like to have a companion in my travels, I can offer you nothing for your service."

"You need not compensate me."

"Scarlett does?"

He gave a smile. "Scarlett does."

"Does she know you have found me?"

"No." His blue eyes flared with certainty.

"Why not?"

"It is only recently that I did find you." He focused on her mouth and ran a fingertip over his lips, as if…as if he could taste her. "The other reason should be obvious."

"You don't have an associate who can run the message to London?"

"I work alone. And as long as I know where you are, how you are, I have no need to risk any informant falling into Vaillancourt's hands."

She gripped her stomach. The possibility that Vaillancourt might haul her away felt like a punch to her gut. She was caught. And for now, persuaded. "You propose to accompany me around France?"

"If that is what you wish, yes."

"How?" She sniffed. "That looks odd."

"For one woman to travel alone in shabby men's clothes, changing horses and carriages constantly? Yes."

He had her—and she called him a very bad name.

His gaze grew hard and dangerously lethal. "For a man and his wife to travel together in comfort and style, not at all."

"Doing what?" she demanded, trying to call his bluff.

"Touring the country. You and I are, after all, English invited here under the peace treaty."

She scoffed. "I do not collaborate with neophytes to gain ground."

"Madame, I know what you did in Paris—but now you run. Furthermore," he said, smiling with a hand to his heart, feigning insult, "'neophyte' stings."

She raised her glass. "*Non, je ne regrette rien.*"

"I gather." He shrugged. "Regrets are a waste of time. Better to do a job the right way the first time. Face it. You are better off with me."

"Very well. I will play. Why?"

"Yesterday you asked residents if they had heard about shipments to military depots in the eastern border towns."

That stilled her. Her inquiry was a whim, an attempt to learn something useful. "Many expect that."

He smiled pleasantly. "Many men discuss that. Odd for a lady to do so."

She crossed her arms.

He tipped his head. "Did you learn anything?"

She bit her lip. He'd pricked her pride—and her curiosity. "No."

"I did not think so."

He was too confident, this dashing British devil. She raised her chin, defiant, wounded by her failure to learn anything in the cafés or the wine cellars about a fact so valuable. "I suppose you have the answer?"

"I do. We will go to a town where such talk is usual, even for a lady."

That made her mouth water. "A depot?"

"We visit a town that sends supplies to many depots."

Her nerves sang with excitement. "What town?"

"Charleville."

"The armory north of here that makes muskets," she said, admiration escaping her.

"And pistols. After we have an idea of numbers manufactured, we travel to towns that receive the shipments and confirm receipt."

"Such as?" she led him on, excitement thrumming in her ears at knowledge of the numbers of all those weapons.

He shrugged. "Sedan. Verdun."

She huffed. He spoke of dreams. "Impossible. You and I will be obvious. We will be arrested by a gendarme and sent to Paris for Fouché and Vaillancourt to throw us in prison!"

"Two are always better at subterfuge than one."

"Say you!" She shook her head at his self-importance.

"I do." He inhaled, his sky-blue eyes so menacing with his intent. "I have devised a ruse."

"More than pretending to be married?" She had to pick at him.

"One must. Marriage is such a small lie. I have a distant cousin who lives in Charleville. He was, years ago, the mayor. He owns the green grocery, the blacksmith shop, and a saddlery. He is gregarious, well respected. You and I will visit him and learn all we can."

Her heart leapt at the prospect. Yet she knew the next problem. Even if she got information, what would she do with it? Her own network was gone. Destroyed by her flight from Vaillancourt. "Why? Why do that, unless you will take the information to London, to Scarlett?"

"My primary job is to keep you safe. I go nowhere unless you do. Until and unless you decide to go to London, the information about pistols and muskets and uniforms and anything else remains right here."

She was torn. "Then why go to Charleville at all?"

"Unless you decide to go to London, going to Charleville is a journey to pass the time or to amuse you. But eventually on our journey, I predict I will meet one of my colleagues and give him what we have learned."

There were others here in France, spying on the government. She had long thought it so, but it comforted her to hear it from another. "Just like you."

"*Oui, madame.*" He gave her a sad smile. "And you."

Without doubt, his presence was a gift. He had the same objectives, and he worked for the country most opposed to Bonaparte's regime.

She knew how valuable his suggestion was. "That kind of intelligence about supplies is what every foe would want."

"Exactly," he said, "it is the kind *you* would want. The kind you would love to pass on to whomever is your control agent. In lieu of that, what better to do than aid me in my investigations?"

Wild with regret that she had to leave Paris and her work, she clamped a hand to her mouth. A sudden sob rose and tears fell from her eyes. She dashed them away.

His expression fell to compassion, and she had the urge to fall against him and accept all his help and succor. But she stood her ground, sniffing back her remorse. What was wrong with her? Crying like a girl? She hated the appearance she was weak and frightened. Once more in control of herself, she said, "Vaillancourt has ruined me."

"On the contrary, I am here," he declared with a blunt finality that froze her tears, "and I will ensure he never does."

She believed him. Why it was so came to her with the hot blue flame of truth in his eyes. He decreed it would be so, and thus her future was changed. She was part of what he envisioned, and she walked amid his truth. His inescapable command.

At least for now.

"Tell me what else you want of me, Amber."

That shocked her.

But he went on and surprised her more. "The night grows deep, and we must sleep to begin our jobs with vigor."

Persistent cuss. He had won. She shook her head, then rose to get more whisky. Instead of rising to serve her like a gentleman, he watched her like a rogue. His gaze scorched her mouth. Her throat tingled as if those perfect lips of his pressed her there. Her breasts filled; her nipples grew hard as if his large hands held her and his fingers plucked her. Her loins gushed with a desire that had no place in this discussion. This man was pure temptation to women worldwide. But she shook her head. She had years of practice denying men sensual advantage.

She would agree for now to Charleville. Later, she would find a way to leave him. "Very well. You and I are colleagues only. To alleviate any threat. And to investigate Charleville."

"Of course," he said without a hint of duplicity. "And?"

"We will not be intimate. Not for sport. Not for affection. Nor for comfort."

"Agreed." He nodded once, as indifferent to her as a vicar giving a benediction. "Such emotions detract from one's ability to think clearly and act quickly."

She wanted to sputter. "What a fine fellow you are. Your mother must be proud."

"She is. My mother is a darling. I love her. She is worthy of it, for she understands that when one loves, one gives everything, expecting nothing in return. For now, I take your compliment. And I agree. You and I will not be lovers."

At his words, a tiny part of her heart shriveled and went away to pine. She had insulted him, and he had found the means to diminish her for withholding a divine emotion.

Stripped of her independence, she itched to get away. "Concluded, then. Good. I leave you. I am tired. I will return to you at nine in the morning."

"No."

"Don't be ridiculous."

"This is no polite act of chivalry, madame. I am here now to order your days and nights. You will never leave me."

"No! That is—"

"How else can I protect you?" He seared her with his quick and blinding anger.

"I will not sleep here with you. You need only reach over and—"

"I promised you I will not. Like my mother, I give all away not always for love, but for love of my mission. You are not mine to ravish, but mine to protect." He rose to his feet slowly, like an enormous god from the sea. "Give over. We will not argue." He pointed toward the small alcove. "I know you had a few minutes to check my belongings, but you may not have probed them all."

He had so defeated her that she could only question him with knitted brows.

"I see not." He grinned, then marched to the adjacent dressing room. She heard him rustle about. He returned with a sturdy white muslin, a nightgown. "I prefer you in women's clothes. Especially because we will travel as husband and wife. Greens, amethyst, and royal purples, I think, are best for your coloring. We will visit a modiste in Buzancy when we stop along the way to Charleville."

She opened her mouth to express her delight and dismay at his presumption. He had planned so very much that she was impressed and humbled. But she had her own ideas. "I will visit friends of mine here in town tomorrow. The Vernes are loyal to my family, old retainers. I will ask to borrow a few ladies' garments from them." She grabbed the stack of clothes from his hands. "But we have two other problems."

"What are they?"

"I do not have a wedding ring." She would not wear the precious one that Maurice had bestowed upon her. She lifted one hand to wiggle her fingers at him.

"Alas, wife, I fear that you have lost it. It was always too large, too loose. I will have one made for you when we arrive in Charleville." He looked pleased with himself. "And the other problem?"

"I do not know your name. You know much about me. Yet I am left without a clue except that your mother loves you…and so does Scarlett Hawthorne."

"Enough to put you in my care. *Oui, madame.*" He bowed artfully. "I am Godfrey. Godfrey DuClare. Viscount Ramsey. Twelfth of my line. Now please avail yourself of your new night rail and robe."

"No armor, I assume?"

All hauteur fell from his maddeningly handsome features. "None will be necessary, Amber."

"Good to know. Godfrey."

"Ramsey. Or Ram, if you like." He pointed toward the dressing alcove. "I wait there while you disrobe."

"And bathe."

"If you wish."

"Oh, I do." *Especially if we are to sleep together and I am to retain my dignity.*

"I will request water for your bath."

"Thank you," she said, gauging the extent of her true gratitude, which would come only later, after he had slept beside her—and not touched her.

"You are welcome, Amber. Your worries are fewer tonight. Tomorrow is a new day."

Chapter Four

RAM HAD NO trouble falling asleep. He'd done his duty to find the elusive Amber St. Antoine.

But he awoke in the dead of night. The warmth of her in his bed within reach startled him. She was a new phenomenon. He'd not had a woman next to him in a very long time. Never for hours in his bed, certainly. He did not sleep with women he hired. Few as they were. Fewer as they had become over the past few years.

Odd, definitely, for him to say to himself that he did not care to take a female to his bed. He liked women. He had always liked them. His mother was a sweet soul, feline as a barn cat. Particular in her tastes in friends, fashion, furniture, and cuisine, she was also pushy in her desire to see him wed, especially lately. But at twenty-eight, he was getting older, wasn't he?

However, he had found no one. No one. Odd that, for a man who had always had his choice of the *ton*, young, old, widowed, bluestockinged.

Silently, he chuckled. *Was that even a word?*

No matter. Definitely a concept.

But the challenge was complex. He found debutantes a bore. Older women—either blue of stocking or not—pedantic, opinionated. A few widows he'd enjoyed in bed and out were also set on sampling his friends (which did not thrill him), and never marrying anyone ever again (which did not say much for men). Some women were well read and intelligent. (That was excellent, as one did not wish to be bored for forty years.) Others were gorgeous. (And were far too proud of it to add any other assets to their character.) But Ram was far from the age when looks alone drew him. Certainly money never had. And he needed no one to run his household. His mother did that well enough. And their estate manager and solicitor were excellent retainers. Ram had no need to marry to keep the servants in line or the house in order.

Blowing out a frustrated sigh, he removed his blankets and rose. Grabbing his quilted banyan, he cast a glance at his bedmate.

She thrashed like a carefree child who took all the bed.

He bit back a chuckle. She was not used to sleeping with anyone…or if she had slept like that with St. Antoine, it was no wonder the poor fellow died suddenly.

That was unfair. From what his friend Whit, Lord Ashley, had told Ram, Maurice St. Antoine was a very fit fellow. That he died suddenly was what often happened to men over fifty.

His heart gave out, most likely.

Ram shook his head, the errant thought that the man had died after exerting himself loving his second wife bringing a laugh to his lips. But that was also unfair to Maurice.

Because the lady who slept like a two-year-old in his bed could inspire a host of angels to want her. Take her. Day and night.

Even me.

And that is foolish.

He padded to the small window that overlooked the rough country lane running along the back of the inn. Rolling fields stretched out beyond that. Stars twinkled in the deep black of night. The moon was somewhere out of his view.

At the edge of the copse, deer sat in shadow upon the earth in a protective circle. Even dumb animals knew how important it was to form a phalanx against those who would assault them.

That was now his job for this woman. To form a barrier, provide direction and comfort. Her fear had sent her rushing from court, Paris, friends, and her role as an agent of espionage.

How drastic her panic must be.

"Do you worry?" the sleepy voice behind him asked.

She ventured so close to him, he felt her body heat, sweet from their bed. He smiled to himself as he inhaled her fragrance, soap and lemon from the bath she'd requested before she climbed into their bed. "No. I have no reason to. I hope you don't."

"I wish I knew why I don't," she admitted with laughter in her tone.

"You trust me," he concluded, and faced her, the sight of her drowsy, sensuous—and totally at ease in the drape of the thin white gown he'd given her.

"That must be the reason." She tipped her head to one side. "I was good at what I did because I had a sense of others. Their veracity. Their desires. I feel the same with you."

"I'm honored."

"Don't be. My acceptance is not one I confer, but one I see." Her gaze traveled over his banyan and his knee-length white shirt beneath. He'd worn only the shirt to bed. Why not? She knew what accoutrements a male possessed—and he had promised not to use any of them with her. "Come back to bed, Ram, and tell me about yourself. We'll be warm, and you can lure me to sleep with that bass voice."

She beamed at him and turned on her heel for the bed. She climbed in, plumped up a few pillows behind her, pulled up covers to her collarbone, and sat back against the tall oaken frame.

He followed.

"What would you like to know?" he asked when he was settled.

"Why you are really here. Aside from the need to help Scarlett Hawthorne in London and others here in France. One who does this kind of work is no ordinary man."

"I beg to differ."

"Why?" she challenged him with a toss of her bouncy red curls. God in His wisdom had granted her looks as vibrant as her person.

He cast his eyes away. He'd watched her much too long. She must not think him attracted to her. Yet he could spend hours eating up her color, her drama, her valor.

She arched two long, elegant red brows. "What?"

"You have the means to become a leader of society. A woman of substance. Yet you have chosen to become a woman of danger. Why?"

"This discussion was to be about you." She was not irritated, but amused. "I don't like agendas being turned."

"I am not attempting to hurt you," he told her as he plopped a pillow over his lap.

"If that pillow is there for the reason I think it is," she said as she slid him a knowing look, "then I am glad you are not turning the agenda even more."

He cocked a brow. "I find this position comfortable, madame."

"Very well." She applauded him even though he fibbed, then clasped her fingers together atop the covers. "Me? I am easy to understand. I grew up with my Aunt Cecily in Paris. We were condemned to Carmes Prison because my aunt was the mistress of the old Duc d'Orleans who became so liberal. Guilt by association tarnished us. In Carmes, my aunt became Josephine Beauharnais's friend. There, guilt by association saved us. So those who wished for my aunt's favor in Carmes merged with those who found Madame Beauharnais lovely and talented."

"And skilled at attracting powerful men," he added.

"My aunt once was good at that. No longer does she seek that. But Madame Bonaparte is definitely skilled at being passed around from one man to another—or was." She said it all with disgust she could not hide.

"But your aunt lives off her past reputation in court."

Amber was pleased he knew that. Her aunt was very different from Josephine. She would explain it as best she could.

"My Aunt Cecily has long since stopped trying to charm important men. Perhaps if I had recognized that she truly loved the old Duc d'Orleans when I was young, I might have a different opinion of how women gain influence in a society where they have little to begin with." She sighed and toyed with the cotton fabric of the coverlet. "But I have seen how Madame Bonaparte gained influence with Paul Barras after he helped to overthrow Robespierre. She is beautiful and intelligent."

He arched both brows. "Wily."

Amber nodded. "So was Barras. After supporting her for a while, he needed someone to take over Josephine and assume her mounting debts."

"Bonaparte fell for it."

"For her," she said. "Sleeping with a man has its benefits."

"Just as your sleeping with me does," he joked.

She grinned at him and his attempt to lighten the mood. "Exactly. Like talking at four in the morning, eh?"

"A way to welcome sleep."

"Or dredge up old secrets."

His handsome visage went dark and tight. "What is yours, Amber? Why do this dangerous work?"

That touched a nerve. "Ah, you mean the dangerous work I no longer do because one man has frightened me so badly I fled like a coward?"

He reached for her hands. "Stop this self-criticism. Because you have left Paris does not mean you can no longer work."

"No?" She snatched back her hands. Warm and strong though Ram was, he was very wrong. "Kind of you to say and help me keep my self-delusion, but the reality is I have left. Abandoned my role. My mission. Few know, I do hope, where I've been or where I've gone. Heaven knows how you found me. How did you do that, anyway?"

"Whispers. Rumors. Society was full of conjecture why you had gone. Many spoke of where. It was one of my jobs to keep track, to learn why this town or that one. I followed all the possible stories. Coming to Varennes made sense."

"Why?" she demanded of him.

He gave a shrug of his shoulder. "Far away from Paris. Not your home in Reims. Not your aunt's home in Compiègne."

"Who mentioned Varennes?" She had to know. If it was Vaillancourt who spoke of this, she was a dead woman, if not tonight, then tomorrow.

He knitted his dark brown brows together. Shook his head. Looked away. "Madame Fouquet? Marie de Soissons?"

"Never them." Amber cursed the names of the two females who led Paris salons, even as she scoured her memory for others. She had never shared with them that she knew anyone in Varennes. Had Maurice ever talked about his former winemaker? That he had retired? Moved from Reims? To Varennes?

She squeezed shut her eyes. Nothing came to her. What did it matter who had said what? If such words had sent Ram here to Varennes, then it was more than probable that Vaillancourt had sent some one of his men here to look for her.

The chill that ran through her shook her. "We have to leave in the morning."

He tucked the blankets up to her shoulders. "We will."

"I have to say goodbye to my friends before we leave."

"We should not linger—"

"But I came to wish them well." She glanced up at him and caught his scowl. He did not know all her actions here. "To go is not smart, but I must."

He sighed and shook his head. "Where were you all this time since you left Paris in mid-March?"

"Compiègne," she said, giving him a few crumbs of truth and feigning resignation.

Beneath his breath, he cursed. "For all those who beat a path to Compiègne to find you, you tested their abilities. They failed to find you. How?"

She swallowed loudly and licked her lips. "I lived beneath the city."

"*What?*" he said, his blue eyes wide.

"Aunt Cecily's house lies between the palace and a church. Her home was once a convent, and during the religious wars, the nuns took refuge beneath the buildings. I lived there for many weeks."

"I have heard of people living there, but never considered it possible for any length of time."

"I stayed as long as I could, but I became so cold." She shivered and drew the blankets higher to her chin. "I...I could not bear the dark either, and I had to leave. I had to see someone's smiling face. And...and besides needing the sun on my face, I knew I needed clothes, a bath, money. I had to get out. You see that, don't you?"

His look of astonishment drifted to one of compassion. "We were not meant to live beneath the earth, but on it, with the sun and wind and rain and snow on our skin."

"That's when I left. I took money from Aunt Cecily's safe. It was not much, but it got me to Reims. There, I knew I had hidden so much more, and I needed it. I awakened the servants one night, did what I had to, and left. I hoped to God I left no traces for Vaillancourt to seize my two maids and my old butler and haul them off to prison." She cast a glance at Ram. "Tell me they are well. Untouched."

"Frankly, I do not know. I did not come through Reims."

She pouted at that news. "My servants are wonderful people. And here, too, the Verne family deserve only the best. Maurice benefited a thousand times over from Monsieur Verne's expertise with the vines and the blends. The family fed and housed me here."

"Their barn?" Ram chuckled, but was aghast.

"Of course."

"Hideous." He grinned, then frowned.

"Don't wrinkle that marvelous brow of yours, sir. I did what I had to."

He shook his head in exasperation. "You will *not* be the end of me."

"Drat!" She had to tease him. "Why not?"

"Be good! Now go to sleep. We have much to do. You need your rest."

She believed him.

This man would not lie to her. Would not make her do anything she refused. She looked into his cool blue eyes and saw there an honesty she had not glimpsed in many others. Not in any virile men. Not in anyone whom she should question with every breath she took.

Yet she believed him.

He sent her a solicitous smile. It did not reach his eyes. But she understood him.

He was hers to have, to command. He was here to protect her, and if he could not protect her from herself, he would do all in his power to make her see an alternative he favored.

So much was his own dedication.

So strong was her dedication to her own work.

She turned away from him and urged herself to sleep. But her mind churned with questions she would soon have to answer.

How long can I stay away from Paris? How long can I deny I yearn for my work? Even at risk of Vaillancourt and death?

Chapter Five

June 12, 1802
Charleville, Ardennes Forest

"WHEN HAVE YOU been here before?" Amber asked Ram as the coachman took his time opening the door to their carriage. She could not wait to climb down and put her feet to the earth. The two of them had traveled via public coaches the past week. This particular conveyance could not have been more rickety, the squabs more lumpy, and the horses any older. The journey from their last town of Buzancy had taken eight miserable hours, stopping for one very ill, retching coachman and one damaged wheel. All of it made her aching bones feel as if she were eighty.

She fidgeted, happy to be in a new place she'd never been, freer each day from most of her worries about her safety, serene at odd moments when she forgot her predicament—and that in itself was attributable to the jovial company of the man who had found her and vowed to aid her. Posing as his wife, she gradually threw off her care of discovery.

As she gazed at his amicable expression, she admitted that their journey now was more dedicated to him and his pursuits. She welcomed the change.

She needed it. After all the years when she had devoted herself to the ruin of corrupt officials who jailed her and her friends, she hailed this reprieve. *Even though you feel guilty that you've abandoned your mission.*

Guilty? Yes. But at threat to my life.

"Don't fret," Ram said, as if he'd read her mind. He grinned in solace at her impatience and covered her hands in his. The embrace of his large, strong fingers was a comfort she'd learned to admire. To accept. To want. "Once, years ago, I visited here. My distant cousins live just near the edge of town."

That explanation warmed her. They had good reason to be here, not simply Ram's desire to learn about the production of muskets and nails and whatever else the townsfolk produced in their forges. She smiled at him, grateful for his ease, his *savoir-faire*. She breathed more easily each day, each hour. Today, when she was farther from Reims and Varennes, she rejoiced that she was sheltered from those who wished to haul her back to Paris and death.

And this man made it possible.

"Come now." He smiled and the world awaited, happier than she expected.

She squeezed his hand and scrambled out. Breathing the crisp air of the north, she was grateful for her new half coat, for her new clean clothes. Amber also appreciated the deep hem in her coat into which she had basted her remaining coins and her wedding ring from Maurice.

She and Ram had left Varennes the afternoon after he discovered her in his room in the auberge. They had taken a coach west to a small village, where the carriage inn offered bad food and straw beds. The next day, they had left for Buzancy. There they had paused for four days while the local seamstress sewed Amber three new gowns, two hats, and two petticoats, and fashioned new slippers. Amber had happily donned one new travel gown in favor of the borrowed gown, petticoat, felt hat, and knitted shawl Madame Verne had given her.

Amber smiled as she remembered the Vernes fondly and hoped no gendarme came to bother them. The four gold Louis that Amber had left in the old Verne family coin jar was small remuneration for the generosity the family had shown her. They had offered their barn, their hayloft, and their kindness to her when she had been alone, afraid, and in need of friendly faces.

Now their succor had been replaced by this man. This man who surprised her with his knowledge of her, his dedication to helping her elude Vaillancourt, and his surprising turn of character from demanding agent of the British Crown to debonair foreign traveler—and her fake husband.

She trained her gaze away from him, trying to ignore the tug he gave to her heartstrings. His attentiveness was so gallant. So…friendly. She could only applaud him…and thank him.

But that was becoming—

"Unnecessary," he had said to her more than once when she expressed her gratitude.

He wished no thanks. He performed a service. Nothing more. Nothing…

She sniffed and turned to survey the quaint village streets of Charleville as Ram paid the coachman. Stone and red-brick cottages with decent tiled roofs and a few spring flowers blooming in little wooden boxes near the front doors spoke of some prosperity. People waved and stopped to talk to others. Everyone here seemed to know everyone else.

A shiver rippled through her. It could be a bad thing to be a stranger in a small town. People had looked at them oddly in the last village. They had claimed to have caught the wrong coach. Here, however, Ram and she could say they knew townsfolk.

"Tell me about your relatives," she said as he took her arm to assist her over the cobbles and direct her along the lane toward a carriage inn. A faded white wooden sign, carved in the shape of a *fleur-de-lis*, swung to and fro in the breeze and proclaimed it was *Le Roi François*. "I came here years ago with my grandmother. French, she was."

Surprise inspired a smile on her lips. "From this eastern part of France?'

"Yes. She was the youngest daughter in a large family when my grandfather saw her from afar."

"And why was he in France?"

Ram slid her a silly grin. The humor stunned her. He too was becoming more carefree these past few days. His ease transformed his stark masculinity into a radiance of magnetic allure.

She longed to taste his charm, and foolish as she was, she pressed his arm against her breast.

Ram set his jaw, blinking away his notice of her seemingly innocent embrace. "Simple. My grandfather was traveling. It was his grand tour."

"But this is so far into the countryside," she said, relaxing her grip on him. To lead him on would be unkind. He was so chivalrous. In that, he resembled Maurice. Her dear husband had been a man of manners and restraint. She had been enraptured by his tender regard of her. So few men had treated her like a treasure. To most, her red hair marked her as a hussy. Her ample breasts and hips said she belonged in a whorehouse. Ram treated her as if he must protect her from the rabble. As his prize—and his wife. And she loved his devotion. She had to pretend nonchalance. "What is there to see here in this town that your grandfather included it on a quest to see fine art and architecture?"

"My grandmother's beauty."

Amber chuckled. "Her fame had spread that far and wide?"

"It did. My grandmother is not so much vain as she is notoriously proud of my grandfather, who grew to love her other qualities."

"The lady still lives and tells everyone of her fame?"

"Not shy, my nana. My grandfather was with his own father, and both had beauty of all types on their minds. The story goes that the two men introduced themselves to my grandmother's father. My paternal grandfather, not shy himself, praised the

Frenchman's daughters. Then he quickly wooed the youngest, married her, and took her home to England. The art the family possesses is notable, too. A painting by Leonardo da Vinci and one of his machines. A flying machine, as I remember."

"But I thought Leonardo lived in Rome? How did the family gain possession of his works?"

"One of my grandmother's ancestors had lived at the royal chateau of Amboise when King Francis resided there and invited Leonardo to come live and work there. The painting and flying machine were gifts from the artist to my grandfather."

"I would like to see both of them."

"Tomorrow," he said as they approached the entrance to *Le Roi François*, "we will knock on the door of the family Boyer and see if my grandmother and I are remembered—and hopefully you and I are admitted."

"How will that aid us in learning what you wish to learn here?"

"It will," he told her. "Everyone knows the product for which the town is famous. You and I will keep our ears open and perhaps learn from gossip any useful news."

It was not until the *propriétaire* had shown them to their room that they spoke again.

"My wedding ring? I need one, remember?" There had been no goldsmith in Buzancy.

"We can stroll around town after we dine and hopefully find one. Tomorrow morning, we will go early to have you fitted, and as we go, we will examine the layout of the town. We'll go to the city hall and stroll along the river."

"The armory should be easy to find."

"I remember where it is. I just don't want to appear too eager to examine it. We must tell any and all that we have stopped here to visit my family."

"When do you want to go see them?"

"Tomorrow afternoon. Then we tell them that we are on our way to Sedan to visit a friend of mine."

She set her new little reticule on the bed and opened the straps. "A geologist like you?" Ram had told her that was to be his unique reason to travel around the countryside.

He set down his own small travel case and put a hand to his chin. "I think so."

She laughed. "You do lie so well."

He gave a small bow. "Thank you."

"Now explain to me what reason you have to visit this mysterious friend of yours?"

"Ah, *Madame le Vicomtesse*, I am a noted expert on French chalk and rock, and I write a treatise on the natural geographical formations used by one of Louis XIV's military generals to build fortifications."

"Vauban." She nodded. The famous engineer had built defensive rings around France on mountaintops and along coasts. He had even dug forts into rock to store supplies. "Of course."

"You know of him?" Ram paused, surprised.

She winked at him. "Every woman does, don't they?"

Hands on his hips, he threw back his head and chuckled. "Just those who have lived under their aunt's house in the tunnels of Compiègne."

"Exactly." She resumed unpacking her reticule. "You are so fortunate that you have such a knowledgeable assistant."

His laughter gone, he looked at her with respect—and an enthusiasm tinged with sweet desire. "I could not do it without you."

JUST AFTER NOON the second day Amber and Ram were in Charleville, they had walked from town up to the residence of his distant cousin. The old white stucco chateau they approached was a sedate beauty.

Ram expressed his concern that his cousin might not be alive.

If he were, he might not be keen about meeting him or welcoming him to his home. "My cousin Georges was a member of the first *Estates General*. He remained for two years until radicals took over and the Terror began. I heard that then Georges left Paris for home and remained here, running his shops and writing his travel books. While many from the National Assembly were hunted down and thrown in prison, he escaped notice. I do hope he lives here in peace."

Amber took Ram's hand and squeezed it in sympathy. It was the first time in their relationship she had sought to comfort him. His hesitant nod showed his surprise, but his arresting blue eyes showed his gratitude. "As do I," she said.

Ram turned and lifted the knocker.

It took only minutes for hope's transformation to joy.

At once upon gazing at Ram standing in his foyer, Ram's relative beamed and opened his arms. "*Monsieur le Vicomte.*" He patted Ram's cheek.

"*S'il vous plaît*, Georges—to you I always was Godfrey. Let it be so once more."

"*Naturellement, mon ami.* Allow me to introduce to you my children. Since last we met here, I have had two girls and a son. They will be delighted to meet you. Sadly, my wife, Corrine, died last winter. She would have loved to have met you. But we gladly welcome you to us!" He motioned to his children to come forward from their observation spot at the end of the hall. "Come meet your cousin, *mes chers enfants.*"

She and Ram greeted the man's offspring with the same enthusiasm he and his children showed to them. Adele was the oldest girl, shy and polite. Edouard was Georges's son, pensive and quiet. Sophie was the buoyant one, resembling her father in his joyful character.

The Boyers took the two travelers to their bosoms with ease and laughter.

"A success," Amber said to Ram, waggling her brows at him as they sank into their comfortable bed that night.

They had eagerly accepted Georges Boyer's invitation to spend a few days.

"YOU CANNOT LEAVE us Tuesday, but must remain for the June festival," Georges insisted the next day at luncheon.

"Especially for the ball Friday night," the youngest daughter, Sophie, declared. "It's the town's grandest occasion."

"I planned to be finished with my rock samples before then," Ram claimed. He was privately overjoyed to stay, because from Georges last night at dinner he had learned nothing about the production of muskets at the old armory.

Amber joined in. "We will not be a burden to you for so long, Georges."

"Nonsense!" The man was determined to be a good host and the finest of relatives.

Ram gave in. They would stay.

A good thing, too. Because they had learned little from local residents about production of weapons. Their visit to the local goldsmith had resulted in a lovely, if simple, wedding ring for Amber, but that man did not gossip. Neither had the *propriétaire* of their auberge or the pretty town boulangère. Georges Boyer concerned himself only with pumping details from Ram about their recent journey to Buzancy. Ram said he needed any changes in the town so that he could include them in his updated travel guide. Georges's three children shrugged, confessing they knew little about the armory. The only fact they learned was that two of Edouard's friends had fathers who worked there.

LATER THAT SAME afternoon, Sophie tugged Amber up into her lavender bedroom and took up her favorite subject, gowns for the town's summer ball Friday night.

"It is to be a grand occasion on the plaza outside the *hôtel de ville*. You are so lovely, madame. Everyone will be in awe of you."

Amber thanked the girl for her sweet compliment. "I must think on this, Sophie. I have no gown for such a grand occasion."

"Anything you wear will make it grand! Besides, what if you borrow my blue gown?" The girl clapped her hands. "I am an excellent seamstress, and you will never know the dress was altered."

Amber could not refuse such generosity from so sweet a child. The girl regarded her as a lady of taste. Why that was, Amber didn't know—she showed no hint of her life in Paris. She was dressed in her simple attire sewn by the Buzancy modiste.

When Amber mentioned the conversation to Ram that night as they undressed for bed, he waved a hand and dismissed her concern.

"Ah, fear not, *ma femme*." Calling her his wife these days in increasingly endearing tones, he took up her hand and kissed the back. "Sophistication shows in everything you are. The way you walk, the way you speak, how you look at the world as yours. Sophie sees a woman who knows what she wants—and who she is."

"I hope not all of who I am!" she joked, but reveled in Ram's words, including his reference to her as his wife. She was his co-conspirator, a stranger whom he had adopted, a woman whom he'd vowed to save. Since they had united, they had become friends who truly enjoyed each other's company. In that, he played the part of her husband as deftly as an actor at the *Comédie-Française*. But the past few days, when he gazed at her across the Boyers' salon or smiled with her at breakfast, she saw him transform by tiny increments from the man who acted as her mate to one who became the husband she laughed with, planned with, plotted with—and slept beside.

He had become so natural a mate to her these past few days

that she had no answer for the question that had begun to form in Buzancy. Was Ram, this British spy who had invaded her life, becoming more than he claimed? Was he more than her protector? Was he at once her conspirator? In subtle ways, also her confidant? Her friend?

And if he was all of that in so little time, was she lax, careless? Or wise?

Prudent. Ram had used that word. And she liked it. Favored it. Told herself many times a day as she glanced at him and smiled or nodded in agreement that she was being prudent to accept his kind offer of his attention, his care, his body as her bulwark against the misfortunes those like Vaillancourt could cast against her.

I am prudent. Aren't I?

"What do you think, madame?" The next day, Sophie held up for Amber's inspection another garment she had altered for herself. But the girl's question helped Amber avoid answering her own. "Is my stitching good enough for the alterations to the blue gown for you?"

Sophie was bubbly and lovely. With pale blonde hair and woodsy-blue eyes, she was the epitome of youth and positivity. All of which Amber had never been. Only once had she approached that much joy for life, and that had been in the eighteen months when she was married to Maurice. Now she had begun to accept the help of an agent of espionage to help her escape the price of her own acts of spying. *And my acceptance of Ramsey does not challenge what I still feel for my darling Maurice. For Maurice, that was love. This for Ram is gratitude, delight...and friendship. Just friendship.*

She regarded Sophie with a broad smile. "*Merci beaucoup,* Sophie. Your stitching is expert, and I am so honored you will allow me to wear the gown."

"It's not grand, like a Paris gown, madame. But—"

"I love it," she assured the girl.

"Even after I finish, it may not fit well," Sophie said worriedly.

"I think it will be superb." Sophie was a chubby girl, and as tall as Amber. So the length would be right and the wealth of fabric around Amber's large breasts would fit. If she were not in the height of fashion, she was not in the city, in Society, nor in the mood to be *au courant.*

She took the shimmering icy-blue charmeuse, dotted with tiny embroidered white peonies, between her fingers and rubbed the smooth silk that flowed like water from her touch. "I think it is from Lyon."

"It is. Papa ordered it for Mama, but she was never able to wear it."

"I'm sorry." She put her arm around the girl's shoulders. "It is difficult to lose your mother at any age."

"Is yours alive?" Sophie asked with hope in her eyes. "I apologize. I should not have asked so personal a question."

"Of course you could. I do not mind." Amber looked away for a moment. "I do not remember my mother well." *She is a ghost to me.*

"*Non!* Terrible!" Sophie caught Amber's hand. "I am so sorry."

"My father was a duke's aide and became very ill. When he could no longer take care of me, my aunt came to London. I was nine when she took me with her to Paris. I lived with her until I married." Amber paused, another thought of beloved Maurice bringing tears to her eyes.

The girl's brow furrowed. She did not understand Amber's emotion. "But *Monsieur le Vicomte* is a very handsome man. You must be proud. I would be so happy to have such a wonderful man by my side."

Caught in the moment when she reflected too much on the past, Amber remembered the present danger—and her growing affection for her "new" husband. "*Oui, oui.*"

Fearing that Sophie would ask more—and that she had told the girl too many facts—Amber hurried to change the subject.

"Now," she said with a brightness she did not feel, "fetch your sewing basket. We will tend to this gown."

As they cut seams and basted new ones in the luscious silk, Amber saw Godfrey DuClare's flame-blue eyes and pondered the words she had let slip into her consciousness. Yes, she admitted, she did have affection for her new husband.

Chapter Six

BREAKFAST IN THE small strawberry-painted room off the kitchen was always a cheerful, chatty affair.

Ram today was in no mood to appear bright and affable. Rather, he could easily chew the hefty circular table down to wood chips. Frustration had him trying to plaster on a smiling face. Acting for once in his life took too much out of him.

"Good morning," he bade Georges, his three children, and Amber. He took his usual chair beside his supposed wife, uncommonly gorgeous in muslin violet at eight in the morning.

One cause of his grumpiness was his failure to learn much about weapons production in town. The other, bigger, cause of his sour mood was that his back was killing him. He had volunteered yesterday to help Georges and the men of the town to build out wooden planks in front of the *hôtel de ville* to create a dance floor. All for the fair tomorrow and ball Friday night. But his shoulders throbbed because he had slept on the floor of his and Amber's bedroom last night. It was not the first night of such rude incapacitation. It was his third.

Oh, Amber had argued with him last night as he grabbed a pillow and threw it to the floor.

He had barked back.

Drawing in her pretty chin to her neck in shock at his growling, she'd appeared chastised. "I wish you wouldn't sleep there," she had said in a pout.

"Well, we don't always get what we want." He knew that too damn well. If he had his wish, his hands would be full of her every night. His cock would be buried inside her mouth-watering flesh and—

"I wish I didn't sprawl out so much. I could learn to be a more polite bed partner. Honestly—"

"Polite, my arse." More tempting, she could never be. He blew air from his lips. "Hardly the major problem, *ma femme*."

"I could say we had an argument and ask for another room—"

He shook a finger at her. "That you will not do."

"Come now, Ram. I am safe here. No one can hurt—"

"I said no." Then he threw blankets to the floor.

"You'll not be able to help tomorrow with the woodwork. I see how you stoop."

"Will you leave it alone? If I stoop, it is not from working with wood. But from working wood."

She had blinked. Hard. Began to form the word *what?* But never finished it—instead she'd clamped her lips together and turned away to the bed, giving him her back and her silence.

She was no innocent, and she jolly well knew now that his aching back did not give him a problem as much as his aching cock.

This morning's conversation, thankfully, turned to the musicians for the ball. Adele played the violin and would be among those playing for the dancers. Edouard, who had helped with the planks for the dance floor, had hurt his hand yesterday.

"I know they will be without a drummer, but my wrist hurts," he said.

Amber piped up. "It looks swollen, Edouard. Will you allow me to bandage your wrist? If we keep it secure, it will heal more quickly."

"If you think it wise," the boy agreed.

"I do. My husband had an injury like that, and we healed it

with good, firm bandaging."

What she had said about Maurice had Ram holding his breath. But he, in the process of buttering bread, heard no gasps of surprise. They all assumed it was he who had hurt his wrist. He glanced at Amber in kind regard to cover the story, and she sat, unmoving, realizing, he supposed, what she had almost revealed.

Edouard was not bothered. "I can dance now. I wished to."

Georges locked his gaze on Ram. "Edouard has a *tendre* for Suzanne Moreau. The lovely daughter of the new director of the armory."

Beneath the table, Amber nudged her foot against Ram's.

"She has many suitors, Papa." Edouard shook his head, accepting his lot. "I'm her age and she pays me no mind. Besides, when I go to Paris in September, she will just have one fewer man calling on her."

Georges frowned. "She would be lucky to have you. But I say you are too young to think of courting. Go to university and you will find many pretty young women."

"Your papa is right," Amber told the young man with a smile. "Paris is filled with many lovely ladies who enjoy men who have a good education."

"And those," added Sophie with a jab of her elbow to her brother, "who can play the drums."

"Oh, phew," Edouard replied.

"Suzanne Moreau doesn't want any man from Charleville." This came from the oldest girl, Adele.

"No?" Ram joined in this little family debate as he helped himself to eggs. "Why not?"

"She wants to return to Mauberge, where they lived before. Her father was transferred here last autumn to increase production, and she hates being here. That's because she likes a man who works at that Mauberge factory. She hopes her father will fail here and they can return. Then she can encourage the fellow she favors."

"Can her father?" Amber asked that as casually as if she simply discussed a young girl's frivolous affair. "Return?"

Ram knew the man could not. If he failed to ramp up production, he would find himself in prison.

Adele drank her coffee. "Suzanne says she is stuck here until her father helps the old director figure out where to hire new workers for the factory."

"They need another forty at least," Edouard added, and asked Adele to pass the platter of ham.

Amber looked bewildered. "That is a lot of men. But then, wouldn't there be enough men in the next town down along the Meuse River to come work here?"

Ram regarded Amber, his brain ticking like a clock. The town of Mézières was around the bend of the river, and many traveled between the two towns by boat. But it was just as easy to journey between them by coach or horse. Still, that town was far enough away that if men from Mézières wished to work here, they would have to come here to live. They might not wish to unless they were offered fine wages as incentive. But Ram dare not speculate aloud.

"Too many in Mézières are free thinkers," Georges added with a shake of his head. "A garrison with more than five hundred soldiers is stationed there. The townsfolk don't like it, and they certainly would not want to come here to work in an armory that makes weapons for the consulate. Moreau will have to import men from other villages or increase every current worker's hours to make the new quota of muskets Bonaparte wants."

Ram shook his head, saying nothing so he could appear uninterested.

But the subject died a normal death. Soon they were on to the weather for the fair and the ball. Minutes later, everyone in the Boyer family left the room.

Bursting with the first clues about production at the armory, Ram bided his time until he no longer heard their footsteps in the hall.

Amber met his gaze with excitement in her own. "Shall we

go upstairs to talk?"

When Ram closed their bedroom door behind him, he strode to her.

She stood in the center of the room with a grin on her face and reached for his hands. "We finally have useful news."

"God loves Suzanne Moreau." He opened his arms wide.

Laughing, she went into his embrace to kiss his cheek. Her gesture was all too quick. Her lips too inviting. Her body too lush. He squelched a groan.

"We know why they need forty more workers, don't we?" she asked him, pulling back.

"They have received orders for increased numbers of muskets and need additional men to make the quota."

"Don't they have to be skilled?"

He nodded. "I can't say. But I tell you one thing—Mauberge is a bigger armory. Which is why Suzanne's papa has come to advise. He knows what he's about."

Amber tsked. "Poor Suzanne."

"She'll have to give up her young man in Mauberge." He tapped Amber on the nose.

"I think she'll be here for a long while. Ah, can true love stand the test?" she joked.

Love has too damn many tests.

The thought shocked Ram. He'd never been in love. How would he know that?

HAMMER IN HAND, Ram joined six men from the town and sidled up next to the mayor. Charles Dejean was sixty and a talker, the type who never failed to tell you about his mother, her foibles, his wife, now gone to her maker—and most likely glad of the silence. In addition, he had five children, grown, talented (weren't they always?), and all had moved to Paris. *Smart of them.* Ram smiled. All of that was sprinkled into a lively recital of Dejean's life story, worthy—the man was pleased to say—of a memoir.

Ram bit his tongue and pretended to admire every word. In between whacks of nails and lifting the thin wood into place (because Mayor Charles Dejean did not lift more than he must), Ram easily measured the man's pride as bigger than the height of his achievements.

"Your family has lived in Charleville for centuries, then, eh?" Ram asked him, after a recitation of Dejean's great-great-great-grandfather's achievements.

"We are recorded in the church records here, in Sedan and in Verdun." The portly man stood up straight, a hand to the small of his back. "We have fought for every king since Henry, the first Bourbon. Now we work in the new government. Even for Bonaparte. A good man."

"He has done much for France," Ram said. Indeed, Bonaparte had fixed corruption in the army and quelled rampant inflation. More than that, Ram knew it was not wise to criticize the glorious new military man who was the first consul.

"He will do more. *Pardon, monsieur,*" Dejean begged, a hand out. "You are so much younger, and my poor back cannot take more."

"*Oui,* I understand." *More than you know.*

After a few minutes, the silence could not hold Dejean. "Monsieur Boyer tells me you are a teacher and writer."

"That is true." Ram sat on the ground, fitting the stubborn board snugly against the next. He wrote often, not tomes but letters, and he did once teach his butler how to juggle bottles like a jester at a county fair. Ram had learned the talent at Eton, when he should have been studying his letters.

"You write about the land, Georges says." Was Dejean drawing him out?

"Geological formations, *oui.*" *Best not to become too specific.* The subject had appealed to Ram since a child, and he read about natural phenomena whenever he could.

"And you were able to get a passport to come to France when

the treaty was signed?"

"That's correct." *How else would I be here?*

"Here in the country, we are usually skeptical of strangers." Dejean went on to tell tales of Germans and Russians who had come to visit lately. "They were here to learn about our famous Charleville guns."

"I'm sure they were." Ram made himself sound uninterested. He knew how inaccurately the musket fired if one aimed at a person over too long a distance. But with a shorter range, the gun did better than many others, as it could maim and kill quite a few who stood in close proximity. "I understand even the new American government likes your guns. You shipped many of them over for the colonists to fight against the British."

"We won their war for them, too. Those guns are the best in the world." Dejean was then kind enough to discuss the manufacture of the iron and wood components, and the need for the bore to be made very smooth.

Ram let him run on. An uncle of his had fought with the British in New York. He often talked about the French muskets that were the best of their kind. Even given that the powder could jam in a hot bore, so that the only way to cool it was for a soldier to urinate down the muzzle.

"Now Bonaparte wants to increase the supply," Dejean continued, "and we are to lead the world once more with our superb muskets. Bonaparte has ordered two hundred and fifty muskets shipped each month, beginning in October."

"Is that so?" Ram stood. The act, he hoped, covered his shock at the number. "We need another board for this row," he told the mayor. "Then you and I can quit and have a glass of wine."

Dejean liked to drink, Ram had learned yesterday when they worked together. He really did not care what Dejean liked as long as he could keep him talking. After all, two hundred and fifty muskets each month, three thousand a year, was real news. From one factory. To his knowledge, three armories produced this musket. Nine thousand a year was a lot of muskets. The only reason a country needed that many that consistently was because they planned to use them. Bonaparte had pointed his army and their guns at the wily Parisian politicians of the directorate. He'd overcome many in Italy—failing, yes, in Egypt and Palestine, but that did not stop him from rallying and returning still a hero to France. Now he had ordered more guns.

Ram doubted three thousand muskets from this one armory would sit in a supply depot for very long. The guns were expensive. A government spent such great sums to defend the country. The survival of soldiers depended on their excellent weapons. After all, a soldier might be shot or wounded, but his musket could survive. To kill another.

The knowledge turned Ram even sourer than he had been this morning. Now he had a problem.

It was one thing to learn the details of such an order of muskets by a famed armory. It was another to realize those details must be conveyed to Paris to his friend and head of mission, Kane Whittington, Lord Ashley. But how could Ram possibly get the information to Whit? He was far from any major city where he might meet another British citizen visiting the countryside of France. The chances of his meeting a fellow British man who might discreetly carry a message, coded as it would be, to Ashley was even less. Ram could not simply send such vital information by post. But the biggest thing that prohibited Ram from sending word was that it was his primary duty to protect a lady who was too frightened to return to a city where she would be arrested. And die.

What could he do?

He removed a handkerchief from his waistcoat pocket and wiped his forehead.

He would not write.

He would not go to Paris.

Nor would he ever think of posing the problem to Amber.

She'd want to go to Paris immediately. For his sake, but also for the sake of the very same duty she once had to her own work, she would urge him to leave. Her loyalty and her devotion were as great as his.

But loyalty could kill. Devotion ensured it.

He shook his head. Flummoxed, he followed Dejean to the local *oenothèque*. In the shade of the café, Ram sat down with the other men to order the local *vin rouge*.

Espionage was a dirty business.

He'd be damned for a fool if he never went to Paris with this information—but he never would. He'd walk the earth with Amber, wandering forever, if that was what she wished.

He sat drinking, laughing with the men of Charleville as he must. Losing himself in his conundrum. In the memory and lure of Amber's flashing dark-brown eyes.

Amber St. Antoine was too important to him to risk her life. He wanted her to live a long and a happy one. He even dreamed in odd moments that he'd prefer if she lived the rest of it with him.

If he could persuade her to that, he'd be one hell of a good talker.

But he should save his breath. Because she had no reason to agree.

THAT NIGHT AT family dinner, Amber noticed Ram's preoccupation. She doubted others did, but she had grown to know him better.

She liked him. Or *admired* was the better word. He was a man of tempered emotions, and the wild rush beneath the calm river of his exterior was a flow she detected now. She was glad she did. That granite core of his personality was what she relied upon. What she had needed from anyone—any man—who sought to help her. And Ram had. Did. Quite well, too.

Here he sat, conversing with the Boyer family as if he were

their old dear friend. In many ways, he was, but he, by his *joie de vivre*, added a depth of honest tenderness that made his affections welcomed and returned.

But tonight there were lines of concern from the corners of his eyes. They had not been there this morning. She could not imagine what might have happened to create it. This morning, with news of the muskets' production, he had gone off to his chores with the men of the town in hearty good attitude.

She had helped the women of the town finish the sewing of many mummers' costumes. She had not seen him before all the family gathered for a glass of *vin blanc* and tiny savories in the salon before dinner. But the meal dragged on, everyone so primed to enjoy the next two days of games and fun. Finally, they each drifted off to their beds.

Ram hung back. "Go up. You must be tired." He begged off retiring upstairs to their rooms. "I need to walk."

"May I come with you?" She probed his gaze. "I won't talk if you don't wish to."

"No. Do come. Although I am not good company."

She smiled in apology. "I am certain that I myself have not often been the best companion."

He put his hand to her waist and opened the dining room door for her. "I forgive you your poor manners, madame."

She could see he jested. "I am better these past few days. You must agree," she teased.

"I do." To her words, he sounded strangely resigned. Yet, trying for levity, he gallantly offered his arm. "The back garden?"

"Let's."

They strolled down the long central hall toward the large double-glass doors at the rear of the house. There, the stables, the carriage house, and the gardeners' house swept around a cultivated area in a half-circle. To the right, by the kitchen door, a red-brick fence enclosed the flourishing vegetable garden.

Corinne—Sophie's mother, Amber had learned from the girl—had been devoted to her roses. A small, neat parterre bound by chalky-white stones held the dark, green-leafed bushes. They sat in long rows and bloomed in all colors, shapes, and sizes. What filled Amber with awe and a heady inspiration was the mix of the rosy fragrance with the gentle night air.

"One day I would like to have a rose garden," she confided quite spontaneously, taking the stony path among the bushes. "I'm sorry. I said I would not chatter."

"My mother grows them." He bent to cup a fat white bud and inhale.

The look on his face endeared him to Amber even more. To his mother as well, she was sure. "Does she enjoy other activities?"

"Cards. Few ever play with her. She is a wizard."

Amber snorted. "Counts them in her head, does she?"

"Indeed. Mind like a mousetrap."

Amber burst out laughing. "I would like to play her."

"Oh, no," he said with a grimace, his hands clasped behind him as he walked beside her. "You count them, too?"

She nodded, satisfied with herself. "I do. Aunt Cecily taught me."

"Dear me. The woman is a legend."

Amber grinned and bent to inhale the delight of what wafted up from two red buds tightly bound together. "She is. So many call her ruthless, not just in cards, but in so much more. Her dealings with Josephine. Her defense of all her friends. And then, of course, she has been so very good to Augustine and to me. She took me in at nine, and she took Gus from her parents when she was just a baby. They were ill suited to raising a child, and Aunt Cecily was intolerant of their excuses. They were, she told us both, wild things and libertines. Aunt would not allow them to have Gus, neglect her, nor corrupt her."

"Your aunt is not really related to you, is she?"

"No. But to Gus, yes. Distantly, somehow. We do not ask. She does not say. Aunt saved us both when she learned of our plights. And I am forever grateful. She gave us a good life. She would have given the same to another young girl, another daughter of a youthful friend of hers."

"What happened to her? Why did your aunt not save her?"

"She was to come to us. An heiress to an English barony. She disappeared when she was sixteen. Ran away from home. Aunt Cecily never found her, though she sent out scouts to search for her."

"Every time I hear about your aunt, I do admire her more."

"She is worthy of it."

In the moonlight, his blue eyes glistened with sympathy. "Before you left Paris, did you say goodbye to her?"

Amber sucked in a breath. "No."

He waited, searching her face, and she understood he wished an explanation.

"I knew it was best to say nothing to her or to anyone, Ram. I could not risk a messenger getting captured. I dared not write a note to fall into anyone's hands. My aunt knows me well. Once I did not appear at my normal social calls, I knew she would understand my desire not to involve her."

"And what of your agents who depend on you? What of them? Did you send them word?"

"Never. It is the nature of my chain that if one of us does not appear, the others may choose to return to check on us once at the appointed day and time, but if we miss our scheduled round twice, agents know the chain is broken. To them, so long missing in March, I was gone. I trust them to keep to that agreement."

"It is a good one," he said with resignation.

"It ensures we are safe, one from the other, if someone gives up information under"—she would not say *torture*—"duress."

Then she turned away, upset anew by knowledge she had ruined a fine network that had operated for years. "I left. I was afraid." She clutched her arms. "I am ashamed."

He was behind her in a moment, his arms, warm and strong, binding her back to him. His lips near her ear, he breathed hot, reassuring words: "Sometimes there is nothing to do but the most obvious. If you had stayed, you tempted fate."

"Vaillancourt threatened it." She sank back against Ram's oh-so-welcome comfort. "The deputy police chief is not a man of many words."

"Does he want your network? Names? Methods? Or does he seek something else?"

"Me," she said so low she doubted Ram heard her.

But he growled deep in his throat, and the arms that possessed her grew strong as iron.

"He told me he will have me. For his bed. For his reputation. For his glory. He'll make me his whore and his prisoner. I know not which would come first, but I know he wants my agents' names. The one who reports to me and the one to whom I report. He knows how we transfer information. He told me so the night he threatened me. And if I don't give him all he wants…"

Ram buried his lips in her hair and tightened his arms around her so securely that she could barely breathe. "I won't let him have you. Never."

She spun to face him and cupped his cheek. "I trust you. I have trusted so few in my life. But you, I believe."

"Thank God." He smiled, though the look had pain in it—and she knew not why.

But, she concluded, as he took her hand and led her inside and up to their bedroom, that he knew not how to cope with his issue.

As he undid the laces of her gown and performed the service of a maid and imagined husband to undo her corset, then turned his back as she stripped and donned her muslin night rail, he expressed his simple, gentlemanly devotion to her as he always did.

Yet something ate at him.

Tomorrow, she must learn. For to make him happy was a goal she now had. To do any less would be miserly when he'd given up his whole life to guard her.

In turn, she owed him much to show him her thanks.

She would have to think on what that was.

Chapter Seven

THE COUNTRY FAIR reminded Ram of those his parents had hosted when he was a boy. Mummers on parade, funny costumes, long feathers in their hats. Young girls in muslins, the colors of the rainbow. The village tradesmen in their lean-to stalls, hawking their wares. The revelry of those hoisting high their mugs of fermented cider, beer, and wine.

Ram and Amber strolled through the throng along with Georges. The two young girls trailed behind the three adults. Georges's son Edouard walked along with a young friend.

Ram tried to throw himself into the gaiety. In a quandary, he had no other choice but to do the next most logical thing.

He took in Amber's delight in the festivities. Her carefree attitude had grown in her each day since they left Varennes. Today, it had come upon her in fuller flush, as if dawn slowly appeared over the mountain of her fear and fortitude. It suffused her, mind and body, and endured. In the sunlight that illuminated her flawless skin and dancing, dark eyes, amid the music that had her humming or singing along in a joy he imagined she'd not felt in a long time, she sparkled like a rare ruby.

He warned himself, as he usually did nearly each hour, to take his gaze from her. To fake circumspection. To appear polite. A gentleman. To act as most husbands would to their wives, attuned, bored—indifferent.

He had pretended false emotions before. Apathy, silliness, or enchantment all came easily to him. He could not say why, other than his mother had always enjoyed plays and invited troupes to their country house with such regularity that he could recite Shakespeare's monologues, badly but nonetheless recognizably, by age ten. Such expertise had befitted him in his work for Scarlett.

He could render expert aspects of libertine, misfit, misanthrope, miser, and even clown. He'd polished his impressions of such behavior when he attended Eton. His acting skills were later confirmed by his friend Ashley and that man's cousin, Fournier. Those two men's descriptions of the buffoons, charlatans, and overly righteous who attended Heidelberg University had inspired Ram to further heights. Furthermore, he was no fool about the characteristics, in particular, of men who seduced women for pleasure or on wagers or just for the challenge of it.

Here with Amber, however, over the weeks, he realized he'd been stripped down. He had become invested in her survival. Dedicated to her welfare. Appreciative of her character. Minus the façade of paid guard, he was naked to her. A man who could not let her go. A man who would not leave her. No matter the price he had to pay.

She was a woman who valued truth. Valor, yes. But honesty was her core essential. For him to hide from her that he revered her was wrong. To hide from her that he admired her was sad. To hide from her that he wanted to taste her was vital to his mission and hers. And yet he ached in his bones to take her in his arms and cradle her there. Spirit her away to the coast, or to Flanders, or up the Rhine to Amsterdam and home.

But she would not go.

He had broached the subject in the past, and she had flatly refused. She had no logic for it. She had run from Paris because she was marked for death. But she remained. And Ram wondered if, in her quiet moments, she pondered returning to challenge

Vaillancourt, if only to call herself valiant. If only to lose…and call herself martyr.

That last was foolhardy.

That last he would not allow. She was much too noble to surrender to blackguards who had no higher goal than power. She was too much woman to allow her to sacrifice herself on an altar of politics.

So as she reflected, he served as her guard, her friend—and her fake husband. Each day, he yearned to be more. Each day, he sublimated what he must do to report to Ashley about the muskets, to care instead for his duty to Amber.

Yet there was nothing for it. He was caught in a web he could not escape.

He lived with her, ate with her, slept with her. Each moment was innocent. Designed that way. Decreed that way. Agreed that way. Yet each movement of hers was a tease to his psyche. A charm to his groin. It mattered not what she did, he wanted to absorb everything she was. Each look, each sigh, each bright, shining laugh.

He was a prisoner to her aura. Worse, to his imaginings.

He could watch her slip into her shoes and long to wrap his fingers around her slim ankles. Slide his hands up her calves, caress her thighs, and open her wide and wet and hot to him. He could glimpse her applying a hand cream she'd bought in the town apothecary shop and long to put his lips around her fingertips. He'd nip them, lick them, and suck her into his rabid desire for her. He could admire how she discussed the fine art of whisking a good custard crème, and instead want to eat her up. Put her to the fine white linen tablecloth, ask the Boyers to quickly depart, and spread her legs and arms out for him like the finest delicacy. There he would entertain her with sweet tales of his boyhood, and woo her with wicked adventures of his manhood. He'd take down her bodice, push aside her corset, trail kisses down her deep cleavage and cup the wealth of her bounteous breasts. He would lave her nipples and stroke her silken stomach, make her writhe and want his mouth on her creamy folds. Pet her engorged pearl and sink inside her sweet—

"Shall we do it?"

He stared at her.

"Ramsey?" She always called to him in an affectionate tone in front of the Boyers. She had paused in the midst of the fairgrounds. People danced around them.

"Of course. Anything you want." Whatever the hell it was, he'd give it to her.

She chastised him with narrowed eyes, then grabbed his hand. "Come along, then. Let's see if you have the skill."

If she only knew what skills he wished to offer her, she would run like a deer from a salivating buck. But those sensuous skills had to die a prompt death, didn't they?

He sighed and went where she led.

She glanced at him. "What roils you?"

Dismayed that she perceived enough of his inner turmoil to ask, he glanced toward the flowing river beyond and frowned. "I wish we were somewhere we could truly enjoy this celebration."

"You think we are not?"

He squeezed her hands in reassurance. "No. We are. I am simply being cautious."

"Good," she said, but she glanced around, her joy in the moment gone.

"The dunking contest." He nodded toward a tall tin water barrel before them. Atop a ledge above the barrel sat a young lad on a rickety woven chair. One young woman below giggled as she taunted him, attesting she was going to hit the swinging ball with her own flat club so that he would splash into the barrel. "Can you hit that moving ball?"

"I'd rather win a stein of beer." Amber pointed just beyond to the archery contest. "There."

"Are you any good?" He paused, hands on his hips.

She narrowed her long-lashed eyes at him. "I am the very best."

He blew out a breath, and beneath it he muttered, "Why should I be surprised?"

"I heard that," she scolded with a playful toss of her head. Today, with the new spring-green gown they'd had sewn by the modiste in Buzancy, she wore no hat. Her wild red curls had grown longer since he found her in Varennes. Today, she'd caught them up in jade ribbons, and in the willowy June breeze, they danced. The look transformed her to be years younger. Beside him, she strolled toward the villagers, who took up the offered bows, quivers, and gloves and stood in line waiting their chance.

Four contenders tried their luck at a time. The crowd encouraged them as they took their places, nocked their bows, and took up the proper stance. Then the chief monitor called the mark, the ready, and the go. The crowd oohed and aahed, then jeered and cheered when one of the latest four appeared to have hit the target more closely to the center. When those four moved off, the four in front of Amber and Ram advanced in line.

Amber craned her elegant neck to see what had been posted at the front. "I say, this contest is popular. The beer must be very good."

"If certain people knew you worked for beer," he said with a pained expression, "they'd have the best laugh."

"If only what you and I did were so easy."

"Full of decisions too complicated to be rewarded with simple alcohol," he complained in a deadly serious tone. Vaillancourt was after her, but once he had her in his grasp, he would press for more, wouldn't he? Fouché was Vaillancourt's superior, ruthless in his professional role, but at heart a family man. He was no fool who'd allow his deputy to keep so valuable a suspected agent as his mistress. So, of course, Amber would die once Vaillancourt grew tired of her. Or Fouché got tired of Vaillancourt.

"There are rewards for what we do," she challenged Ram with a hint of humor. "Big ones. You know it."

He scoffed. "Such as?"

She frowned and turned away from him to finger the protective leather gloves upon the nearby table. Woodsmen had donated them for the competition.

The man in charge of the lineup called for the current four contenders to nock their arrows. The crowd cheered and crowed, scoffing at the losers and yelling congratulations to the winner of that round.

Ram moved forward with Amber into the next group of four who would compete. Why would she consider rewards…unless she debated whether to return to Paris? Was she not telling him everything?

He had to know what drove her allegiance to her cause. Whatever it was, it had to be more than an ethereal devotion to a democracy that seemed as celestial as it was unrealistic here in France.

He took her arm. "Tell me one big reward."

She pressed her lips together, frowning at him. "I would get to foil someone who thinks he is superior, capable of anything, everything."

"Who?"

She glared at him with hell in her eyes. "A rapist."

The way she said it gave him to understand it was she who had been the rapist's victim. "Amber—" he began.

"Do not." She put up a hand. "I will win this. Then we will go to the river and talk."

THE CROWD ENCOURAGED the new set of four. Amber took her place at the end of the group, then on cue she assumed her stance and nocked her first arrow.

Anger clouded her vision. Of course she debated returning to Paris. How Ram perceived that of her had her questioning her ability to mask all her thoughts. He should not be able to understand her so well. But then, they were alike, he and she. Deceivers, actors. Yet honest with each other.

The moderator called the shot.

She let fly her arrow.

The center! All points to her!

She grinned and cast a glance down the targets. No other arrows had landed as perfectly.

She primed the next arrow.

The shot was called.

She pulled, aimed, let loose.

The mark—again—was hers!

Ram stood to one side, his gaze boring into her. She tried to close him out. How dare he worm his way into her consciousness!

The call.

The shot.

Hers, off bull's-eye this time.

Miffed, she turned over her bow, quiver, and gloves. To hell with the beer.

She marched toward the rushing river.

Ram strode beside her.

She felt exposed to him. Safe from others because of him, but suddenly insecure near Ram.

Very.

Yet she needed to be satisfied with him. It was a paradox. She knew not how to live without a proper answer…and she knew not how to serve herself. How to approach him. How to go on.

Big, bold, gentlemanly Ram, who stood as a bulwark against the world, was an enigma. Most men she'd encountered since the age of fifteen were assertive, even aggressive, in putting themselves in her path. They'd announced in no uncertain terms their interest. It was sexual.

They said the most ridiculous things to her. Not "You're lovely" or "Would you care to take a stroll in the garden?" but overt, licentious bits that, when she was young, frightened her.

When she grew older and Aunt Cecily had taught her ways to put down a rabid fellow, Amber became more circumspect. She could smile and, wordlessly, tell the man to give over. She knew how, also courtesy of Aunt Cecily, to subdue a more insistent man by calmly insulting his pride and leaving the scene, public as it most likely had been.

Maurice had exhibited none of those characteristics. At an age double hers, he assumed a paternal attitude toward her when first they met. He had come to Paris to meet other vintners to discuss expanding their markets, and her aunt had invited him to a soiree. She introduced him to Amber that afternoon. On the next one, Maurice saved her from one man who pawed her in Aunt Cecily's garden. Maurice's actions were bold, grabbing the fellow by the scruff and throwing him toward the door. His words to her were paternal...until days later, she had kissed him for his kindness, and his lips returned an emotion priceless in its tenderness.

She had been his wife for a little over a year, suffered the miscarriage of their baby, cried in his arms—and, in time, with him she learned to laugh again. Only last Christmas had he turned ill, taken to his bed, and quietly, relentlessly slipped away from her. Alone she had cried, mourning him until she could not stand or eat, until she did not know her name. Augustine and her aunt had urged her back to health, only for her to return to Society and be accosted by Rene Vaillancourt her first night back. Then, with no respect for the dead, he had pulled her into an empty room and threatened to have her.

"Eventually," he had said, his sly elegance a hellish offense to her grief, "you and all you know will be mine."

She had been warned of the deputy's power. Her aunt saw it and had foretold his interest. For years, Amber had seen his desire for her across many a crowded salon, his long-lashed mercenary eyes riveted to her like a lizard, bold and unwavering even when Maurice was alive. Such arrogance she had never met. Shaken to her core each time, she had avoided his every approach. Then when he had the audacity to stride up to her, a woman still in mourning, she had heard his vehement words—and fled.

Without notice to anyone.

Without regret.

With only self-preservation in mind.

After belonging to a man she adored, her flesh froze at the touch of that man. She'd gone to ice at the probability that he could take her to his bed and afterward, himself replete, take her to a cold, dark room and beat from her the system that had fed Scarlett Hawthorne's British government with the information that could save millions from disaster.

And now, when she had relished the safety given by a paragon of a man, she was foolish to consider—even for a moment—that she was strong enough, stupid enough, to return and withstand the storm that Vaillancourt would bring upon her.

No. She would not go.

Could not.

Here with Godfrey DuClare, Lord Ramsey, twelfth of his line, she would remain.

But how was she to go on with him? Honorable and honest, polite, he was now more distant and such a gentleman. Very much like Maurice, but then not at all.

Ram was quite extraordinary. One day, if she ever had the opportunity, she must thank Scarlett Hawthorne for her assignment of this man to her survival.

If indeed that did occur.

It won't. I might die at this espionage business.

And, for protecting me, Ram too.

But Ram must live. I will see to it. Somehow…

Meanwhile, I will learn to live with my own guilt for having left the service I was so proud of.

Live for each day, Maurice had whispered to her as he lay dying.

And today was for living. This moment. With this man.

She took the path to the river. It wended this way and that, the rustle of the leaves in the lush forest like a symphony of tiny violins urging her onward. As those sounds blended with the tinkle of the river as it gushed upon the shore, she felt delightful shivers enliven her. The banks of the Meuse spread gently down. She stopped feet away from the sparkling, curling waters.

She sat, removing her slippers and her stockings. The gown she wore today was one of those from Buzancy, and she did not want to ruin it. Nothing for it, then—she would have to hike up her gown.

She bit her lip, knowing she would display her bare calves, a thing not done by true ladies. But then, she was a woman—a widow, too—who had not upheld propriety in her actions, wasn't she? She was a spy, an agent for the British Crown. She could show a little leg. Her poor partner—agent for the Crown that he was—would have to bear it.

She would push the boundaries of their relationship.

"You are fortunate you can lift up your skirts." He stood beside her, assessing the river rushing past.

"You could remove your breeches," she said with a toss of her hair.

He crossed his arms and peered down his perfect, straight nose at her.

She giggled. "Come in. Remove your boots. Roll up your breeches. You need the refreshment!" She beckoned him with her fingers and gave him a wink. *Oh, I am bad.*

He scoffed, but in those well-fitting breeches his accoutrements bulged beautifully.

She widened her eyes at him. "No pillow at hand here, sir!"

He blushed—and she adored the boy who lived in him that he would honor her so. Then he sat down on a log. "None!"

She threw back her head to chuckle. "Impressive!"

"Go." He indicated the river. "Get in and stop baiting me."

She lifted her skirts and deliberately gave him a view of her legs, from knees to bare feet. "I want to be fair."

"Well," he said, his gaze locked on her ankles, "that ship sailed long ago."

"Have you had many women?" she blurted, taking a few steps to let her toes freeze in the water. She had lost sight of him as she walked, surprised and yet not, at the gush of her own desire for him warm and wet between her folds.

"Enough to know what I am about. And what I am not."

"You are not about anything lately." He had not made any advances on her. Only that one reference to him pleasuring himself. She must not continue with this dialogue.

"By necessity, madame."

"Thank you for that," she said so softly that she wondered if he heard.

He did not respond.

She dared not turn to look at him, but she did want to know more about him. His past, his personal affairs.

"Have you had many men?" he asked her, closer behind her than she expected, his tone wistful, demanding.

"That's fair," she said as she stepped into the bracing water that flowed between her legs. "No. I had only my husband, Maurice."

"I have enjoyed the pleasure of a few ladies."

She smiled to herself. "No wives?"

"None."

"No permanent lovers?"

"None now. In the past, I had one lady, but when I came abroad, of necessity we parted. I wrote a generous pension. She was a very congenial companion, sorry to see me leave."

Amber walked gingerly further into the river, the bottom covered in smooth stones. The cool current added to a new rush of wet desire for him. And yet to want him, to have him, would be so wrong, so against their agreement and the necessity for clarity in what they must do together.

She turned, walking along the grass away from the river and him.

That she was committed to dealing with her guilt for leaving Paris meant she would wander the earth. He could not, would not be, by her side forever. A lifetime of protecting her was too much to ask. At some point, she would let him go, encourage him to leave her.

Now, today, she wanted him. If her desire was simple female lust, she could accept that in herself. She had found immense pleasure in it with Maurice.

But she feared that to want this man meant she might also need him as hers, as permanently as she had needed Maurice.

The price here was higher, harder to pay, yet as needy as she was, she would not lie to herself. She stopped and put her hands to her cheeks. The sun was not that hot. Her body was. To have him would be so...easy. To deny herself his loving again and again would not be.

For she knew, just as a wild cat in heat knows when a male tracks her, Ram desired her.

Facing away from him, she also knew it was right to give him only a portion of what he wanted. Answers to who and what she really was. And why. And so she said, "You asked me before what keeps me devoted to my work."

She felt his warmth as he came up behind her. She squeezed her thighs together in abject want. She had the urge to turn, embrace him, and follow the demands of desire pulsing in her belly. To have him fill her would be the satisfaction she needed.

And so unfair to him.

To me, as well. Taking from him more than he should give.

His arms went around her, and he pressed his body, big and strong, to her back, his cock, long and turgid, against her derriere. She let out her breath, at ease, at her leisure, in his embrace.

"Tell me, then." His voice could melt her. His gruff tones, so resonant with care, bored into her lonely heart like a flaming iron through a block of ice. "Help me understand you."

"My aunt always kept me safe. I never knew what terror was, what nightmares could come to a girl from others. I had no parents. Not really. I remember them hardly at all. Just my aunt saving me at nine. My aunt, always there, always ready with a smile, help, a golden word."

He settled her backward more comfortably. His lips nestled near her ear, his words moist breaths of compassion on her tender flesh. "What happened?"

"Carmes."

He grunted. "Someone hurt you."

Not a question, a statement. But it was wrong.

"Not me. Dear God, no. Not me. But one I did not know very well but whom I saw beaten to death." She gulped to keep the horror down. To speak of the beatings, the rapes, turned her stomach. To speak of how Vaillancourt had stood by watching the brutal death of young Diane Massey was hideous. She deflected to the subject that was less upsetting. "My aunt saved me from the guards. Greedy, insatiable men who took the post to take what they could from women caught in a net. Tangled, stuck. It was…"

He squeezed her tightly to him.

She sighed, her head falling back, her neck arching. My, how she wanted him. Her belly quivered.

He dipped his head and put his mouth to the spot behind her ear. His attitude was reverent, nigh unto a benediction. Tears scalded her eyes as she realized he did not know how her body pulsed to have him inside her. "Tell me nothing, my sweet woman. I should not have asked. I wish not to terrorize you or to make you remember."

He turned the talk from her craving for him to her reason to spy. She shook her head. She was saved. She was damned.

"Many men behind the consulate collaborated with those during the Terror who put innocents in prisons, like Carmes. Barras, Talleyrand, Fouché, and Vaillancourt."

"I suspected," he whispered.

"What happened to everyone in Carmes should not go unpunished. To men and women. To my friends… And most people have no means to do so. But I can." She spun in his arms. "You know as well as I that if all power is given to one man or a few, they grow fat on it."

He pushed her hair from her cheeks and lifted her chin. But his gaze was on her lips. "I do," he breathed.

"You are noble to help me."

"Am I?" He gave a sad little laugh. "Like you, I have my motivation."

"To aid your own network—to protect me."

Now his magnetic blue eyes held to hers. "From others. All others."

"But now?" What did she ask? She should not venture into his mind, his secrets. Men's thoughts were dangerous, and she knew it so well. She had much evidence.

He cupped her cheeks, stroking her skin and thrumming her senses. "My first duty was to guard you. Now it is to save you, and I do believe that means to save you from yourself."

The tears that had burned her eyes escaped her lashes. "Are you telling me we cannot run forever?"

"Sweetheart, you know we can't."

His endearment filled her with a thirst to reply in kind. Yet she could not lead him on. She was now a woman without a cause. One only on the run. "But what else is there for me?"

He inhaled and wrapped her close, her head against his mighty shoulder, his big hand splayed into her hair. "Freedom."

"Boredom," she shot back.

"You would be useful to others with your knowledge of people, customs, language, and the turn of events."

She blinked, struck with the novel idea. "Far away? What good would I do?"

"Much."

"You are so sure," she chided him.

"Look what we have accomplished here. What we could do elsewhere."

"No," she insisted. She would not tie him to her forever and see him die because of it.

"Then Sedan! Verdun," he offered.

"No."

"Karlsruhe."

"No!"

He set his jaw. "Even the Rhine, Amsterdam. London!"

She shook her head. "I don't want to go. I have no one in any of those places. No friends. No family."

"You will have me." He pointed to himself.

I must not take you for such simple emotions as fear or gratitude. "I cannot live off your grace and favor."

"Why not? I am a man of circumstance. I can give all that I have."

His words, so reminiscent of his mother's definition of love, thrilled her—and sent dismay through her.

Ram could not love her. Should not. A woman adrift from herself, she would be his ruin. "You are too generous."

He flinched. "Think on it."

She had insulted him, and in small compensation, she hugged him closer.

He planted a kiss to her forehead. "But for now, we will return to the Boyers' house and dress for dinner."

                              Chapter Eight

T HE FESTIVAL BALL that night began as the mayor took to the
makeshift stage and the village orchestra opened with a
country dance. All in the Boyer family plus their servants, Ram,
and Amber had walked to the center of town at dusk and taken a
table among others around the dance floor. The square glowed
with the fires from huge braziers set at the periphery of the green.

Ram took Amber out for the first dance, and she felt new
warmth flow through her. But she knew it was not the flames
from the braziers that ignited her. The serenity that flowed
through her like honey was Ram.

His tenderness toward her. His words of compassion. His
restraint.

Their minutes by the river this afternoon had been an idyll.
She'd needed the time to confide in him. The memory of other
girls and women being raped and beaten by Carmes's guards was
one she had denied herself for years. She had never uttered the
words to anyone. Maurice had probed for the cause of her
collaboration with the team of agents, but she had told him
nothing. He had known she engaged in the transfer of sensitive
information to spies for the British, but he had not directly asked
her for details. Nor had she spontaneously given them.

Revealing her justification to Ram was unusual for her. An

agent himself, what did her own reasons matter? She simply acted. The same as he, she discovered new information and transferred it. Yet somehow that he knew her motivation was a comfort to her.

She would have gone on forever in her role reporting to her superior as long as necessary, too, if Rene Vaillancourt had not taken an unnerving interest in her. But he had, and in it was more inspiration to defy those who would grab power for themselves at all costs.

All of that had brought her to this sweet moment, this charming town—and this enchanting man.

AFTER THE FIRST set, she and Ram had parted to do their social duty and dance with others. The man who was her protector and guide was a gentleman who would command any ballroom. So tall and dark and convivial, her Ram was a scrumptious devil whom many a girl would crave to have as a beau, or husband, or lover.

I do.

Stunned, she stared at him. It was true. She could want him as her own, if she dared to give up all.

But have you not already done that?

No. No, I have not.

The truth rubbed her raw, and she twirled away to find wine and distraction.

MAYOR CHARLES DEJEAN was no dancer. His sense of rhythm and timing had deserted him long ago, and Amber's toes bore the brunt of those years. He surrendered her to Edouard Boyer, who had more grace as a youth than many a man could ever acquire.

Amber loved dancing with the boy. The two Boyer girls applauded, and when they took to the dance boards, it was clear they too were able dancers.

Throughout it all, Amber would find her eyes on Ram. She kept comparing him to Maurice.

Never were two men more unlike each other. Maurice, soft-spoken, mild, deliberative. A stylish man who tenderly cared for his library, his old chateau, and the rolling hills of his Champagne vineyards. More than twice her age, Maurice had been tempered by the loss of his first wife and viewed his love for Amber through the prism of welcome accidents and complex ironies of life. He had urged her to temper her work—"whatever its necessities"—through the perspective "of the long years you will live."

She'd tried. Ever since she left Paris, she had tried. Now that she had the assistance of this very unique Englishman, she could allow herself a glimpse of what else her long years might offer her. In his world, dancing in a gilded ballroom. In his care, embracing with abandon the safety he provided. In his arms, taking and giving what pleasures they could give each other.

Of all her visions, that last was one that was most possible. Most appealing. In its power to mesmerize her, the promised ecstasy of making love to Ram played in her head like a rhapsody that repeated over and over again. Yet an affair with him implied she would never go back to Paris. In her heart, she hated to let that hope die.

She should not have him. Not now. Not even once. It would be unfair to him. Even though he wanted her, sleeping on the floor, suffering frustrations, avoiding touching her in their bed. He did not make a habit of taking women to his bed. There was no good reason why he should take her.

She sighed as she watched him take another lady to the floor for a country dance. With her every breath she yearned to be that woman at that moment.

He was suave, educated, and oh so manly. Why had he not found anyone to love? In Britain, he had estates and money. He had told her details of his holdings and his family treasures. They included a storied collection of English, Delft, and even Chinese Ming porcelain. She was a connoisseur of fine china, searching in her free time for valuable pieces from Sèvres and the old, small factory up in Montmartre. What was it like, she often wondered, to have time to sit and ponder the origins of such beautiful pieces? She had no idea. Her life had been taken up with the need to save others…and to avenge their torture and loss.

Intriguing that Ram had that time, that possibility of money and leisure, and found time to treasure such things. Yet he was here, doing the same job she was. Saving others.

Saving me.

"Madame." The young friend of Edouard sat down beside her on the bench. "May I get you a wine or cider?"

"*Oui, merci*, Allard. Cider, *s'il vous plaît*." She'd enjoyed three mugs of the local white tonight. She needed no more. Her turn of mind to the fancy of china, Ram's English possessions, and his allure was enough to warn her off another serving.

When the boy returned, she sipped her apple cider and asked him about his future plans. "Do you go with Edouard to Paris to the university?"

"I wish to go, but my mother is ill. She was the village teacher and cannot work any longer. I must go to work at the factory."

"Have you applied, Allard? I understand they need more laborers."

"*Oui*, madame. I was to start last week, but the new director said I must wait for five new men from Mauberge to come."

"Oh?" She was keen to hear that news. "Why are they so important?"

"They understand a way to shorten the time to perform some method during production of the stock." He winced and glanced away, a frown on his young face, unhappy with his lot. "Those five from Mauberge will teach all the new workers their methods. Speed, the director told me, is what they need most to fulfill the orders for new muskets."

"I see."

"I don't want to work there."

Amber stared down into her earthen cup. Sorrow for his lot swept through her.

"But it's better than the army," he added.

"I would say so, Allard, *oui*."

"New conscripts are being called up."

"Here in town?"

He nodded, dismal at the prospect. "We're producing new guns for fresh soldiers so they can go off and kill and maim each other."

She wished she could conjure a comment to soothe him.

"All our guns are going to Sedan, where conscripts from here will train."

Is that right? Sedan, eh? She took a sip of her cider. She must tell Ram. He would love to know that news.

"The government is fortifying the border for war. Word is they sent the last shipment of muskets to Sedan, too. They must expect an invasion from the German states that don't yet ally with Bonaparte."

The boy was very smart, very attuned to the news that many German princes and margraves of small territories were signing treaties with the French, breaking with Austria.

"You may be right," she prevaricated. Better to agree with him and appear an addlepated woman than tell him all she knew of rulers like those of Baden and Württemberg, who conscripted their citizens for the French and even taxed them to give the proceeds to Bonaparte as a gift.

"Would you like to dance again, madame?" Allard had finished his wine.

"No, *merci*, Allard. Go ask a nice young girl to go to the floor with you. I await my husband."

Ram was dancing with yet another older lady of the town.

And Amber waited, her mind racing.

Bonaparte. What does he plan?

He already had hundreds of thousands under arms. Conscription numbers had been high since the directorate began. Each family had at least one male in uniform. To outfit each of them with one musket was one thing, but if weapons numbers were also increased at Mauberge and the other armory of St. Etienne in the south, that meant someone predicted a use for them.

Since the country was not at war, the new guns were ostensibly to replace those lost to mishap. That number had to be minimal.

If Bonaparte's government had ordered an increase in numbers of muskets, the consulate had ambitions to use those muskets.

The first consul was going to war.

She stood, bursting to tell Ram.

RAM WATCHED HER dance with Georges, and later with the man's son. Then he seemed to have lost her for a long while. He liked watching her, agile and elegant Amber. The country sets Ram usually pranced to at Almack's were more sedate than these French roundelays. He seethed with ridiculous jealousy. Their hands on her should be his hands. Their smile should be his. Their joy all his.

Christ, he was quite mad.

He left the edge of the makeshift floor that the local folk and he had assembled on the grass. Seeking out a strong, good red wine, he put coin on the rough bar of the local vintner. The mug he got was tall and full. He drank far too quickly to taste it.

"You must sip it, monsieur." A comely brunette glided up next to him. Her long lashes fluttering in dismay, she reprimanded him with a tsk. "The *vin* does not run away."

He had no reason to be rude, so he smiled at her, even if his effort was halfhearted.

"Your wife enjoys herself. You should, too."

He regarded the young with knitted brows. "She deserves to do it."

"Are you so hard to live with?"

"*Oui*, mademoiselle." He noted she wore no rings and then drained the remains of his wine. "I am terrible."

"Do you not make her happy?"

"Nor myself."

"Regrettable. What is life for, if you do not seize the day…or the night?"

He snorted in laughter. "For one so young, mademoiselle, you are ancient in wisdom."

She drank from her own mug. "I am. You should make her notice you."

"She does. Sadly."

"But not enough, eh?" She put her mug on the counter and took his from his hand. "Come, then. My name is Josette, and we are new friends."

She led him to the floor, and they joined a set. She was twenty at most, pretty and lively. At the end of their prancing, she curtsied and he bowed to her.

"I think we have done good work," she said beneath her breath.

Beside him appeared Amber.

"You have a new friend, *mon amour?*" she asked, her face glowing from her own exertions.

"I do. Allow me to present Mademoiselle Josette, whose family name I did not learn. My Amber," he said, forgetting himself as he caught the jealousy in Amber's brown eyes. "My wife."

Josette did the polite thing and offered a small nod of respect. "Your husband is a good dancer, madame. You should take care of him. He pines for you."

Then she was gone.

Bah! That's all I need. Someone else to work on her. What am I? A boy?

He spun away, furious.

"Wait! Ram!" Amber scurried to catch up with him and caught his arm.

"I'm going home." He faced her but did not look down at her. "You must follow. But do *not* talk to me."

"Why…why not?" She sounded like a fishwife. That pleased him, but he plodded onward.

No one else was in the lane to overhear how she called his name and ran toward him. "What did I do, Ram? Dance? You did, too!"

He did look down at her then. This ravishingly gorgeous creature in the sylvan shadows of the moon. She was everything he desired in a woman and was nothing he would ever have. Silently he cursed himself, then turned on his heel, and off he went.

He was three steps away when she tugged at his sleeve. "You're being mean."

He did not stop. "I am."

"And pigheaded."

He kept walking. "Not *me*."

"Very well. *I* am! *I* am!"

He shook his head. *Let her stew.* He stormed down the lane that led to the Boyers' house. Then he heard her running up behind him.

She pranced beside him. "I will not go to London."

"Good for you."

"I won't live off you."

That was a pitiful argument. "Fine."

She ran in front of him and put out a hand to hold him back. "I'll go to Sedan."

"Sedan! Really? Why not say that louder and tell the world?" he groused, bitter that her statement solved only one of their problems.

"That's what you wanted from me! There is a reason—"

"Wonderful." He walked around her.

"Don't you want to know? No? Well…stop! Listen to me. I do *not* want to tell the world this bit."

He halted and flapped his arms at his sides. "What?"

She walked right up to him, her breasts spilling from that blue silk, heaving and gilded by the moonlight. "Edouard's young friend says the new muskets are going to Sedan."

His face fell. "Good to know." After a moment's consideration, he marched on.

"Wait! Ram! Stop. We must go to Sedan!"

He scowled, then walked around her.

She ran in front of him again.

He stepped to one side.

"Sedan, Ram. I will go to Sedan. You too."

"Really? How wonderful. But in reality, my darling, it changes nothing."

"Because I won't go to London? Or…or all those other places?"

He whirled on her, an arm out, anger in every growl. "*Oui,* madame! Because I can't leave. Because you won't go. Because the night is long and my temper short. Because I am a man who needs to go swimming in the river, and *you*"—he poked a finger at her—"cannot follow."

She looked as if he'd struck her. "I… But… It's night. Not safe."

He spun away and back again, so quickly that she teetered on her feet.

He caught her arms and held her against him. Every sensuous muscle in her supple body rubbed against his. Damn his chivalry!

"*This* is not safe. *This!*" He crushed her against him. "And this!" He jammed one hand up into the thick curls of her hair and, with the other hand, found her arse, plump and hard. "And this," he whispered against her lush lips, brushing them with the most innocent kiss and prying them open to explore all of her with his tongue.

※※※✳※※※

SHE MELTED INTO his embrace as his tongue seized every bit of her mouth.

He lifted away. She hung there in his arms while he squinted at her in the moonlight as if she were a stranger who had shocked him with her presence.

That was exactly what he had been to her. A stranger become friend. A friend who was now dearer. Necessary to her.

Fighting for logic as he took her lips again, she went, lost in the music of sweet security he alone brought her. The rhapsody he created played in her head like a score of violins leading to freedom. Cares gone, love embraced, she drew him closer. Why could he not be her lover? She could not remember, did not want to. She only knew that to clutch him close and sink her fingers in his long, silken hair was assurance of ecstasy. And she had not had that in so very long.

He gave it freely. Always had.

"There is no rule," she murmured to him when he raised his face. "No reason to this."

"True." He let her go so quickly, she struggled to find her balance again, waving her arms in the air.

He steadied her…and left her.

She would not let him go angry and without resolution.

Amber ran and caught him, seized him by his frock coat, and rose on her toes. Her arms around his shoulders, she looped a leg around one of his thighs and nearly climbed him like a cat. He was *hers*. She was his and she'd *have* him. His anguish, his need, matched her own.

And *oh. Ohh.* He felt like every lovely sentiment he'd ever spoken to her. *Allow me to protect you, defend you, guard you from all harm.*

She stared up at him. "Let me," she begged him. "Please let me kiss you. I yearn…"

His face went lax with want, his eyes shimmering with hunger in the translucent light of the moon.

"I want you, Ram. I do."

He did not budge, but waited as she smiled at him, two tears running down her cheeks, and stretched up to claim him once more.

His lips were sublimely warm and firm, his mouth as wide and as generous as she'd imagined. He tasted of red wine and smelled of citrus and sweat. He held her with urgent passion, and shook with a raw hunger that shocked her.

This was real, right—Ram was hers.

✦ ❧ ✦

Chapter Nine

T HEY RAN LIKE children to the house, hand in hand, up the stairs, down the hall to their rooms. Each step jogged more and more sense into him.

He reached their door first, flung it open, and whirled her inside.

She was laughing as he slammed the door shut and fell back against it, drawing her toward him.

She danced forward, a vision from heaven. In the flickering candlelight from the wall sconces, she fluttered before him like an angel in that pale-blue gown.

How could he do this with her? He'd be a cad to take her when he was here only to keep her safe. *Even from me.*

Her smile died as she gazed at him, knowledge of his rejection in her eyes. "You question this."

He shook his head, frowning, then cupped her gorgeous face in both his hands. "It has consequences."

"Yes," she whispered, mashing her supple body to his in an urgent plea. In her undulations, he nearly went to his knees as his cock pressed hard and hot against her belly. "Pleasure."

"Pregnancy."

She blinked, surprise in her eyes. "No, I—"

"I want you too much, and I fear I will not be so controlled with you that I can stop when I should. Even then, it may not be enough."

Desperation on her face, she grabbed his cravat and twisted the ends in her fingers. "You don't need to stop."

"I do!" he growled. "If you were pregnant, do you think I'd want you to remain in France wandering, waiting for one night, one morning, when Vaillancourt finds you?"

"I don't wait for him."

"What for, then? Eh?" He clutched her, giving her a little shake. "Pregnant, mine or not, you won't leave France!"

She gave him the endearing smile of a woman who wanted to be ravished. "He cannot find me. Cannot have me. I am with you."

"Oh, my darling." He shook his head, his heart drowning in a sea of misery. "Be sensible. I am your guard, your protector. I am vigilant, but if he finds us, he can be wily, unpredictable. I am no fool, my sweet woman—and, at best, only one man to fight off dozens. Nor am I a tyrant to force you against your will to leave France. Not even, God help me, a magician to spirit you away with a snap of my fingers!"

She tugged him closer, her hard nipples boring into his chest, evidence of her desire for him.

Hopeless, he could not pull away.

"Sweet Ram." She cupped his cheek. "Fear not. Have me as you will. You cannot make me pregnant."

He winced, confused. "That is exactly—"

"No, Ram." She combed his hair from his furrowed brow. "Listen to me. I cannot have children."

"But you said you had been pregnant."

"And I lost the child." Her brown eyes turned solemnly umber in the shadows of the room.

He crushed her to him. How could he do this and not hate himself afterward? "Sweetheart, you've had so many tragedies in your life. I will not add to them. Certainly not by making love to you."

There. He'd used the word that had brooded at the edge of his consciousness. He did love her. Her strength, her resilience. Her dedication. No woman in the world matched her.

But she shook her head to and fro. "Ramsey, darling. Stop. Hear me. I was damaged in the miscarriage, and the physician said I would never bear another child."

He kissed the top of her head, her hair like gossamer against his lips. Her breasts a plush invitation. Her long, lean legs against his, the lure he could not resist.

She nestled close and raised her heart-shaped face to him. "You are what I want tonight. For the joy of us united. For the passion, incomparable. I know we will be perfection."

Part of her statement he believed. All of her was what he wanted. For tonight and for any of the tomorrows he could persuade her to stay with him.

Oh, yes, it was clear to him he could not coax her to do anything she did not first accept for herself. If he now became an opportunist who took when he should refuse, then he would be the one tarnished—and justly so. But he wanted to show her his regard and needed in return all the vibrance of her in his arms. So he would take her for the time he could. Enjoy her for all the hours she gave him. Devote himself to loving each inch of her delectable body and her valiant soul.

He could do all that and hope that in some tomorrow he could not name, she decided that living was a proper choice—and living with him was the best choice. If he were extraordinarily lucky, he could also allow himself to hope that he might be worthy of her love—and that he was all she ever needed to fulfill her life.

"Oh, Ramsey, forget about what separates us and let us create new reasons to remain together. Make love to me."

Her invitation broke him. He sank his fingers into the blue silk sleeves of her gown and slid them down her shoulders. All of her tonight, he would have and hold and celebrate. Tomorrow, she could change, dismiss him, find the fault in all of this. But for now, he was weak enough to take what she offered and hope what he returned would ease the burden of her cares. He knew certainly that what he did now would never change who she was or what she really wanted from her life.

But this was tonight, and the next vibrant hours held promises of bliss they could share to ease the burden of the days ahead. He would make love to her and pray she did not recognize the fullness of his sentiment. For he knew her well enough to realize that once she saw he loved her, she would leave him. Her sense of fairness would demand she go. That she did not love him mattered less to him than that he loved her, now and always. And so he'd have her.

He grinned at her as he traced his fingers along the edge of her bodice. Those beautiful breasts he had dreamed of would be his. He glanced down at her breaths expanding the lovely globes of her breasts beneath his fingertips. He bent, holding her still as he swept the tip of his tongue over the heaving tops and dipped into the valley. Her hands went to the buttons of his frock coat and his waistcoat. Her eager fingers shook, and she did a poor job of unbuttoning his clothes. That was fine. He had time. Long minutes, hours to savor every inch of her. He had helped her undress every night for the past few weeks. Tonight would not be a problem. He had patience even if his cock did not.

"Toe off your slippers," he murmured beneath her ear.

She wiggled beneath his hands and lips. "I rather like my stockings."

"Nice, they are," he said of the white fine clockwork he'd bought her in Buzancy. "Leave them on."

She shivered. "You'll remove them," she said, an order and a hope.

"I will." He nipped her earlobe. "With my teeth."

She went still and cupped his throat. Her eyes were wide and black with lust. "I want your tongue."

"Turn around." He chuckled. What else could he do without tearing the clothes from her? "You tell me all you want, and I promise you, you will have it until I no longer breathe."

She rose and pressed her lips to his in a frantic kiss with a need he'd never known from a woman.

He caught her shoulders. She shook back her bouncing curls, and he swept her around to the wall. His body flush to hers, he filled his hands with the bounty of her breasts. It was enough to test the resilience of his cock. He set his jaw. "Listen to me, my darling tease. Let me undress you or we will have each other too quick, too faint, standing against this damn wall."

"The gown is Sophie's," she said.

"I know," he replied, and worked carefully. But agility deserted him. His fingers felt like sausages, fumbling and crude. He was full of nerves, a schoolboy—and he bit off a curse.

At last her gown fell open.

"Step out."

She did, and he swept the pale silk to the safety of a nearby chair.

He scowled, eyeing her corset cover. He had to lift that away now. "God in heaven, women wear too many contraptions."

"All meant to keep a girl warm—and lonely," she murmured, shaking with her laughter.

"A good job of it—fie on it all." He struggled.

She wiggled, giving a laugh he did not share. "Hurry."

"I would, my dear," he grumbled, "if you would not grind your pretty arse into my cock!"

She giggled into the wood of the wall. The one eye she had trained on him winked, and, inspired, he got the corset to fall away. Then he spun her around, and this time, he shared her chuckle.

In a flash, she crossed her arms and tore off her chemise.

The shock of her naked, the beauty of all that perfect skin, stopped him cold. His arms at his sides, he could do naught but stare at all the riches bared before him and shrouded in the shadows. Tomorrow in the daylight, he hoped she still cared enough to allow him the full pleasure of her bare splendor. He would treasure and taste her, feast on and thrill her so that she never forgot him. "Christ," he murmured, spellbound, "what am I to do with all this?"

"Love me," she whispered, and stepped forward to fit all that magnificent beauty against him. Her arms around his shoulders, her breasts huge, her nipples hard, her hips flat against his poor, confined, and begging cock, she rubbed her nose along his jaw and up across his cheek to plant tiny kisses on his lips.

She fit him like a puzzle. Plane to plane, arc to arc, round breasts boring into the many layers of his own clothing.

"You feel wonderful," she whispered. She wrapped her arms around his waist and sank further into his embrace.

Oh, he loved her. Had he not for days, for weeks now?

He could bear no more. He sank to his knees. His arms around her hips and thighs, he nuzzled her bare stomach, and her knees buckled and she would have swooned from her joy of it.

But he had her. She gasped as he spread kisses over the skin above her thatch. She sank her fingers in his hair and twisted. Smiling to himself, he kissed her belly until she squealed. Gasping, she trailed her nails against his scalp. He'd be bald, but he'd love her like this for the next century. What did he care for hair when he could savor her crying his name as he loved her?

He needed more, so stood, upended her, and threw her over his shoulder.

She was chuckling and pinching his ass while he strode to their bedroom and the bed that, up until now, had gotten no good use. Tonight, they would fill it with every fond regard he had for her, and she for him.

At the side of the bed, turned down by their maid while they were at the ball, he stood her up.

He paused, a man caught in time. Now in more light from the lit sconces, he stood still, stunned, reverent of the sight before him. Such beauty humbled him. And he was deaf to the words she uttered, dumb to any frail response he could make.

He had long admired the cut of her silhouette. In form, she

was a tall woman with bounteous breasts, fine waist, and long, lean legs.

But standing before him only in her skin and those white stockings, she was the epitome of every woman. Her skin was pale, a red-head's porcelain perfection. Her breasts were large, her huge nipples glossy and faintly pink, hard, and pointed at him in her excitement. Her waist flared at her hips; her thighs were sinuous. The legs he had imagined were trim from riding and dancing were also so nimble that, outside in the road, she had wrapped one around his own.

His mouth watered. His arms ached. His cock strained his breeches. He was a mess of a man, paralyzed by the beauty he dared to take in his arms and hope he could show her how he valued her there.

Her eyes narrowed on him in question, then she reached out and her breasts jiggled. She undid his flies, and his cock could not take the torment.

Impulsively, he stepped backward and found the chair, yanked off his boots and socks, and went back to her. He took her hands and put them to the buttons of his flies. "Be aware, my girl, that I don't want to be sixty when this happens."

Defiant but smiling, she undid each button with a deliberate, slow twist of her fingers. But in a blink, he was standing, his breeches around his ankles.

"Good work," he said as he stepped out of them.

She grinned, her hands on her hips as she appraised his standing penis. "I think you'll do well no matter your age."

"Madam," he said as he pointed toward the bed, "I grow gray waiting for you. Get up there."

She scrambled up on the bed like an eager child. Then she spread herself out on the ivory linens, her arms up, beseeching him to fill them.

He stood, memorizing the moment when the woman he adored was welcoming him to take what he had yearned for— and what he had feared she would never grant.

He loved her.
She wanted him.
For tonight, desire was all she gave.
For tonight, that was enough.

SHE WAS BEING so unfair to him. Chiding him to make love to her. But she was starving for him, and he had so many doubts she had to erase.

Her gaze met his. "You stop again?" she asked.

He smiled, though she did not feel his mirth. He reared back on his knees and took a long, satisfying look at her in her nakedness. "I wish to remember you like this."

She knew what she looked like. Maurice had often delighted in admiring her naked, flat on her back, or posing before him in one of her cheval mirrors. From her riot of flame-red hair to the sculpted lines of her heart-shaped face, to her full lips and neat chin, she had known from age fifteen she possessed the licentious looks of a lady of the night. Her height, her long neck, her heavy breasts and large nipples—all created the picture of a woman who welcomed a man to enjoy her.

Maurice had loved each inch of her, with hands and mouth and cock. In none of that was any shame, he said, but a celebration of the human rite of mating. Though he knew she was a virgin when he first had her, he had educated her slowly and persuaded her to show and tell him whatever she preferred of his caresses. Through hot hours of pleasure in his arms, he had taught her that making love was an art. A couple had to work for their full joy in mating. Now with Ram, she was more than eager to take and give whatever she could to ensure he had his fill of her...and she of him.

Still, he hesitated—and she could not bear the wait nor his questioning of what they did. She took his hand and led him to cover her breast. Beneath his hot touch, her flesh swelled. She pushed his fingers to her ribs, her waist, to her wide hips and to the curve of one inner thigh. His molten blue eyes met hers as he threaded his fingers through her thatch of hair. She undulated, straining for more of the heat of his possession.

"You are so beautiful, and I hate the lack of candlelight," he whispered as his tender fingertips played amid her curls.

"Tomorrow in light of day, I will still be yours," she assured him.

The glance he gave her told her he welcomed that statement. "I should not rush, then?"

"Take all of me. I do want all of you, darling Ram."

He tugged at her hair, and she opened her legs wider.

He made an animal sound in the back of his throat.

❧※❧

WHAT FEW BRIGHT flames the sconces cast off, he would do with tonight. If he were fortunate enough to enjoy her still tomorrow, he would feast on the sight of her then. For this moment, he would taste her and thrill her so she never forgot him.

He'd take his time, imprint her on his soul to savor for years to come. He was done waiting, wanting, pining. She was his gorgeous work, his irresistible woman, and he sent his open palms down her heavy breasts. He lifted both, kissed one nipple, then sucked lavishly the other.

She hummed her delight, and he plucked her nipple as he wended his mouth down her ribs to spread kisses across her stomach.

He sank to his knees and inhaled the sweet fragrance of her desire for him. With a touch to each thigh, he crooned, "Open your legs, darling."

Her stomach quivering at his command, she did as he asked.

He threaded his fingers through her damp curls. "Wider," he

whispered, and she obeyed, tilting up her hips toward him. "Such a good woman, you are," he told her in the silence of the night, where the only sound he heard was her whimper telling him that she approved of his fingers sliding inside her.

Her folds were heavy, slick, and warm. He parted her with ease, found the essence of her with his searching fingers, and bent to draw her pearly sweetness into his mouth. With his lips around her little nub, he flicked his tongue around her so she thrashed in a throbbing bliss. Her cries of delight spurred him on to more.

He rose, proud and eager, his breathless lover with her dark, reverent eyes upon him. He took his cock in hand. He glanced down, placed himself at her entrance, and sank slowly, deeply, sweetly inside.

His eyes closed. His heart surged. She was his. Tight, hot, and wet.

She groaned and wrapped her legs around his hips. She had him captured, hers, spellbound. He was in, lost to her, found in her.

Instinct flooded him. He thrust into her and began a rhythm that left him blind to all but her and how she fast held him. The glorious end came with moans of delight and sighs as they collapsed into each other's care.

⫸⫷

THEIR LEGS ENTWINED, his arms about her, one hand claiming one breast, she grinned and kissed his chest.

He chuckled—and she felt his joy ripple through her own body like an erotic invitation to more loving.

Loath to separate from him, she hugged him closer. "In bed each night before you realized I was against you, I felt the wonder of your body against mine."

"I knew," he admitted. "I was a rogue and dallied there longer than I should have."

She put a kiss to his cheek. "You are no rogue to me."

"I wanted to be a perfect gentleman. What we have done here tonight shatters that façade like the glass it was. I would not have you scorn me later for this."

She put her hand to his jaw. "Ram, never will I criticize you for this. I am many things, dear man, but I am no coy girl who changes her views of her lovers with the change in the wind."

"I did not mean you are—"

"I know you didn't. You wish only to quell your fear. I didn't take you easily. You are only my second lover."

He sank his nails into the skin of her arms. "My darling woman, I want you however you wish to come to me."

For lust. She gave him a watery smile, admitting that she came to him for the same reason. Of that, she was not proud. "I am grateful." He would take her for what she gave. To seek more would not serve him well—and he knew it. What he did not know was that her desire for him held so much more than mere wanting. And that yearning grew tonight with each moment.

She shook her head, running out the budding idea that if she could leave France, she could love him, need him, and aspire to years of blissful peace with him.

She held her breath, hoping that he was so instinctive that he could imbibe that in his touch. As he crawled up from the foot of the bed to hover over her, she panicked. But his warmth spread through her like fire. She ran her open palms over his sculpted chest and sighed. Against her hip, she felt his renewed interest in loving her. "You are the most marvelous creature." *Selfless and honorable.*

At such praise, he laughed. Humility, she'd learned, was one of his assets.

She drew him down to cover her. The thrill of his skin to hers was exquisite torture.

He supported himself on his elbows as he dropped kisses to her cheek, her throat, and the hollow between her breasts. He cupped each breast and laved one nipple to ripe, aching torment, then took the other to do the same. "I cannot stop. I must taste each inch of you."

She squirmed, alive beneath his homage. Her arms around his back, she arched up against him and sought to encompass all his strength and ardor. But she failed. They were boundless. She had welcomed his dedication to her cause, lived to learn each day how potent his promise to her safety was. But here with him, undressed, uncovered to her in so many ways, he became more than the guardian of her body, but the steward of her serenity—and of her joy.

She undulated with fulfillment. He left no part of her un-touched, un-treasured. Her ribs, her hips, her inner thighs. His lips were swift to capture her, his mouth generous and demand-ing. And at her core, he opened her with reverent fingers and found the part of her that yearned for all of him.

He was deliberate and maddeningly attentive. He licked and sucked her until she vibrated with need for his possession and her fingers dug into the muscles of his back.

She moaned. As if her mewls gave him incentive, he parted her heavy folds with his fingers and gave her lush swaths of his tongue. She melted and, mindless, spread her legs wider.

With two fingers, he plumbed her wet depths and dipped inside her with his talented tongue. He was thorough, torrid, sweet or soft. She was gone from this world until he rose, took her fingers, and put them to him to let her guide him. As he slid inside, the delirium turned to heaven.

He paused. His kiss to her lips was a blessing. When he began to move inside her, her head lolled upon the pillows. Lost again somehow in this newest rapture he created, she followed him. Release came, swift, flashing, and hard. He remained for long minutes, their union full of pulsing, pounding aftershocks.

Languid, she lifted her hand to run her fingers through his hair.

He smiled, euphoria in his twinkling eyes.

This was what she had needed to complete her trust in him.

He was a careful and unselfish lover, just as he was a careful and generous man.

"One problem," she said, and raised a finger, a grin on her face.

His head came up. Appalled and curious, he stared at her. "What?"

"I still have my stockings on."

He slid a hot hand down her thigh to her calf and stuck his finger in the ribboned garter. "Give me two minutes, sweetheart, and you'll never want a stitch of clothing again."

Chapter Ten

BEGINNING WITH THEIR fond farewells to the Boyer family the next morning, their journey to Sedan was a jolly affair. Amber and Ram climbed into the coach he had rented in the town earlier. Alone there, not minutes away from Charleville, he chuckled as she joined him on the opposite seat.

"You're too far away, sir." He caught both her hands as they explored the buttons of his frock coat. That she wished to seduce him revealed a new level of trust in him. Joy twinkled in her dark-brown eyes as she put her hands to his cravat. "I get to disrobe you for a change."

He had not allowed her any of that service at night during their time together. Her hands upon him during the day in the normal ways of married couples had been enough temptation. Too much, in fact.

Now, she took her sweet time of it. Untying, unwinding, laughing as she went. Dropping his cravat to the seat. Unbuttoning his frock coat and waistcoat, smoothing her hands over his shoulders and pulling his shirt over his head.

"Oh," she sighed, paused, and marveled at his naked chest. With a faint hum in the back of her throat, she splayed her fingers over the rise of his pectorals. Her touch seared him. Her admiration spurred him to bite his lip and give breathless laughs.

"If you take too long at this," he bit out through tight restraint, "we'll be in Sedan for lunch before we get to dine."

"Oh." She giggled, her eyes that of a mischievous cat's. "Never fear, dear sir. I know there is much here to savor."

He caught one of her hands and put it flat to his erection. "You have no idea how much more." With a few flicks of his fingers, he undid his flies.

She opened them wide and withdrew his already turgid, pleading cock. Her gaze to his very erect penis, she stroked her thumb over the tip. "I mean, really, darling. How do we know if we are compatible, eh? After all, you and I have had only two goes at it."

"Three."

"Hmmm. Was it?"

"Definitely. Three. We could not tarry this morning. We had to leave, you little tease." He remembered the scene at breakfast when she made eyes at him. He had forgotten his hunger for food and wished only to throw up her skirts and have her, wanton and willing, on the broad oak table.

"I wanted you at breakfast," she confided, kissing his cheek, rubbing him to distraction. "Actually before…"

"Definitely during," he added as she began a rhythm she accompanied with panting breaths, leading him to ponder how to maneuver her here on these short, uncomfortable seats. "We will be destroying both our backs…"

She widened her eyes at him. "I like a challenge."

Hell. What she did to him… Her eyes danced as she squeezed him, full and aching to fuck her as he was.

He rushed to match her in artless indulgence. "Rickety conveyances offer a few challenges. Even for a dexterous man," he said as he pushed up her skirts and stroked her satin thigh, minus the white hose he'd torn in their frolic last night, "it is difficult."

"But, my dear fellow, I am not only willing"—she climbed upon him, her knees to either side of his thighs—"I am a dexterous woman."

She sank over him, and he found her succulent center and slid home.

"I don't want to hurt you," he said, his breath harsh and fast as she twisted herself lower on his shaft.

"Darling man," she cooed when she had descended as she could, "you won't."

"But this," he said with a laugh as he caught the straps and the coach tipped as it took a sharp curve in the road, "is not our nice, wide bed."

"All the better here, then."

"I like the way you think." He took her lower lip between his teeth and nipped her. She was a scandal. She was his personal, private, beloved scandal.

"Now," she murmured with wide eyes, "perfection requires at least…ten times."

"After which, we will not count."

"Nor walk."

They laughed as he caught her little chip hat that bobbed on her red curls. He lifted two pins out and threw her chapeau to the other seat. Greedy for all of her, he pulled her closer. "Our journey to Sedan, my darling, will be a luscious memory!"

He was lost to her. His head back against the old, soft leather upholstery, he surrendered to her seduction and gave her all he had.

She did not disappoint a starving man. He took in how she savored this: her head thrown back, her mouth open—unmoving, transfixed, she melted over him.

His darling. His woman.

This was where he longed to be. And where he belonged.

She let her head fall to his chest. "Oh, Ramsey. You are so wonderful."

So simple a word did not convey all he was. Randy. Enthralled. He was all of those.

She put her forehead to his shoulder and spread little kisses on his throat. "You are my new obsession, Ram."

As he reveled in her boldness, he sank his fingers in her hair. "We'll see how well you like me when I never let you rest at night."

"We'll see how well you like me when I match you."

But in one thing, he always exceeded her. He loved her.

To continue to bury himself deep inside her, he would give her all of him she wanted—and demand of himself he let go the fear that she would never love him in return.

RAM ARRANGED A room for them at an auberge on the *quai* of the Meuse.

The inn was not only ancient, but smelled of old hay and mold. Ram groused that the place was not up to his standards of cleanliness. They accepted the faults because the inn was located in the center of town, and he wished to be there to overhear gossip in the streets.

Amber just wished to have him as soon as possible again. Eager for his affections, she felt the prickle of expectation whenever he looked at her. He hid nothing of his desire for her. The man made her feel free for the first time in years. To her surprise, she welcomed liberation from the cares and responsibilities that had always dogged her in Paris.

She certainly had become assertive in her desire for him. She'd never been that way with Maurice. Her husband had always initiated their sexual encounters. But then, this morning it occurred to her that if she did not show Ram how much she wanted him, he would not be the aggressor.

His sense of honor was greater than any other man she had ever known. For that, she admired him—and wanted him all the more.

TORRENTIAL RAIN KEPT them inside that first afternoon. Amber told him she didn't mind. To which Ram replied that they could take the opportunity to stay inside and work on their own special techniques.

She chuckled. "The weather cooperates."

The next morning, he grinned as he rose from their bed. She openly admired his physique. His broad shoulders, slim hips, and muscular legs were almost as intriguing as his tight buttocks. Other parts of him appealed to her even more.

"The sun does shine today," he told her with a peek out the window.

"Such a shame," she said as she threw back the covers. "I was hoping to perfect our methods."

He swung toward her, hands on his hips, and his body showed healthy signs that he agreed with her. "We don't want to miss breakfast."

"Think you'll starve?" she purred, and bent one knee.

His shining blue eyes twinkled as they skimmed her naked form. "Not if we share a little apéritif."

"Not little at all," she joked with an eye on his eagerness. She opened her arms to him as he came to her and covered her with his warm iron body.

It was nine as they wended their way along the twisting corridors down the stone steps to the common room and took a bench in one corner. They relished their fare of oats, eggs, and smoked sausage. Sated by their hearty meal, they gazed at each other so endearingly that the owner's wife commented on it.

"Married recently, are you?" she asked in a mash of French and German.

"We are," Ram replied in French.

"Enjoy it now," she instructed them. "The years wear you down, like rain on rock."

Amber smiled politely, but inside, she resented the woman's dim view. She watched her leave them, wishing the woman would take her negativity with her. "I believe marriage can be joyous and loving for many years in a thousand ways."

Ram reached across the top of the table and took Amber's hand. "Don't mind her."

"I lived it with Maurice. Couples have problems, but isn't it their duty to work them out, like wrinkles and tears in a yard of fabric? I realize many wed for all the wrong reasons. Money, position, power. But if two people begin well, if they admire each other, why can they not improve themselves as they improve the whole?"

Ram examined her frown. "Don't allow her to sour your day."

"You're right." She twirled her fingers on the table. "I am…opinionated. And irritable. But we have work to do."

He squeezed her hand. "Let's get to it."

She batted her lashes at him. "Afterward, we can adjourn once more to our bedroom."

"I like the way you think. We'll find our answers quickly."

But if they did—certainly when they did—they would once more have to discuss what to do with all that information.

Amber knew the conclusion they must both draw. To return to Paris so that Ram might disclose all they knew to his friend, Lord Ashley, was the right course of action.

Ram would fight it.

There had been a day when she would have feared it and the threat to her safety. But she understood the value of returning. And she valued his protection. In that, she had safety.

After so many weeks together, after so much delight in who he was as a man, as her protector and now as her lover, she'd thought long and hard about a return to Paris. She was no naïve girl who knew not how to ascribe responsibility for that change of heart. She was a widow, a worldly woman who had grown up amid the machinations of men and women who strove for power. She knew why she was changing her mind about her old role. It was not simply her understanding that her network was most likely gone, destroyed when she'd run from Paris and Vaillancourt. It was that she cared for Godfrey DuClare. Caring more each day in new and novel ways in bed and out of it, she valued him more.

Valued him more than she had wished.

But she would never stand between him and his duty to his country and to his colleagues. His honor demanded him to report any vital information. Just as hers had.

AFTER THEIR BREAKFAST, they emerged from their room onto the sunny cobbled path. She had shrugged off her questions. She had no answers to them. Not now. Not yet. What she could do would be to help Ram discover the information that would be valuable to the British. "What do you suggest we do?"

"Let's find a popular café and sit with coffee and pastry."

"Coffee for me. No food. After that breakfast, I won't eat again for a hundred years."

Strolling the city, she carried a sketchbook she'd purchased in Buzancy. She was no artist, but carrying it gave her an excuse to gaze overlong at scenery—or people. Today, when they stopped to dine, she did not take it out.

"You don't care to draw today?" Ram asked with mischief in his blue eyes.

"The tables," she explained.

"Ah, yes. I see. Too close together."

"Exactly."

He chuckled as he pulled out the small chair for her. "We don't want anyone questioning your talents."

She wrinkled her nose. She could draw stick figures very well and had shown Ram her inglorious examples. "I am dedicated, if nothing else."

He took his own chair, a rueful frown on his features. "God knows that's true."

On the nearby dock, two fishermen argued, and it appeared they were soon to pummel each other. When the café owner appeared at their side, he was officious. Bounding off to get their waffles and coffee, he muttered about foreigners.

"You would think," she said beneath her breath, "being on the border, he'd be used to new people coming and going."

"On the borders, life is tenuous. Your Parisian French and my poor hack of it does not endear either of us to him."

She rolled a shoulder. "He fears what he does not know."

Ram tipped his head. No one else came to patronize the establishment, even though at this hour many emerged from their cottages to walk the *quai*.

"Do you miss home?" He closely watched her reaction.

"I miss the peace." How well did she wear her heart on her sleeve? Most likely her views about marriage and about intolerant people gave it away.

He stared at her. "Care to explain that?"

"What I mean is that, I loved my house, Aunt Cecily, Augustine, and our social life. I resent the circumstances that drove me from it. I favor good food and fine bedding, baths, and my own clothes." She pulled at the cotton gown and shawl she wore. "These fit well. The modiste in Buzancy was skilled. I don't criticize her. But if my preferences make me sound superior, I don't mean it to be. I have had education, wealth, and many opportunities that others have not."

She looked away. She would tell him the truth. "I'd like to think that one day I could live a normal life. Not worry about who will knock at the door. Who will come to call and wish to take me away."

That confession had him raising his brows—and she was not surprised. It was her first indication that she tired of her role and her flight from it. He reached out and, across the small table, raised her hand and kissed her palm.

She tried for levity. "So there you have it. I am not as fierce as I appear to be."

INDEED. HE TURNED away to look at the river as it rushed along the banks. He would not reiterate his exhortation to leave France. He'd done that too often. Now he had learned the power of leaving well enough alone.

She would decide as she would.

He could wait.

Chapter Eleven

T HEY STAYED IN Sedan only four nights, then Ram hired a
carriage and off they went to Verdun. In those few days, she
and Ram had learned little new. The townsfolk expected a
shipment of muskets, but had heard the number was small. A
new big shipment was to go to Verdun. Ram and Amber took the
gossips at their word.

Their journey was southeast to the city that, like Sedan, sat
on the Meuse River. Here they learned their first day that many
spoke not only French but also German.

The town was nestled in the rolling eastern hills. As they
strolled up to the old tower gates, looking for a place to dine,
Ram told her what he knew about the star-shaped citadel of the
ancient city of Verdun. At the turn of the last century, Louis XIV's
famous old Marshal of France, Vauban, had added to the
medieval city wall. Like other fortifications Vauban was famous
for constructing throughout France, this here he had built as
steep black stone walls struck deep in the wet soil. The ramparts
stood so tall that they created narrow, sunless, mean streets
smelling of the stagnant water left from countless floods, Vauban
ordered hydraulics to push out overflowing water from the
Meuse.

"Still, it's a pretty town." Amber noted the half-timbered

houses, some with brightly colored family crests carved into the heavy wooden doors and elaborate Gothic windows dotting the second and third stories.

Their accommodations were a set of rooms in a small guest house. The proprietors were a man and his wife who were pink-cheeked, jolly folks. They spoke a mix of German and French that made for interesting misunderstandings among them.

"I wonder," said Amber in poor German to their hostess, Greta Mercier, "if *mein Mann* and I could have potato cakes?" She turned to Ram, and in French asked, "How do you think one says 'potato' in German?"

"*Kartoffel*," he said. "I know a few words from my friend, Lord Fournier."

"Fournier?" Greta perked up and grinned. "We have many here in the family Fournier. *Verstehen Sie?*"

But then the woman rambled on about a good-looking young man who, Ram translated, had stayed with them for a full week. "He was very handsome. Tall, white-blond hair, and very polite."

Ram asked her more about this man's looks and concluded she had met his friend and colleague, Diederich Fournier. "*Ja*, he is my friend, *Frau Mercier*."

Ram had left Paris with Dirk, Lord Fournier, weeks ago. They had journeyed together toward the east. In one of the small villages where they stayed in an inn, Dirk had become very ill. Ram and he suspected Dirk had eaten something that was rotten. Ram had accompanied Dirk nearly to Verdun, but when his friend rallied, Ram had left Dirk and went north to track Amber. Dirk had continued onward to his family, who lived in Baden. Ram was surprised Dirk had stayed so long in this city.

"He was very ill," she said, and made a face. "You know," she tried in French, "sick."

"Is that right?" Ram was surprised. Dirk had told him he felt better and persuaded Ram to leave him to go north and do his duty.

Ram had developed that issue to his own advantage. "Perhaps

you have met another friend of mine? Tall, hair like my wife here." He made up a name. "Monsieur Lucien Albert?"

The lady thought a moment. "Lucien Albrecht, *oui,* monsieur. *Nicht Albert. Nein. Albrecht.*"

"*Merci beaucoup, madame. Das ist eine Schande.* That's a shame. I had hoped to join him here. He was a friend of the commander of the citadel. He came to visit with him."

The woman frowned. "*Nein. Nicht herein.* Not here." She rattled on in her mix of two languages. What he got from her discourse was that the French commander of the citadel was too busy to receive guests. He was receiving too many shipments of muskets to pass the time with others in frivolous ways.

When the woman left them to their coffee and apple strudel, Ram could not suppress his grin.

"Now," Amber said, picking up his lightness of being, "that's progress. All we need is more detail."

"Such as the number of muskets."

TWO MORNINGS LATER, sitting in a different café closer to the citadel, Ram and Amber were about to leave when he motioned that he wished to remain. Two guards from the citadel had had hard night duty. They grumbled about new shipments that had arrived at two o'clock in the morning. The soldiers had stacked crates of muskets all night long. They were weary and resentful, because the muskets would have to be reloaded into wagon trains soon.

"Sending them off to Baden and Wurttemberg, my captain told me," said one.

"Krauts," added another Frenchman. "Can't trust them."

"I'd not give the bastards one, let alone five hundred," put in the first. "Plus two new cannon."

"Five hundred new muskets and two new cannon," Ram said

later, after he had closed the door to their rooms, a grin on his face.

Amber shivered at the mere idea of so many. "Many more than we expected."

Ram took her in his arms. The information had come to them easily.

THAT NIGHT, ON a veranda facing the flowing Meuse, they dined leisurely on good white wine, veal, potatoes, and sauerkraut. Amber ate, preoccupied with issues that had clouded her mind since they'd begun to get such vital information about weapons in Charleville. She may have come to terms with the fact that her own network was ruined by her departure from Paris, but she knew what they learned now about weapons was very important. Furthermore, such news was crucially vital to Ram and his network. His responsibility to his friend and colleague Lord Ashley remained strong. After all, Ram was doing the work assigned him by protecting her, wasn't he?

She knew it bothered Ram that he had no way to inform Ashley of what they knew about increased manufacture and distribution of muskets. He would not bring up the topic. Yet raising it to him was necessary. She would not shy from it. But she would carefully choose her words.

Amber initiated the topic of the need to leave Verdun. Her past reluctance to travel with him had gone long ago. She would go anywhere with him now. She could even go someplace dangerous...like Paris.

"Talk to me, Amber. You are too silent, and I worry," he said with compassion in his gaze.

"You and I cannot stay here," she said to him, and put down her fork and knife. "I know it. So do you, Ram. We have more information than we ever dreamed. And we must report it." All he did was shake his head, and she had to lead him to the topic. "Do you not have any friends posted elsewhere here in the east? Perhaps in Strasbourg?" That was the next largest city south of them.

"My original duty before I was assigned to find you and protect you was to come here and learn if two British men who were reputedly prisoners here in the citadel were still alive."

She sat back, shocked. "You never told me that."

"You did not need to know."

"Why not? I could help you. My French, darling man, is much better than yours. And I know the lie of the land."

"You do, sweetheart. But I have asked around. I hear nothing of any of our men detained in that monstrosity of a building." He nodded toward the tower of dark green and black stones.

She smiled at him. "Well, I am glad of that. One good thing done."

He reached over to pour more white wine into her glass, and she smiled.

Then she froze in her chair. Four men who had just arrived took a table closer to the café's entrance. Three were dressed in well-cut street clothes, and the fourth was attired in military garb. By his insignia, he was a captain in artillery blues.

"Ram, we must leave. Quickly. Please." She fished in her reticule for a handkerchief and wished to heavens it were larger.

"Of course." He got to his feet, a hand to her elbow. "You're pale."

"Please. Pay for our meal. I am ill." She put the handkerchief to her mouth and slumped, pretending illness.

The proprietor expressed his sorrow that madame had taken a poor turn. Might he do anything to help?

Ram assured him his lady needed to rest. With an arm around her shoulders, he led her down the lane to their auberge.

Within minutes, they were back in the safety of their rooms.

"Tell me what happened there," Ram urged her.

Amber paced the floor. "I had to leave. I know those four

men who came to sit at the other table. The three in street clothes are Vaillancourt's men. I have often seen them with the fourth one, the captain. He is Armand Galhard, an aide-de-camp who brags he is an expert in muskets and cannon manufacture. He is young, ambitious, and the son of an influential Paris banker. His duty is to inspect factories when they finish making certain armaments, then to visit depots when they are to receive supplies. He must count the deliveries and report back to Paris that they have arrived in the right numbers and on time."

Ram was wide eyed with the thrill of her news. "Bonaparte keeps his military plans very secret. Only he and his generals, usually engineers and artillery, know real plans. For the Italian campaigns and later, we know that Bonaparte was always careful and never revealed his tactics by supplying a city or town with too much of any item all at once."

"He delays delivery of necessary supplies?"

"Yes, it is all a ruse, Ram said. "Bonaparte tells only those who need to know well in advance, like the engineers and the artillery, what he requires. Aides-de-camp are used as couriers of information from certain cities, and they never know the entire plan of supply. Nor do they know the plan of attack."

"They don't have to," she concluded. She sank in misery to sit on the bed.

"No. They report only what they see. That young aide can ride back to Paris tomorrow morning and inform his general that two cannon recently came to Verdun, plus muskets." Ram paused and frowned. "Tell me about the men in regular clothes."

"I have seen them with Vaillancourt. I do not know their names. Somehow they must know the aide-de-camp from Paris." She put a hand to her throat, terrified. "I don't know if they remember me, but I remember them. Oh, Ram. They might be looking for me."

Ram sank to the edge of the bed and reached to embrace her. "I wouldn't be surprised."

She felt the prick of fear. But she knew what they must do.

"Looking for me is not so important as the knowledge that Bonaparte increases the number of armaments and puts them in the border forts."

"It is important, but not as important as your life."

"I cannot look away and ignore it!" She looked up into his brooding eyes. She did not like what she had to say, but do it she must. "We must return to Paris."

"No."

"HE PREPARES FOR war, Ram."

"Yes. Against Austria. Which means Bonaparte's attempt to pry German princes from their bond to the Austrian empire will have teeth. He gives them guns to protect themselves."

"And to fight for him." She raised his hand and put it to her cheek. Tears gathered in her lovely eyes. "Godfrey DuClare, listen to me—I will not be the cause of your failure to perform your duty."

He kissed her hand and rose. This time it was he who paced the floor. "I had thought I must send someone to present the news to Ashley. But I know no one I can trust. We are too deep into France, far from Paris. I know Ashley has more men and women arriving to help us gather intelligence, but I know not who they are. Or if any are here in Verdun."

"Darling Ram, I have taken you far from the center of your network."

He returned to stand before her and ran his hands up into the wealth of her curls. Silken red waves tangled in his fingers. Her hair had grown from the shorter crop she had when he found her in Reims to frame her face around her ears and throat. "You are my work. You! And now, yes, you and I will take a short trip to Paris to inform Ashley. But we will do it carefully."

She hugged him, her cheek to his firm stomach. She was

proud of him. So proud. He was her stalwart protector, her finest lover, her everything. This man she would not lose. "Paris is a big city, my darling. I know it well. I will do all I can to help you do what you should."

"You must agree that you will stay hidden. Not go anywhere."

"Ram, please. Do not stay my hand. You have done so much for me. I want to help."

"You will help me by staying hidden." He brushed his thumbs over the rise of her plump cheeks. "You are too precious to me to ever lose you. You are my finest work, darling woman."

She kissed his fingers. "What if I promise to be careful? Hmm? Stay out of the streets and disguise myself when we must go out?"

He snorted. "You'd need to cut your off your hair. Wear clothes that disguise all this beauty." He waved a hand down her torso. "In other words, no."

"Ram, please. Ashley needs to know this information."

He damned his lack of choices. This news was too important to send in any letter. But he must let Ashley know, without question. If he failed to report this then Parliament would howl with outrage. The army, the navy, had to know what Bonaparte planned. The Treaty of Amiens had been a plan of little value to Britain. Clearly, the Little Corporal from Corsica valued the treaty even less than paper it was written on.

"Ram, listen to me. Any help you need, I will provide."

"What I need you to provide, my sweet, is your kiss." He cupped her face and bent to take her mouth. Amber had convinced him. "I will tell Madame Mercier you are ill. We will remain here and plan well our trip by diversion, lest anyone try to follow. But I will go out into town to assess if the four we saw tonight have gone. Only then will we leave."

Chapter Twelve

"YOU DID WELL!" Amber whirled around in the parlor of the house Ram had rented on the left bank of the Seine. The five-story townhouse was small, built at the turn of the previous century, and had sparse but tasteful furnishings. "Did you ask the man you rented from anything about his family?"

Ram stood by the window overlooking the rue du Four. The rich, heavy damask drapes were pulled back. The curtains beneath, trimmed in delicate ivory French Chantilly lace, obscured a clear view of the street. Ram had told Amber he would not open them completely. It was best to keep the view to the inside obstructed.

He and Amber had arrived in Paris late yesterday afternoon. Fortunate to find a sign for a rented house on the front door of a townhouse near the Saint-Germain-des-Prés Abbey, Ram had pressed the owner for the name and location of a registry where he could find good, strong men. He needed three, one for the front door, one for the kitchen entrance, and one to follow Ram wherever he went. The three whom he met, he hired immediately.

"This house is now owned by one of the banking family of Jarre." Ram turned to look at her with a smile. "Before that, it was owned by the Vicomte de Neufchateau for his mistress."

"How quaint." She smiled, pretending she was easy in her skin to be back in Paris. But she had heard rumors about the end of the vicomte's family during the Terror. One young daughter named Diane had been in Carmes when she and Aunt Cecily were there.

"What's wrong?" Ram asked.

"The vicomte's family were robbed by their bankers."

"The Jarre who own this house?"

She clutched her arms and nodded. "So many turned on others during the Terror. Often without provocation."

"Do you not wish to remain here? If so, we can go."

"No. No, of course not." It was irrelevant what had happened here. The city was her home. Everywhere were stories of those who had done evil to others. She was here, no matter that she could not take up the reins of her espionage work to correct old wrongs. She was more than content to help Ram do his duty. "Good that the house comes with a man-of-all-work."

"Monsieur Jarre's man assured me our new *majordom* is trustworthy. Still, you and I will be discreet around him."

She went to Ram and put her arms around him. "Always. This visit here is for you. I am so heartened that you will do this. I see in your attitude that you are happy we've come."

He drew her flush to him, his eyes bright with humor. "I wish to please you, madame."

"Ba! Please yourself, my darling man. Let's see if we need anything for the larder. Or sheets or covers for the bed."

"Why don't you do that and make a list? I'll go shop for your needs."

Hands on her hips, she had to try to persuade him to her thinking. "I cannot stay here all the time."

He gave her a wry look. "You can."

She pouted and batted her lashes like a coquette. "You cannot keep me caged."

"Honestly, you should not go out at all, and you know it. You cannot go out during the day." He cupped her nape and brushed his lips over hers. "Please don't try me."

"I won't. I promise." But living so very close to the old abbey, the very place where she had met her superior each month for many years, called up her sense of responsibility. Her chances of her control agent going to their meeting places again after so many months were small. But Amber had a spark of hope he might appear. She could then assure the man that she was alive and well. Useless, yes, but alive and well.

"At dusk," Ram said, and tapped the end of her nose. "We will walk out as the sun sets. Only for a few minutes."

She gave him a big, wild kiss. "Wonderful. I will wear my trousers."

He rolled his eyes. "Don't. You look nothing like any man I've ever known."

"Not even a skinny youth?"

"No. Parts of you are not at all skinny. If you wear trousers, people will stare all the more. But I will buy you a wide-brimmed straw hat. We will try to conceal all of this excellent bone structure." He tipped his head as he stroked the arch of her cheeks.

MINUTES LATER, RAM went out the kitchen door. His list for groceries in his inside his frock coat pocket, he went first to the nearby café to which their new *majordom* Gaspard had referred him.

Casting a glance down the *ruelle*, Ram smiled. Pleased that he did not see his hired man assigned to the back door, he began to walk away to his errands. He was even more pleased that he did not detect how his third man followed him.

Yet a sixth sense ruffled his composure. Ram had always been able to tell when someone tracked him. His third guard did a good job and was definitely not following him. Did someone else?

He would take care. So he proceeded, felt safe doing his shopping—and began to wander and crisscross the streets. If anyone attempted to follow him, he would learn before he headed for the market in the corner *place*.

A few streets away from his house, he paused at a printer's glass window. The man specialized in history books about Paris. Surreptitiously, he looked at reflections in the glass. No one followed him. Then he dropped into a small café for a coffee and pastry—and took his time. Satisfied he saw no one loitering outside waiting for him to appear, he asked for *l'addition* to pay his bill and emerged into the bright July sun. Outside, he stood a moment and raised his face to the sky. He rejoiced that he and Amber were in Paris, and safely so. It was time for him to buy items they needed at home. Off he went to the market.

The street *vendeurs* had erected their tents and stalls earlier. They were farmers or craftsmen from beyond the Periphique city zone who came to the city to sell their produce, animals, and wares. This market attracted about ten families from the distant *faubourgs*. They sold everything from freshly butchered beef and pork to live chickens. Others offered ripe red strawberries, honey, jams, and a rainbow of assorted vegetables. Ram bought much too much, but he was glad he could. He and Amber had eaten very sparingly the last two days as they traveled to Paris in the most uncomfortable carriage he'd ever sat in. His arse was sore from the jostling.

But all of his wares were purchased for a good cause. He could not be more pleased that Amber was cooperating with his need to keep her safe, hidden from any of Vaillancourt's men.

"I LIKE THIS one." Amber pointed to two small perch in the *vendeur*'s wooden box.

She had come out with Ram at dusk, wearing her new straw

farmer's hat that he had purchased for her this morning. She felt refreshed to breathe the sweet summer air and stretch her legs in the city she loved.

Ram promptly paid the man, took the fish in its old paper, and dropped it in Amber's basket. They strolled leisurely toward the abbey.

The old church stood proudly among the lesser shops and houses. She was majestic, a survivor of the Terror, but she bore the hideous marks of that time. Her outer walls were falling apart. The buildings were pocked with stones that had been thrown, and marred by blackened walls where some had tried to set the whole on fire. At one point, a mob had broken into the abbey prison and killed more than two hundred people.

Amber paused before the west door, knitting her brow and biting her lower lip. This looked so different than when she had been here last. The heat of deep July did not change a place that much. She wondered if the change was only in her mind. She'd been away from here for so long that she'd forgotten how it looked? She did not think that was so. Instead, she wondered how her superior had taken to the news that she had fled Paris in fear for her life.

Did you come to meet me at our appointed time more than the required twice?

Were you here, wondering about me, worrying about me?

I worried about you. I still do.

Ram was beside her, regarding her. "Shall we go home now?"

"Yes. I am so sad that the whole complex looks so old and ragged," she said to Ram as they turned away to head back toward their little house.

"All the churches were attacked during the Terror and many have not recovered," he replied.

"Yes. Many were sacked. Others burned. In Compiègne, the churches were robbed of their altar pieces. The lovely Cathedral of Reims is now taken over by city lawyers. Even the archbishop's residence there wears battle scars." She shivered.

"All that is finished." He put his hand to her back.

"But what we have in its place are men who are just as greedy as those the mobs swept away." She nodded toward two young women who stood on the corner hawking news sheets. "Let's buy them."

This part of town was notorious for harboring and hiding those who wrote pamphlets and news sheets that criticized the government and those who ran it. While the government harassed many who printed them, they were too prolific and popped up everywhere. People bought them for news of the day, but many delighted in those that were gossip sheets.

Ram dug coins from his pocket and paid for both copies. "The news will be interesting."

"When in a vacuum, always buy scandal sheets." She opened one of the sheets and skimmed the tiny print but stopped at once when she saw Gus's name. "Wait, here is a story about—" In the fading light of day, she squinted and read the story. "Ram," she said to him in a hushed tone when she was finished, "Gus and your Ashley are married!"

"What?"

"Look here." She gave him the paper.

He stood reading for long minutes.

"They went away as lovers, and when they returned, they had the British envoy marry them." Amber had a hand to her chest. "I hope to heaven she loves him. That she didn't marry him because of rumors that she was his mistress."

"It says they were away for weeks and visited many towns in the north." Ram glanced up from the sheet, folded the papers, and stuck them in her basket. "Among them, they went to Reims."

"Reims," Amber murmured, thinking about why the couple would go to the city where she and Maurice had lived. "Dear God, Ram. They were looking for me."

He nodded, his face dour with concern. "He had to find you. So did she. And they put the news of their wedding in the sheets.

You and they are popular."

"I am too popular, it seems." She gave a forced laugh.

But when she turned, she was looking straight into the faces of two people across the street. Two she knew very well. She could not move. Nor could she turn her back on them.

Ram paused. "What's wrong?"

Then Amber sensed him following her line of sight. He landed on the tall, dark-haired, handsome man and the golden-haired beauty by his side. Neither took their eyes off Amber.

Both appeared to be shopping, dressed in finely tailored clothing indicative of their status as merchants of good wine.

"Ram, you have no cause to worry. I know them well and I cannot ignore them. They are Aunt Cecily's vintners from the Loire. Please. Come. We must greet them."

Amber sailed forward, her manner that of one who welcomed the sight of them.

"Madame!" The young lady beamed and dropped into a curtsy.

"Madame, it is wonderful to see you," said the man.

Amber embraced both with gusto.

"Allow me to introduce you," she said to Ram, hoping he might appear less fierce and more friendly. "This is Mademoiselle Inès Bechard and her brother, Monsieur Luc Bechard. My friend is Lord Ramsey, an Englishman attached to the British delegation. My dear," she said as she turned to Ram, "the family Bechard live near Amboise on the Loire. They grow very fine grapes and produce excellent white wine, which Aunt Cecily stocks in her cellars for all occasions."

Luc took a step nearer Amber. His manner was careful, his expression that of alarm, as he murmured to her, "We are pleased to see you well, madame. Never did we expect to see you in Paris. I assume my sister and I are to say we have not seen you."

"You are correct, monsieur. This happenstance is one you must forget. Please."

"We understand," said Inès with a nod.

"The news of your disappearance has frightened many. Changed much in the city," said Luc with troubled gaze.

"Too much to state here," his sister added.

"I can only imagine," Amber said with regret.

Ram intervened, a hand to her elbow. "We must return home."

"Home?" asked Inès.

"None that you know, Inès," Amber replied.

"Ah," said the girl, her large umber eyes on Ram as if she understood he was her guard and protector.

Luc took his sister's arm. "We are thrilled to see you well."

"*Merci beaucoup*, Luc. Inès." Amber had a smile for them. "We must go. *Adieu*."

She and Ram had gone no farther than a step when Luc appeared at her side. "One thing. You must know this. We have problems, madame."

Ram cast a withering eye over Luc and the restraining hand he had placed on Amber's forearm.

"Please," Luc said to him. "I know madame is sought by…" He looked around before he continued to speak. "You know to whom I refer, madame. Please listen to me. He promises to bring in any and all of your friends to question them about your location."

Amber gasped. "No. No."

"How do you know this, monsieur?" Ram scowled at the man.

Luc turned to Amber. "I was with your aunt at a dinner party last night."

His sister attempted to appear normal, as if the four of them were having a pleasant conversation.

Ram stiffened. "We must go."

"Amber," Luc beseeched her, "listen to me. He told your aunt he has a list of those who will go to prison. He says it is his goal to strike each name off permanently until you reappear."

"Oh, Luc." She could not breathe.

"He is the very devil, Amber. Take care."

"And you as well, Luc."

She and Ram hurried to their little house.

"THAT WAS CLOSE," Ram said with distaste when they were safely at home in their kitchen.

Amber removed items from her basket and only shook her head. She was the very picture of a frightened woman, pale and solemn.

Ram was bursting with anger that Amber had been recognized, and outraged that the four of them had stood in the streets like deer ready for the hunter's shot. If that man and his sister went to anyone with this story of Madame St. Antoine's appearance in a market on the left bank, word would spread. It always did. "Do you trust those two not to say anything?"

Amber plunked herself down in the old kitchen chair. "I do."

Ram paced the floor. "How? Why?"

"One of them participated in our network."

"Which?"

"Luc."

Ram lost his breath. "You report to him? Or he to you?"

"No. No. Not him. Another."

Ram sank to the opposite chair. "But I thought you said no one knows anyone else but the person who reports downward or upward?"

"I did. That is true. But I once saw him quite by accident with the person who reports to me."

"And there is no other reason for Bechard to speak to this person?"

She winced. "One other reason."

Ram wiped a hand across his mouth. "Should I know this reason?"

"I prefer not to tell you, Ram. Not because I don't wish to, but… I have learned the less anyone knows, the less they can give under torture."

He trained his eyes on her. "I don't intend to be a guest of the inimitable Rene Vaillancourt."

"We never know, Ram. I always fear anything." She flung out a hand. "Here in France, things are so different. Life is cheap. A man who wants power will gladly lie, cheat, steal, or kill to get what he wants. It will benefit you nothing, my darling, to know this."

"I see." He had good reason to worry over this. But it would do him no good. Worry clouded one's judgment. "Very well. I take you at your word."

Ram wished he had another man under his employ to go and follow the Bechards. Amber might trust her friends, but he had no reason to.

BUT AS AMBER began to dress the fish they had purchased for dinner, she worked over in her mind the full import of what Luc had shared with her.

Her network was broken. She had no one reporting to her. She'd come to terms with those two facts long ago. But it was serendipity that Ram had chosen Saint-Germain-des-Prés to take a house. She was so close, so very close to the spot where she'd met her control agent. She could walk to the place where she had always met him. If her agent came to check on her occasionally, that person would be thrilled to find she was still alive. He could repair Amber's chain. He would be happy to do it. He'd get her another report. Gus was gone, her chain broken by her own flight from the city, pretending to be in love with Kane Whittington, Lord Ashley, and seeking her!

Amber's superior had means. And Amber had motive. She

would not see her friends or associates die at Vaillancourt's hand for working with her to save the republic of France. She would not.

But then, there was this other man in her life now. This dashing, stalwart, heavenly creature who made love to her like there was no other woman in the world. This man, this defender of her life, this force of nature, this bulwark, this ram who would not see her hurt. Who stood by her though life and threat of death. *Godfrey DuClare, my Ramsey, who would rather die than allow me to do this.*

Amber glanced up at the man who had saved her. The man she loved. Yes, loved. The one who would never let her seek out her superior for fear Vaillancourt might appear there instead.

Vaillancourt. Damn him to hell.

She forced back hot tears and made her plan.

She finished dressing the lovely, fat fish and brushed and washed her hands. She had potatoes to quarter…and a wonderful man to help her.

She would finish making their dinner. They would enjoy the fish and potatoes and the frilly lettuce salad. Ram had bought good white wine from the Loire vintner in the square, and they would make a celebration of the meal.

After they ate, Ram planned to go to Ashley's house to announce his and her return to Paris. He would deliver the vital news about the weapons, then return to her, and they would enjoy the satisfaction of his having done his duty. They would celebrate that in word and deed and in their bed upstairs. She would not harm this night filled with so much success and joy.

Tomorrow she would discuss with Ram her need to go to the meeting place of her superior. She had no choice but to try to persuade Ram to allow it.

For what else was the finest love composed of, but the duty to be true to yourself and offer the one you adored the finest person you would ever be?

Chapter Thirteen

July 11, 1802

RAM STOOD BY the fire in his friend Ashley's parlor, his hands behind his back. He waited impatiently for minutes before he heard Kane's footfalls come down the hall toward him.

As the door opened, Ram smiled and greeted Kane.

"Good God, am I happy to see you!" Kane strode forward, arms out to embrace him. Lines of worry on his face eased. Ram had known his friend would fret about him and his efforts to find Amber these past weeks.

They patted each other on the back, then broke apart.

"Come sit down," Kane said.

Ram took a chair, as did Kane. His friend gave him a once-over, and Ram knew his clothing told a certain tale. Purposely tonight, he wore dark, modest clothes resembling that of a bourgeois merchant. He had not wished to call attention to himself and prepared well to see Kane in secret. He wished to put his friend's mind to rest about the chances he took coming here.

"I came in the back door," he said, "through the gardener's shed and up into your orangery." Ram arched a brow in humor as he crossed one leg over the other. "We are newly arrived in Paris, and I wished you to know."

"Madame St. Antoine is with you?"

"She is. And has been in my company for many weeks now. She is healthy, whole, a challenge—and at times a real hellcat."

Kane burst into a short laugh. "Whatever the circumstances, I am overjoyed that you found her and that both of you are well. I feared for you. But then, I am sure you know what misery that was. I am thrilled you are here and well. You look, dare I say, happy?"

"Please!" Ram grimaced. "Grace me with no flowers, Whit. The duty to find the lady was nothing to the challenge of persuading her to allow me the honor of protecting her."

Kane gazed at him as if he saw a new man. Perhaps he did.

"Amber and I arrived in Paris day before yesterday." Ram fixed his friend with a generous smile, something he knew Kane had not seen on him very often. "We read in a scandal sheet you recently married Augustine Bolton. I bring you congratulations from Amber and from me, my friend."

"Thank you. We are, I am pleased to say, very happy."

"I am thrilled for you. It is what you needed."

Kane arched both brows and grinned. He seemed a different man as well. Could it be he was a man in love with his wife? Ram knew the power of caring for another now, how it changed a man's perspective and made him anxious and eager to protect the woman he adored.

Kane gave a sharp laugh. "I did. But no man voices it, does he?"

"Never good for one's image." Ram ran a hand down his thigh. "Let me get to this. I come for a few reasons. I want them said quickly, and then I return to Amber. I do not want her without me for long. I have hired men as guards, but you know how that goes. You have five, your opponent has ten. It's never safe for long."

"Do you fear Vaillancourt knows where you are?"

"I gather your wife has told you how he hounds Amber."

"She has. We encountered one of his men in Varennes."

Ram sat forward, frowning. "You were there?"

"After the two of you left. We talked with Madame Verne and her daughter, Solange. They were helpful. But we met one of Vaillancourt's men in the town, and he is dead now."

Ram went stiff with shock. "How?"

Kane inhaled deeply. "My wife has a very special skill with knives. He attacked us, but she got the better of him."

Ram blew out a breath. "Good that these women have talents. Amber can handle a knife and pistol."

"To your advantage."

The hall door opened, and Gus stepped in.

Kane and Ram rose. But her appearance meant Ram could not speak about the weapons going to Sedan and Verdun. She was Amber's friend, but Ram doubted Amber shared all her secrets with Gus. He had to be prudent here, and was glad he had penned a short note with details about the muskets and cannon going to border towns in the east. He just had to find a way to put it into Kane's hand before he left.

His friend stepped forward. "My darling, you may remember my friend, Lord Ramsey."

Gus walked toward Ram and thrust out her hand. She was a lovely young woman with dark hair and bright green-gold eyes. "I do. We are so very happy to see you here, sir. Thank you for coming."

They shook hands. Gus indicated they should sit down again, her to the settee, the men to their chairs. "You are very welcome. I come with loving regards from Amber."

Gus breathed deeply. "She is well?"

"She is. So has she always been these past weeks. I like to think it is I who have kept her well, though she would not tell you that."

"I'm certain," Gus said with a sympathetic smile. "I hope you will tell me all. We have been very worried about you both. So is our Aunt Cecily. Have you been to see her? Will you? Will Amber?"

"That, I doubt."

Gus shook her head and frowned. "But…may we tell her?"

"Do not. Amber has her reasons. Not all of them does she share with me." *To my regret.*

Gus sighed. "I know. That is her way. But then, she must have approved of your coming here."

How much did Gus know about what Amber did to weaken the government of the consulate?

Ram chose his words carefully. "She did not want you to worry any longer. She was certain you had. Especially when we learned that the two of you had gone away on a lovers' escapade. Amber saw through your ruse. She knew you would not go away with any man without excellent reason."

Gus scoffed. "How good of her."

"She is a very fine woman."

Gus smiled. "She is indeed, Lord Ramsey. Now tell us, why are you here tonight?"

"I was just informing Whit that we arrived in Paris only day before yesterday. We are getting settled."

"In her house in rue Dauphine?" Gus asked.

"No. We are in a small house on the left bank in Saint-Germain-des-Prés."

She shook her head. "Why? Do you not wish to announce you are in the city?"

Gus knew about Vaillancourt's interest in Amber. Was she pressing him for more information about Amber's intentions to return to her espionage? "Exactly."

"Wise," said Gus with fear in her eyes. "But then, why return here at all?"

She knew Amber faced danger with Vaillancourt near. Ram would have to test to see how much she knew about Amber's so-called "work." "Amber insisted we return because she had lost the threads of her work."

"She has been away from Paris since mid-March," Gus said with anger and a harsh note of despair. "Of course she has not worked."

"When we heard that you both were looking for us in Reims, she considered returning. But doing so only if she were still invisible to Vaillancourt."

Kane looked at Gus. "The man is relentless in his pursuit."

Ram nodded. "And Amber is determined he will not stop her."

"And you agreed?" Kane asked.

"Only if I were her companion. Yes, we live together. We have developed a trusting relationship." Ram looked at Gus. "I hope I do not offend you when I admit that your friend and I are intimate?"

Gus smacked her lips. "No. Amber would not do anything unless she believed it to be right. Will she remain incognito? Indefinitely?"

"She says she will. I encourage it. Three of the deputy police chief's men found us at various points along the roads. They are ruthless creatures. I do not want Amber in public. They would take advantage at their chief's command. I think him capable of anything." He looked to Kane. "I will keep her by my side for as long as is necessary. No one will hurt her."

Gus let out a shaking breath, gazing at Ram with sad eyes. "So I conclude, then, that I will not see her."

"I came alone. I will go out with her on her journeys and I will not come here again. She congratulates you on your marriage and hopes you are very happy." He turned to Kane. "I bring you my own fond regards for a happy life together."

With a nod, Kane accepted Ram's kind words. "Ramsey, we fear Vaillancourt's orders to do anything to find you both and take Amber from you."

"That is not news. Amber has told me the same for weeks."

Gus whispered, "He wants her to reveal her network."

Ram held his breath. Gus knew so much about Amber's activities. She even called it a network.

Gus continued, agonizing over her words. "Perhaps he wants

more than that."

"He does," Ram replied. "But he will have her over my dead body."

Gus stared at him. He remained silent as she absorbed the full meaning of that statement.

A knock at the door came, and Kane called to his *majordom*, Corsini, to enter. The man had a tray filled with cakes, glasses, cups and saucers, a teapot, and a carafe of brandy.

"Would you like any refreshment?" Kane asked Ram.

"None for me, thank you."

Corsini took his cue and drifted away, closing the door behind him.

Ram got to his feet. "And so if you will forgive me the brevity of my visit, I return home to Amber."

"You will let us know how and where you are, I hope?" Gus pressed him.

"I would like to say yes, my lady, but I cannot. To come here taunts the devil. It took me hours to change course and defy anyone who might have discovered me. I return now by different routes." He took Gus's offered hand and bent to kiss it. "No news will be good news."

Kane said, "I will walk to the orangery with you. Pardon me, my darling. I will have a few words with Ramsey."

Ram had a few things to divulge to Kane, too.

"LISTEN TO ME, please, Ram," Kane said when they stood amid the fragrant orange trees in the warm room at the back of the house. "I have men here to help you. If you need assistance, I can send them to you now. Also, if you need money, I have that too. Scarlett was more than generous. So whatever you may want—"

"I have men enough, Whit. Money is a challenge. If you can deposit an amount with my *majordom* in my house off rue d'Orleans, that would help."

"I gather you are not pleased to return to Paris."

"God help me, no." *I'd rather be safely away in London with Amber beside me. Yet she substitutes my duty for her own, even as it helps assuage her guilt that she cannot do hers.* "But Amber will not listen to reason. She is beside herself that Bonaparte makes way for himself to destroy the consulate. Dirk Fournier thinks the same."

Kane was shocked. "You've seen Dirk?"

"No. Not since he and I parted weeks ago." Ram paused. In the hallway, he thought he saw a shadow move. Kane employed trustworthy staff, but one could never be totally sure of loyalties. If someone were there listening, Ram would not chance saying anything more. He was glad he had committed the details of military supplies to paper. "Rumors there are that Bonaparte wants the territory along the border with German Baden. He offers land and money to the margrave. That man wants to be a grand duke."

"Dirk's grandmother's territory."

"Exactly. When I left Dirk in late May, he was in a hurry to get to Karlsruhe. Unless you have heard from him, I assume he is still there."

"I have no communication from him. So he must be still in Karlsruhe."

They embraced, and as they did, Ram stuck his small paper in Kane's hand. It detailed the new production number of muskets in Charleville and the numbers of new weapons sent to Sedan and Verdun. As per their usual method of communication of detailed information, Ram knew Kane would read the note, then burn it.

Kane tried to smile and failed. "Despite the pressure of protecting an independent woman, you look happy, Ram."

Ram could only chuckle at the truth of that. "Let me say the same for you."

"*A bientot*, Ram."

"*A bientot*, my friend."

Chapter Fourteen

THE NEXT MORNING, Ram rose early from their bed. Careful not to disturb Amber, he wrapped his banyan around him and headed for the small library downstairs.

Sleep had eluded him—and he knew why. Though he and Amber had begun the night with kisses that satisfied and fulfilled, afterward Ram had Luc Bechard on his mind. Or rather, what Luc had told Amber in the streets danced in his memory.

Ram had seen her become distracted at that news. Only during the hours when they lay together in their bed did she not think of the other man and his words. Ram feared she took Bechard's information as evidence she must return to Society. He could not let her do that. Vaillancourt was devious, and his ploy to compel her into Society again was so obvious—and terrifying. The man would imprison her and kill her.

In the cozy, wood-paneled library, Ram strode to the bellpull and summoned Gaspard, the man-of-all-work, who lived here. The fellow acted as *majordom* and all else. The man who rented the house to Ram had assured him of the fellow's utmost discretion. "After all, we have had refugees of all kinds renting this house for more than a decade," he'd said. "Gaspard will not betray you in any way. He can, in fact, aid you in almost any endeavor."

Gaspard appeared quickly, pulling his own robe around him. He still wore the stocking cap that he'd slept in. His wiry gray hair stood out at odd angles. A funny-looking fellow with a long nose and bulging eyes, Gaspard was quick to laugh, quick to nod, quick to suggest a better alternative. *"Bonjour,* Monsieur Algernon." Gaspard had accepted without question the name Ram gave him. Ram and Amber were to the *majordom* and anyone who asked, including the man from whom Ram rented the house, known as *Monsieur et Madame Algernon.* "You wish breakfast?"

Ram requested a pot of coffee and an omelet. "I will take it here. Ah, Gaspard. One moment, *s'il vous plait.* Do you know of anyone who knows their way through the tunnels of Paris?"

"Oui, monsieur. Would you wish to meet her here?"

A woman! Ram snorted. "No, in the *place.* By the clock, shall we say? At ten?"

"This morning, monsieur?"

"Oui. Have her wear a green scarf around her neck."

Gaspard bowed. "It will be done, monsieur."

Newly arrived in Paris, the couple known as Monsieur and Madame Algernon were from Arles and visiting Paris for the first time. The *mascarade* worked for him and Amber. No one would call upon them. No one would be invited to their rented house. They were safe from discovery. Save for Luc and Inès Bechard, who had recognized Amber at once in the street.

That incident flooded Ram's mind with the fear they'd be discovered by someone else. Anyone else who came to the left bank for...what? To see a friend. To buy a pamphlet or book from one of the many publishing houses. The chances were few, but Ram felt the odds had just worked against him with the appearance of the Bechards.

There was no hope for it. He was left with the conviction that he and Amber had to leave Paris soon. He would begin the intricate preparations—choose a convoluted route, multiple carriages sent out at the same time as couples to act as decoys. A day or two and they could be gone from Paris.

If Amber would go.

He knew how her mind worked. What Luc had told her ate at her. He heard it in her voice, saw it in her stance. Her sense of responsibility was strong. He and she would be back to the old argument in which he pressed Amber to go to England—and she refused to leave France.

Yet now, with Luc Bechard's words of warning, it was clear that Vaillancourt would not give up. He wanted Amber. Lie, cheat, kill, the man cared not. He would have her.

AMBER REACHED ACROSS the bed to tug at Ram. When she came up with only the sheets, she opened her eyes.

Early and gone again. She smiled. Although she preferred when he slept late with her and took her in his arms, she knew him well enough now to know he was disturbed by Luc and Inès discovering her yesterday.

At once, her delight in the day died to her own worry about Vaillancourt. The man was her nemesis. How could one man not give up his obsession with a woman who had been married to another and who clearly did not care for him?

She flung back the covers and marched off to the alcove to do her ablutions. She scrubbed her face and her hands, lost in the labyrinth of her poor choices to deal with Vaillancourt. She had to get hold of her reason. It was the only way to foil the man.

She had questions she must answer. Had Vaillancourt told Aunt Cecily that he planned to find her? Did he truly have a list of people to harass to find her whereabouts? Who was on that so-called list? Her friends, innocent and not? Her allies? Complicit or casual? Her supervisor?

No, that last he could not have. That person was too good, too secretive. Nor did anyone know the one who had reported to

Amber. No one knew Gus reported to her. Or had done.

That was one reason Gus had induced Lord Ashley to go away with her. Their friendship was the other. But under the guise of having an affair, Gus had searched for her. Otherwise, she'd had no reason to go to Reims.

Did Amber's superior know that Gus and Ashley had searched for her? She shut her eyes. Of course he would. He knew so much, seemingly everything and everyone of any importance.

"And what of my superior? Are you still active? What has happened to you, dear sir, since I've been gone? How have your operated? With such a hole in the reporting system, is the whole team disabled, or worse, defeated?"

Amber ran two hands through her hair. Gazing at herself in the full cheval mirror, she took in the woman in the sheer muslin negligee.

"It's time to tell the man you adore your plan. He won't agree."

But she would do it anyway—and he knew her well enough to know that was a certainty.

He would not like her plan, but he would let her go.

He loved her that much and more.

⫸⫷

"GOOD MORNING." AMBER sailed into the library. Ram sat at the desk, his blue-velvet banyan gaping open to his naked waist. "Are you studying here so early in the morning?"

"I am." He stood and opened his arms to her. In a pale pink morning gown with a matching robe, her long red hair billowing around her shoulders, she came to him, fresh-faced and kissing him. "You smell wonderful."

"You feel wonderful," she whispered, and squeezed his torso. "I missed you this morning in bed. You have spoiled me by awakening me with kisses."

"Can I make up for the lack now?" He teased her lips with little touches of his own. He never tired of kissing her.

"Always," she cooed, and stood breathless, her eyes closed, as he spread little kisses across her cheeks and nose.

"Mmm. If we continue with this, we'll have to scandalize Gaspard and return to bed."

"Why not?" she teased him with a wicked smile. "Let's."

"I wish I could, darling." He brushed tendrils of her hair from her plump cheeks. "You are ripe temptation. But no, I have a few things to do."

She nestled closer to him. His banyan opened wider, and she, in her thin gown and robe, was nearly naked against him. "I want to do again what we did last night."

"Oh?" He looked at the ceiling, innocent and dumb. "What was that?"

"You know very well."

"I do." He outlined her lips with the tip of his forefinger. "I like how you cry my name when I have made you come."

Her cheeks blushed bright pink, and he gave a chuckle. "You had me, sir, body and soul."

With my tongue on your most sensitive spot and my fingers inside you, you came with a force that shook me. "I loved it."

"I loved it," she said too with a broad smile, wrapping one of her legs around his, placing her most intimate part to his rigid cock. "You are such an inventive lover, my darling, that I wonder how some lady has not made you her own before now."

"Never," he said as he plunged his hand into the wealth of her hair. "Never has anyone enchanted me as you do. There was no one before you. There will be none other ever after." He knew he danced on the edge of his admission that he loved her. But God in heaven, she had to know the truth by now anyway. He adored her.

She sank one hand between them and cupped him.

Sweet woman, he'd have her on the desk. He moved them

toward it.

But then Gaspard knocked at the door.

She dropped her head to his chest and moaned her displeasure at the interruption. Still, she stepped backward and turned away from the door.

"Monsieur." The man sounded apologetic, as if he realized he had interrupted them in a tender moment. "I regret to report that your meeting with the person you wished will have to be an hour later."

"That's fine, Gaspard." Ram turned to Amber. "Would you like to have your breakfast, darling?"

"Please. But I am in no rush."

"There you have it, Gaspard. Thank you. I appreciate your promptness in that scheduling matter."

"*Pas de probleme*, monsieur. I shall pass on your agreement."

She strolled away from Ram and finally took a chair facing him.

"What bothers you this morning?" he asked her.

"My contact."

He sat back down in his chair and tipped his head, not understanding.

She licked her lips. "The person to whom I used to report all my information."

Ram grew wary. "What about him?"

She met his eyes. "I used to meet him at the abbey."

"Is that so?" He would be careful. A sixth sense told him where she wished to take this conversation. "Is he a priest?"

"I don't know."

Ram put two hands to the desk and calmly folded them. "What is he? Who is he?"

"I don't know."

He stared at her. "What is it you are telling me?"

"I would usually meet him at the abbey on a Monday."

Hmmm. Today is a Monday. "And?"

She swallowed and leaned forward. "I want to go today to see if he will be there, looking for me, expecting me."

"Why would he?"

"Because he valued my work."

"I see. And after no word from you since March, he would still arrive to hope you might appear?"

She sat back. "I know it sounds illogical."

He leaned forward. "My darling, it is worse. You said it was not the rule."

"I must try. I am here. By accident, yes, but so close, and I must try. He could still be looking for me."

Ram did not blink an eye.

"Oh, I can see you think me foolish."

"No, my darling. Too hopeful."

"What if… What if he sends someone else to see if I appear?" She ran a hand through her hair. "Well. No. I take that back. He wouldn't. That would mean his report would have to know it is me he sought. And the rules do not allow others to know, save those in the line."

Ram hated to do it, but he knew what her work meant to her. And he knew that she would regret every moment that she had not gone to check if her man appeared. "We will go."

She jumped up. "Ram!"

"We will," he confirmed. This small thing he could do to make her happy. One of his three guards would follow them.

"At two."

"Two o'clock. That's when you would meet?"

"On Mondays. This is the perfect! And you will come with me."

"I will." He smiled. He'd not let her out of his sight.

She ran toward Ram and flung her arms around him.

He held her to him, this woman he loved beyond anyone or anything he'd ever known, and prayed that what he did today did not mean the end of his affair with her.

For if this contact of hers appeared, Ram knew deep in his guts she would leave him for this man, this phantom, this agent who had recruited her, kept her, and used her for years before Ram ever set eyes on her.

But he had to agree to this. It was indeed the last thing she could do. It was also futile.

But to love someone completely meant one had to let them fly free.

He buried his face in her shoulder and feared she would fly away from him today at two. If she did, his world would shrivel, become small and foul, done in grays and blacks without her.

And so before they did this frivolous thing, they would have the one true thing that existed—their desire for each other, a living, daring ecstasy that he would give her as long as he had breath.

⇛⇚

THAT AFTERNOON, AMBER and Ram set out for the abbey. Their walk was brief. The weather fine. Pedestrians few.

Ram walked with her toward one door of the ancient church.

"At that bench," she told him with a nod toward the stone garden seat, "we would meet."

"I will remain here." He stood by the corner of two old buildings damaged, most likely, by the same mobs that had attacked the abbey during the Terror.

Amber nodded and left him. They would remain no more than fifteen minutes. She had promised Ram that. Her hopes were high, even if her chances of success were few.

She sat on the old bench in the shade of linden trees. She inhaled the fragrance of the last blossoms mixed with the allure of flowering jasmines. She waited. The minutes ticked past. But no one came. No one stepped from behind the large evergreen. No one wore a face veil incognito or a sweeping hunter-green cape edged in red braid. No one walked with a limp of the left leg.

Her contact was not here. He would not appear.

She stood with a sigh and approached Ram. Without a word, he put his arm around her waist and drew her toward their house.

Her time as an informant was over.

Her remaining challenge was how to get word to her superior that Vaillancourt kept a list of those whom he wished to kill.

THE NEXT MORNING, Ram left Amber after breakfast to do a few things to prepare for their journey out of Paris. First, he'd go to his own rented house on the right bank, then he'd seek out the woman Gaspard had sent to help him the other day. Today, he did not need to learn from her about Paris tunnels. This morning, he needed her to help him with another detail of his flight from Paris. He needed a coach.

As he caught a fiacre for the ride across the Seine, he sketched out in his mind an escape plan. He was taking Amber to Amboise, to the Loire River. If she refused to go to London, that was fine—he would suggest the south. Provence. Arles. Nice. A ship in the Mediterranean to any place she wished to go. Constantinople. Jaffa. Anywhere in the world out of reach of the deputy chief of police.

Minutes later, Ram left his own house in rue d'Orleans, smiling. He had enough money, thanks to Ashley, who had sent thousands to his *majordom*. He'd need every bit of it for their journey.

Back on the left bank near their rented house, Ram ordered a coffee and bread at a bustling café. He sat waiting for Gaspard's friend. Down the street came three urchins selling today's gossip rags. He dug coins from his pocket and bought one of each. Gaspard bought a copy of all he could get each morning. Amber and Ram read them to each other for amusement. She knew the people whose names appeared in the sheets and would tell Ram about them, their characteristics and their escapades. He had not read this morning's so-called news. He'd had better things to do than waste time on frivolities.

Drinking his coffee, he enjoyed the momentary peace. He raised his face to the July sun and breathed in.

He raised his cup once more, and his gaze fell upon the stack of printed sheets. His cup midair, he paused…and reread the first sheet.

Then the next.

And the third.

Heart pounding, he stood, paid, and grabbed the sheets in one hand. He told himself not to run home, forcing himself to walk at a normal pace.

However, in Bonaparte's France, under Fouché and Vaillancourt, nothing was normal.

Nothing.

His only hope was that he might persuade the woman he loved to accept the news he gave her—and finally, *finally*, leave France for England.

Chapter Fifteen

From the moment Amber saw Ram enter their salon, she knew there was trouble. Somewhere. Somehow. Whatever it was, it was horrid.

She gulped as he came to a halt, closed the salon doors, and fixed his gaze on her. In his pale, handsome eyes, she saw fear, sorrow, and, to her despair, death. He came forward. In his hand he held short, ragged sheets, the kind publishers used to print their gossip. He led her to the settee.

Biting her lip, she looked at him and sought what he could not give today. What no one could give. Peace would be destroyed by whatever was in those rags…

He pressed into her hand the sheets.

She read one with large print. *Attempted abduction of niece of comtesse and British envoy!*

No. Not Gus. She read another one. Skimmed another. But each one repeated the same story. Different words, but all the same meaning.

*Last night after a social gathering, Monsieur le Comte Ashley
and Madame la Comtesse Ashley were accosted by bullies in the
streets. Dragged from their own carriage, the attackers
attempted to separate the comte from his wife and carry
her away.*

Rumors have it on good authority the criminals were hired by a certain official in the government who wished to bring misery to the comte, who is a British envoy living in Paris since the signing of the Treaty of Amiens.

Fortunately, Monsieur le Comte employs his own guards, and it was they who were able to free the envoy and his lady.

Good Paris Citizens are eager to learn precisely who is responsible for this outrage and ask who will be punished for such a black mark on this city and its citizens!

Amber sat, paralyzed. One thought rang through her head. Vaillancourt had done this to show her how powerful he could be. How perverse.

"Gus and Ashley," she finally managed to say, "are safe. It says so. Are they?"

Ram cupped her chin and directed her to focus on him. "Yes, it says so in one of the sheets. Whit has guards he hired."

"Like you do," she murmured.

Ram nodded.

"But they could not stop the abductors."

"Amber, they did. Whit and Gus are safe. At home. Unhurt."

She ran her gaze over Ram's face. "But what Luc said yesterday is true. Vaillancourt plans to destroy all my friends. Seek out all my acquaintances. Abduct them. Torture…" She clamped a hand over her mouth, lest the sobs that rose to her throat fill the whole house with outrage.

She was on her feet. The papers fell to the carpet. "I won't let him do it."

Ram rose and took her against him. His large hands to her spine, he stroked her. "Amber, sweetheart. You cannot stop him."

She shot back and stared at him. This marvelous man was kind and considerate, irresistible. She loved him. She ached with it. The joy he gave her, the unequaled bliss of being his beloved, she would always value—and never fully enjoy. "I can, Ram. I can stop him. And I will."

His eyes turned dark and frightful. "No. I will not let you throw your life away on him."

"Oh, my darling man, I will not let you throw your life away on *me*. Give over, Ram. You cannot stop me. I will return to Society. I will return to who I was. What I am. And the man who will not let me live without him."

He stood frozen. "That is madness."

Yes. She stepped out of his arms. "I dress to go to see Gus and Ashley. Please, Ram. Come with me."

His face showed a man hollowed out, ravaged by her declaration. She loved him. But she could not have him. Could not save him this torture of her loss. She would deal with her own as days wore on, for never would she have that serene life with him she had but glimpsed in the rapturous moments in his arms.

Tears in his pale blue-gray eyes, he said, "I'll have Gaspard hire a carriage."

Then he spun away.

Chapter Sixteen

July 14, 1802

AMBER CLIMBED DOWN from their fiacre, wild to have this interview done. Ram had sat opposite her, deathly quiet. She had no words either. What was there to say now that she would leave him?

She climbed the steps to Ashley's house and rapped on the door before Ram could raise his arm.

Ashley's swarthy *majordom* came at once. Ram asked for Ashley, and the butler told them he was in his study. He could announce them, he said, if they would please wait.

"I cannot," Amber told him. "Lead us to him, please."

The butler asked for their coats. She saw no need for him to take her pelisse. "No. I have no time for niceties."

The servant nodded and headed toward the stairs. Amber and Ram followed. After stopping briefly before an open door, she rushed around the butler and found herself gazing at a man as tall as Ram, dark and muscular, and with the same gravitas as the man she loved.

Behind her, Ram bade his friend hello.

"Good morning, Lord Ashley." Amber folded her hands before her and summoned composure. "Forgive the intrusion, but I know you will receive me."

Kane eyed them both, then came round his desk to approach her. "I am pleased to meet you, although, I do believe, not in these circumstances."

"You have that right, Whit." Ram bit off his words, sour as they were. "I have fought this, but she will not listen to me. I hope you can persuade her otherwise."

Frowning, Kane nodded. "Please sit down, Madame St. Antoine. Ram. Corsini, please ask my wife to join us."

"Yes," said Amber as she took a chair near the fireplace. She was chilled by her own actions this morning and gravitated toward a warmth that did not exist. Sitting on the edge of the chair, she intended to do this quickly, cut to the quick and leave. "Do summon Gus. I wish to see her, congratulate her on her marriage. I do hope, sir, this is a love match."

Ashley gave her a stiff smile. "None other than that, madame."

She flicked a hand. "Let us dispense with formalities. We are too much in each other's pockets to be otherwise. I am Amber. You are Kane. Save for Godfrey here, who remains Ram." She gave Ram a small, intimate smile.

She recoiled at the sight of his unrelenting bitterness. Lest she fly away to their home and run with him to anywhere on earth he wished, she cut to her purpose. "Let me begin by telling you that we've seen the scandal sheets. Our servants collect them each morning. It is how Ram and I have avoided the gendarmes of Vaillancourt. A very thorough job done on that man in those broadsheets today." News of very recent events, such as this of last night's attempt at abduction, meant someone with all the details had informed the publishers of the story. She wagered that had to be Ashley. "I assume the work is yours."

Kane admitted to nothing. "What you read in those sheets is rumor," he said as he braced his hip on his desk and crossed his arms. "Not all is to be trusted."

"Very well," she said, noting his failure to admit his actions.

She knew that many in and out of Parisian Society paid the publishers on the left bank to print *libelles,* damning stories against anyone. Such methods had worked public sentiment against the Bourbons and now criticized the consulate and all who ran it. If the printed word weren't bad enough, balladeers strolled the Pont Neuf singing scandalous ditties and earning for themselves sizable remunerations. Amber had heard them singing as she and Ram rode here. "Define it as you will. I am not here to argue with you about your work."

Kane gave no quarter. "My work is to negotiate commercial contracts for British citizens and, when I can, to buy agricultural products for them."

"Of course it is," she said with the politesse of a smile.

"Amber!" Gus flew into the room, her morning gown of white muslin aflutter beneath her heavy purple damask banyan as she ran to her friend, arms out. "Oh, you look wonderful. Healthy. I was so worried about you."

She hugged Amber, who rejoiced at seeing her friend well. But she was here for reasons more vital than reestablishing a friendship. She braced herself for the argument she was undoubtedly about to create here.

Gus stepped backward, a bewildered look on her face at Amber's cool façade.

Kane put his arm around his wife's waist. "Join us."

Amber resumed her chair. She had much to say here.

Gus welcomed Ram, who merely frowned. Then she took a seat across from Amber and said, "You come unannounced."

Amber pressed her lips together and glanced down a moment to trace the folds of her pale-yellow gown. Ram gazed at her, his dark hair falling over his brow, but could not cover the despair in his blue eyes.

Gus grew wary. "Tell us quickly why you are here, Amber."

"I know what happened to you last night."

Gus inhaled. "Newssheets on the street, I suppose?"

"A new song, too, tells the tale of the Englishman who married the comtesse's niece, both of whom were attacked by peasants hired by Vaillancourt."

Gus added nothing.

Neither did Kane as he sat beside his wife in his own chair, his gaze never wavering from Amber.

"This," she added, "comes on top of other reports that you, Augustine, did away with a fellow in Varennes. He, sad to say, died of a severe cut to his groin. He bled to death."

Gus held her tongue.

Amber grew testy. "I see neither one of you will admit to these acts."

"Why should we?" Gus replied. "You seem to have the facts you want."

Amber regarded Kane. "I have a plan."

Silence enveloped the room.

Very well. "I return to Society," she told them. "I open up my house again. Announce I am ready to receive once more. Then I send out my invitations to dinner parties and balls."

Gus set her teeth. "No."

Amber countered, "You have no say in the matter, Augustine."

Gus seethed. "The same way I had no say in your departure from Paris? Your extended absence? Your failure to perform your duties?"

"My duties," Amber blurted, "did not suffer."

Gus scoffed. "I beg to differ."

Oh, I am being a harpy. But I must be to push all of them from me. If they find one crack, they will find another...and stop me. "No catastrophe has befallen anyone in my group in the time I have been gone." *A lie, but I must be brazen.* "While I take no credit for it, I take no offense either. Neither should you."

"Oh, yes," Gus offered with sarcasm. "The only catastrophe is that the man in Varennes is dead...after he tried to kill Kane and me."

"Exactly," Amber said with vehemence. "And now nothing

like that will happen again."

"You will stop such things from occurring?" Gus taunted her.

Amber gave them a secretive smile. "I will."

Gus fumed. "Even you cannot have the audacity to expect a dinner party and a ball will set any of us free from Vaillancourt's determination to have you as his own."

Ram, who had stood in the same spot throughout this scene like a marble statue, closed his eyes.

"No," Amber said. "It is the beginning."

"Of what?" Gus asked.

Amber had always known who she was and what she wanted. Today, what she wanted was far from her ability to obtain. Life and love with Ram would never be hers now. She had lived too long and worked too diligently for the overthrow of greedy, rapacious men. They now returned to destroy all whom she loved. Her friends. Her sister, in all but name. Anyone else she had worked with, they would kill. And now, given this chance, she would stop them. For if she ran, if she went away with Ram and turned her back, Vaillancourt would eliminate them all. By torture, by any means, the man was capable of the most heinous crimes. She would not allow that to happen. If she could stop him, delay him, at worst mollify him, she'd do it. She would find his list of her associates, steal it, destroy it. Then she would encourage any to run, to hide, to await his total destruction—or with her, to work toward it.

She got to her feet. To her dismay, she did so with a hesitation that gave away her despair at what she did now.

Ram saw it and growled at how she wavered. She could not allow him to see any more justification.

She licked her lips. "I will open up my house. Receive guests. Return to the work only I can do. Examine what is left, what needs repair, what needs addition. I will invite Society to my door."

She blanched, suddenly weak.

Ram cursed, then shot forward and took her arm. "Tell them.

Do it quickly and we will leave."

Amber raised her head, blind to their outrage—and her own deathly fear. She would never tell anyone about the list. Only the means to obtain it. "I will become Vaillancourt's mistress."

Gus was out of her chair. "No."

Kane was beside her, ferocious in his disbelief. "Why that, of all things?"

"Because it is the only way the man will leave everyone alone. Because it is what he has wanted for years, even before Maurice and I met. I have refused Vaillancourt time and time again. He grows more ruthless as he grows more powerful. He will not be denied."

"Amber," Gus pleaded, "do not do this!"

Kane looked at Ram. "What say you to this?"

Ram stood, angry and hopeless. "Whit, whatever can be said, I have argued. To no avail. Amber refuses. In this matter, I am without power. Though I wish to God I had it all."

Amber looked each one of them in the eye, then turned and walked away. She could do no more. Say no more. Drained, she had to leave this house and all in it.

Behind her, she heard footsteps.

She had gotten to the landing when Gus caught her arm and spun her around. "Don't do this. Do not throw your life away. You are young. Vaillancourt will hurt you. Defile you. Destroy all you have built. Do not reappear. Someone will rebuild the network that you and I can no longer serve. Trust in that. Live your life. I detect Lord Ramsey wants you to live it with him."

Amber stood her ground, unable to stop the tears that silently streamed down her cheeks. "I would do it, too. Accept Ram's offer of...life and love. Especially love. But I know of what Vaillancourt is capable. You only know a small bit. I will not have you hurt."

Gus tugged at her. "He cannot hurt me now. Kane will not permit it."

Amber rounded on her. "Do not believe it. Where evil lives,

it is capable of destroying the finest, the fairest, the worthiest of any of us. Each of us fights with the weapons we have. You have your own skills, your knowledge of what you and I and our network has done. You have Kane, who has another entire cadre to support him. Use it. Employ it. Never abandon it. As I will not abandon what I know, what I have, what I must do to strengthen the work I have done and what I will leave behind. I must fight as I can. For the love of a freedom I can only imagine. For you to live in the love that can bring you peace and joy."

"Amber, you told me once never to fail to take love where you find it."

She caught Gus close and ran her fingertips through her friend's hair. "I did."

"You can again."

"Could? Might. Should not. Cannot." She felt a stab of weakness and gazed back in the direction of the study and Ram. Oh, if she could have him and her good conscience as well, she would leave all others behind without a second glance. "Perhaps one day I might take the love I'm offered and live in peace. But that day is not this one."

She gave a final nod and took the stairs down.

At the last step, she stopped and turned to bid *adieu* to Gus. "I love you, sweet Augustine. You have been my dearest friend, my colleague, my collaborator, and my darling sister. Go seize your love and live in peace. You deserve Kane and all the happiness you both will find together."

Then she picked up her skirts and fled outside, beyond friendship, beyond love.

RAM STARED AT Kane, but saw nothing. "She does not listen to reason."

Kane looked as downhearted as he.

"I have tried everything."

Kane put a hand to his shoulder. "Find yourself."

Ram blinked. "What?"

"Find yourself and then you will find a way to help her."

"I doubt that."

"Don't," Kane insisted. "You will find a way."

Ram exhaled, dumbfounded. The one thing in his life he needed to change…and he had no means. "Never easy, is it, loving another?"

Kane winced. "Never. But then the rewards are more than you imagined."

Ram embraced his friend once more. He knew not how to claim those rewards. He knew not how to change her mind. That Whit could believe Ram could change even this was sweet, but foolish.

He would have to watch Amber leave him…and grieve that he knew not how to prevent it.

Chapter Seventeen

RAM HOOKED THE leather straps of his valise and did a visual sweep of the bedroom. He had left nothing here.

He had given all he had. Someday, that would be enough for him. Enough to bring him peace.

But today…

Today he would not conclude anything. That would happen another day. He knew not when.

He swung toward the door and took the hall and the stairs down at a clip.

Gaspard stood in the foyer, his hands folded before him. The poor man knew not how to take the attitude he perceived in Ram. Upon their arrival from visiting the Ashleys, the *majordom* had opened the door for Amber and Ram. At once, she had adjourned to the salon upstairs. Ram had gone to their bedroom suite to pack. Neither had words for the other.

There was nothing left to say. Only the sorrow was palpable.

Ram took the last step down. "Gaspard, hire a carriage for me, *s'il vous plaît*."

The man snapped to attention, his gaze assessing Ram with dour concern. "Monsieur, is there anything else I can do for you?"

"No, *merci beaucoup*, Gaspard. You can close the house properly after madame leaves. I know not when that will be. You must ask her."

The man's pale eyes went soft with worry. "I will. May I say, monsieur, I hate to see you both leave. You have been a pleasure to serve."

"You are kind, Gaspard. Please notify the house agent after madame's departure. Send the invoice for the rent to this address. I will pay the sum." Then Ram pressed a piece of paper with his address into the man's hand along with a few sizable banknotes. "A token of my appreciation."

Gaspard glanced at the denominations. "Monsieur! You are very kind. This is not necessary."

"It is."

"If I may do anything for you in the future, I am at the ready, sir. You will call upon me, I do hope."

"I will remember that."

"Ram," Amber called to him from the top of the stairs.

"Pardon me, monsieur." Gaspard opened the front door and went to the street to hire a hack.

Ram heard Amber descend the stairs. Her skirts swished as she came.

She stood before him, and he summoned the ability to gaze at her one last time. She appeared pale, fragile. "I want to thank you—"

He shook his head. "You have chosen."

She put a hand to his forearm. "I—"

He seared her with his gaze—and she dropped her hand. Yet in spite of it all, he gave her one departing gift. "If you need me, you know where I am."

Her brown eyes opened wider at his words. She stepped backward. Tears dribbled down her cheeks. Her lips trembled. "I do."

He needed air, the street, solitude. "*À bientôt.*"

SHE WAS ALONE again for the umpteenth time in her life. She had no idea why she had thought she'd be different, more assertive, even bold this time. That was not the case.

For weeks after she returned to her own house in rue Dauphine, she went nowhere. She could not manage the stairs down but remained secluded in her boudoir. She did not cry. She did not laugh. She simply sat, stunned at what she had done, leaving the possibility of happiness with Ram. And here she thought she knew herself so well.

Oddly not. Her staff were still there, doing as they had always done. After Maurice's death and Vaillancourt's pursuit of her, she had ordered her banker to pay her servants whether she was in residence or not. All of them were loyal and discreet. She wanted for nothing. She wanted only Ram. Pined for what could not be. Yet she had chosen to save others. Somehow sitting alone, empty of all emotion, she pondered how she had come to this—and had no conclusion. She knew only that she must do this, appease Vaillancourt's need of her. Become his friend, if that were possible. Become his lover, if that were necessary. Though she recoiled at the mere thought, curling into a ball of misery alone in her rooms.

But as day after day eased her nothingness, she forced herself to her duty. As Ram had said, she had chosen. So she dressed, she dined, she feigned happiness before her mirror—and knew it was a farce.

Two weeks after her arrival at her home, Rene Vaillancourt sent her a missive. He was thrilled she had returned to Paris. He would be even more delighted when she returned to Society. She did not rush to respond, but waited a week. She wrote him she was pleased to be home and that she would soon rejoin Society. When she did, she looked forward to seeing him once more. If the man understood the lies in her words, he accepted them with a response that said only, *I will wait for you.*

By mid-August, Amber ventured out to see Aunt Cecily. The lady had written often and asked to host her, but Amber had begged off. She told her aunt that she was recovering from her trip to the countryside. That was true. But also false.

She recovered, if one could call the aching longing for Ram she felt in the pit of her stomach an attempt to recover. But she'd grown accustomed to his presence, his charm, his love for her. He had remained in Paris. Amber knew because his name appeared often in the *libelles*. He still worked for Ashley as one of his envoys. He was linked with numerous friends, new and old, British and French, but none of them were ladies. For that, she rejoiced.

The autumn gave way in Paris to a resumption of regular court sessions with Josephine presiding like a queen. Madame Bonaparte received wives of envoys and Napoleon's military with a graciousness noted by everyone. The lady was the little, coarse Corsican's finest social asset. She appeared at the opera and theater. She stunned in the finest gowns and inspired all of Paris to ape her in donning expensive high couture.

Amber went slowly and deliberately back into Society. A dinner party one week, a ball the next. A theater performance. A friend's garden party.

She also returned twice to Saint-Germain-des-Prés Abbey to her bench. No matter—her superior did not appear. She was well and truly done with her work. What remained bright and hot, however, was her need to foil the man who was determined to hurt her or love her, lure her friends and kill them. She took special care to learn all he did, all that was written about him too in the gossip sheets.

Rene Vaillancourt was a bachelor whom many women wished to make their own. Why not? He was attractive, if one liked the looks of a tall, sleek, dapper fellow with handsome sapphire eyes, a sun-kissed Provençale complexion—and the aura of a snake. He had had mistresses. Over the years, each woman fell by the wayside in a month or two. For the past few years, he was said to have only one-night rendezvous. But he put it out that the woman he would have as his very own one day was the ravishing widow, Madame Amber St. Antoine.

Bah. Amber cursed him and wished he'd find a new obsession. Alas, that was not to be.

Now that she was in Society once more, Vaillancourt appeared often at events to which Amber was invited. She was the very model of the merry widow enjoying herself. She presented as a leader of Society, happy in her role. Rumor had it that she had mourned her husband, and she had mourned the end of a secret affair with a certain British envoy. She accepted the compliments and flowers from a few men in Society, but none did she honor with smiles and a certain *joie de vivre* more than the illustrious bachelor Monsieur Rene Vaillancourt.

The man approached her in tiny increments. A glance across a crowded room. A smile another night. A bow and a brief conversation during one of Aunt Cecily's afternoon receptions. At a ball, he approached her and asked for a dance. She agreed.

At the next occasion when they met, Vaillancourt joined a general and his wife in their theater box. Amber too was a guest. Vaillancourt sat beside her, a perfect gentleman.

They grew closer, said the *libelles.*

It was a ruse. Indeed it was. No man—certainly not the deputy chief of police—could match her darling Ram. But no one knew any of that. Not her maid. Not her aunt.

Add to that, in all these months, Vaillancourt had not arrested any of Amber's friends. He did not go near Augustine, Lady Ashley. Nor did he appear anything but congenial to the contingent of British envoys attached to Lord Ashley.

In November, the British ambassador had finally arrived in Paris to assume his role formally. That man was an experienced diplomat, cool, composed, a man of delicate sensibilities with the ability to talk a person to death. Bonaparte was not impressed.

Meanwhile, the city bulged with British. Hundreds crossed the channel, eager to see the sights of Paris now that the radicals had been eliminated. Charles Fox had come and gone. So too the notorious Earl of Egremont had come, along with his gaggle of lovers. Other British—delighting in strolling the parks, carousing in cafés, and attending the opera and theaters—extended their holidays.

As Christmas approached, Vaillancourt sent Amber little gifts. Hothouse roses one day. Confectioner's chocolate almonds the next. A handkerchief of delicate Norman *Alençon* lace. The morning of December 24, he sent her an edition of *Candide*.

Alone in her library, she snorted. The man could read, could he?

That night, Amber was to attend the opera with her aunt, but her heart was not in it. She had been invited on occasion to the Ashleys' for social events, but she had declined. She predicted that Ram would be invited to most events hosted by them, and she did not wish to see him. She doubted he wished to see her. Amber declined to attend Christmas Eve dinner with the Ashleys and their friends. They had enough friends to enliven the evening—and she was in no mood to act as if she were enjoying herself.

The New Year brought with it the ice and snow that Amber hated. But she was invited to Vaillancourt's house for dinner parties and garden soirees. At first, she feigned frail health. The cold, you see. Then it became apparent to her that to find this list Vaillancourt kept, she had to accept his invitations and go. So she found reason to disappear to find the ladies' retiring rooms. Or feign a headache and ask for a quiet room in which to retire.

She always took the wrong directions and searched in his study, his library, or his *majordom*'s rooms.

When, at last, she did find a bit of news at his house one evening, it came from a source rather than Vaillancourt. The occasion was at midnight among a gathering of Bonaparte's generals, their wives, and other assorted dignitaries. A general was newly promoted and wished for more honors. His family had money and connections. His wife was dead. No children cluttered his halls. The man had ambitions to find a Society lady to help him secure his future. Poor fellow had not read the gossip rags before he pounced, and he had the gall to try for Amber.

She was gracious in her polite acceptance of his favors. Of course, she watched as Vaillancourt examined the military man with the slitted eyes of a jealous man. She soon found herself in a worthy discussion of the value of the Charleville musket. Lightweight, easy to use.

"Indeed, we have increased production numbers." The new general puffed himself up, so proud of himself that he could boast of such things.

"Sound," she agreed, and fluttered her eyes like a vacuous female. "One can never have enough, eh?"

"Exactly." He grinned, showing all his bad teeth. "Especially since we have ambitions."

Do we? "I hope so," she told him. "We French are so much more civilized than many."

"Especially the Germans and the Austrians."

"Oh, but don't we like those Germans close to us?" She pretended affection with a hand to her bosom. It was printed in the *libelles* and sung in the streets that Bonaparte had asked for troops from German princes, one of whom was the former margrave of Baden, now for his services anointed a duke. "Those in the Alsace and Lorraine."

He smacked his lips. "They are really Frenchmen. But those in Baden and Württemberg, a few others in the south, come close. That's why we have a new shipment of muskets going to Baden and Strasbourg."

"Really. How good."

"It is. That city sits on the Rhine, and we must use it to march into the northern plains to Prussia. We will be shipping many munitions to that city."

"So wise," she said, bursting to leave this hideous man. Now she had to figure out how to convey the information to someone who could use it and forward it to those who needed it.

Kane would welcome it. But she could not go to him easily. She'd be noticed, even followed.

Soon she'd be in Vaillancourt's house more often…and she'd have more information to send onward.

She must choose another.

"YOU DISLIKE THE new general for the Rhine," Vaillancourt said to her with a smile when all had gone home. She'd stayed behind, as she usually did lately. It burnished Vaillancourt's reputation to say that the widow St. Antoine favored him more and more. She wanted him to see how necessary it was to go slowly with her. To get into his house often, she wanted him primed, beside himself with lust. Drooling would be best.

"Dislike? Hardly!" She *adored* the new general who had a loose tongue and a poor opinion of women's understanding of weaponry. Accepting her glass of cognac from Vaillancourt, she took a sip. "I hope I was not obvious."

"No. Never. You are such a good actress."

"Thank you," she said with hope Vaillancourt never thought that of her with him.

He took a chair opposite her, dangling his snifter from his fingers, his reptilian eyes all over her. "Do you tire of your solitary life yet?"

God, yes. May you never know how much. She could only bite her lip and gaze at him with all the sorrow in her heart.

"I would like to make you happy."

You could if you told me if you have no list of my associates and friends ready for arrest. "You are too kind, Rene."

"Not with presents, *ma chérie*. But with my company."

She swallowed the bile that rose in her throat. "Rene…"

He sat forward. "You have known for a long time that I cannot get you out of my mind."

She tipped her head. "Rene…"

"Your coyness thrills me, my darling. Do not take me for granted."

Believe me, I do not.

"I want you to allow me to court you, Amber."

She gave him a devastating smile. "Rene, I am no *coquette.*"

His eyes flashed, brilliant and hard. "You are finished with your previous enchantment?"

Ram. Never. Lest words betray the truth, she merely lowered her lashes.

Vaillancourt reached for her hand. His skin was cool. Bloodless. "Allow me to thrill you. Thrill you regularly. Will you?"

I cannot go to bed with you. Not yet. Not ever. If I can stave that off...I will. She forced herself to appear torn but tempted. "You could begin, *oui,* Rene."

"Begin, then, I will." He grinned at her. "I want you to act as my hostess."

That is marvelous. "You plan to entertain more often?"

"I do. I want you by my side for that." He raised her hand and kissed her fingertips. Christ, he was cold.

"Let us begin, then."

"Soon. I give a party for a few on the staff of the first consul. Friday evening."

"Wonderful."

"Will you come consult with my chef and my housekeeper?"

"Of course. When would you like me here?"

"I'd like to have you here often." His eyes lit with a salacious glint.

He took her question as a double entendre. She fought shutting her eyes to the very thought of him *having her often. Alone.* "Day after tomorrow, then? Say at two?"

He looked like an eager schoolboy. "Two it is. I will be ready for you."

She lowered her lashes. Blushing was not in her repertoire any longer. But she had to feign it, didn't she? "Please, René. I may not seem like a delicate person. But I am. I truly am. Please don't expect that I can rush into a relationship..."

He stood and led her to stand, too. Against his hard, slim

body, she forced herself not to scream. He lifted her chin and began to kiss her.

She turned her head. "Please, René. I beg you to allow me to decide the time and place."

He kissed her cheek. "Of course, my darling. You will be my guide."

⤜⤜⤜✕⤛⤛⤛

RAM MOVED THROUGH his days a man outside himself. Riding a particular stallion he favored and rented from a stable nearby. Dining *al fresco* in his own gardens. Perfecting his aim with his pistol—knowing his real target was a certain deputy of police.

In the beginning, he declined invitations to social events. He had no ability to carry a conversation. Nor did he dance.

He would take himself to cafés on the Champs-Élysée, idling for hours examining those who passed him by. He drank coffee. Avoided alcohol. If he started, he would never stop.

He wrote to his mother and grandmother. The letters were perfunctory but kind. He knew how to hide his feelings in print. He performed his work for Ashley, traveling to northern towns seeking more information on supplies and increasing military standards at depots and forts. The increase in Charleville muskets was only one such.

More cannon were ordered, cast, and sent not only to northern and eastern forts but also to Bordeaux, Lille, and Amiens.

By September, he was able to attend dinner parties without grinding his teeth at the vacuity of conversation. He read the scandal sheets. In late autumn, Amber's name had begun to appear. Ram found it intriguing that she had not jumped into the role of mistress. Instead her name was not linked to any man. Some speculated she nursed a broken heart.

God knew he did.

In January, Ashley assigned him the duty to follow a French

émigré who was sent to Paris by Scarlett Hawthorne. Ram's duty, said Ashley, was to track if she met with any officials in the government. Scarlett had questions about the trustworthiness of the woman.

Ram trailed the lady to the left bank one afternoon, and she disappeared into the old church of Saint-Germain-des-Prés. Bonaparte had made peace with the Catholic Church and all churches were open to the public once more.

As Ram sat in the sun that rare warm day following the suspected double agent, Amber walked across the street. The sight of her was like a shot to his heart. With narrowed gaze on her, he watched her casually stroll to the church and take a turn toward the bench where she had waited for her contact. He stood, paid for his coffee, and walked along his side of the street. Amber sat on the bench, spoke with no one, stayed only a few minutes, then stood to leave.

When she turned her back on the meeting place, he caught a glimpse of her face. She had changed. Determination that had once etched her features in bold lines had waned. She wore a vulnerability on her softened features. Was it real? Was she using that to appeal to Vaillancourt? Or was the change a reflection of something else?

Whatever it signified, she was no more the woman he had held in his arms.

Lest he put too much stock in that, he strode quickly away. To see her with her guard down surprised him. Had she changed—or did he merely wish it?

If she had, he did not know how much. Nor why.

For that, he would wait…bide his time, follow her, and assess any lasting shifts in her behavior.

ONE EVENING AFTER a theater dinner party, Amber wandered in

Vaillancourt's house as she usually did. His house was orderly. No elaborate furnishings were there. He was a bachelor, and the house reflected that, well appointed and comfortable as it was. The colors of upholstery and draperies were blues and whites, cool and indifferent. In his library, his bookshelves were orderly, the books in such strict alphabetical order that she perceived he never read them.

Tonight to justify her wandering, she feigned a horrid headache. She found in his library, in a small drawer of his desk, a set of two keys. He kept all his desk drawers locked. One of the two keys fit the small drawer at the top right. At the noise in the hall, she replaced the keys and scurried to a chair. One hand to her brow, she grimaced.

The footman who entered found her thus, apologized for his intrusion, and departed.

Three nights later, she returned.

The prize she found, not in the top right compartment, but in the blind drawer behind it, was a small leather folio with names.

Dozens of British. Kane and Gus, Ram and Fournier.

Scores of French. Two of her dearest friends.

Many émigrés. All of whom she knew well.

She memorized one list five at a time…and returned home to scribble them down.

She just needed a way to transfer the information. Some discreet, reliable way.

Chapter Eighteen

February 18, 1803
Paris

RAM CLIMBED DOWN from his hired fiacre and hesitated on the steps of the stylish theater. Tapping his hat on his head, he buttoned his greatcoat against the chill of the winter night and resigned himself to this required bit of public display.

"I need you out tomorrow night at the theater," Ashley had insisted yesterday. Ram and he met every other Monday in a café on the Champs-Élysées. "Gus and I host Lord Appleby to introduce him to Society."

Tonight's party in the Ashley box was to include many for the sake of appearances. Lord Manning was one. He came alone, his wife curiously indisposed. The Earl and Countess of Chiltern had arrived in Paris, intending to spend the winter.

All did this to show off handsome widower Lord Appleby, who was an expert in finance—and in warding off young ladies who wished to marry his fortune and esteemed title. The Earl of Appleby was from Norfolk, and Ram and Kane had first met him at Eton. Appleby had the formal role to improve the exchange of currency between Britain and France. No small task was that, especially because Bonaparte became increasingly belligerent toward the British ambassador.

Rumors even flew this morning that the first consul had met privately with Ambassador Whitworth last night and they had not gotten on well. Many feared it portended more trouble.

But setbacks in diplomacy were normal, especially with a temperamental man like Bonaparte at the helm. Ram had no illusions about the wiliness of the little Corsican.

The crowd around Ram urged him up the steps. Tonight was an oddity for Paris because the star of the show was a returned émigré. It was said that Josephine had personally asked Talleyrand to authorize the young actress's return to her homeland. This woman was a twenty-three-year-old who had been the rage in Drury Lane for the past few years.

Hundreds around Ram talked of their excitement as they surged toward the entrances. Many mentioned they hoped Bonaparte and his wife would appear to honor the Frenchwoman. The first consul loved the theater and attended often and without prior notice.

Tonight's play at the Gaîté starred the London sensation who performed the Bard's plays as if she were born to it. Though she was known for her abilities as a comedienne, Charmaine Massey had lived a frightful and tragic life. She had fled Paris and the Terror in the middle of the night with her younger sister, her father's mistress and that lady's illegitimate daughter.

Charmaine was the oldest daughter of the guillotined Vicomte de Neufchateau. A notorious minor member of the royal house of Orleans, the vicomte had stepped out of his usual role as roué to espouse a strong republican government. Once a friend of Louis XVI, he had fled to Brussels but been discovered and hustled back to Paris so that his old enemy Robespierre could condemn him to the blade.

The vicomte had preempted his radical foe and dispersed his large family, legitimate and not, to the four winds. Charmaine, the vicomte's mistress, and that woman's daughter had escaped the Paris mobs that night. But one other sister had been abducted from their carriage. The gossip sheets proclaimed that the girl had never been found.

Charmaine had made a living in the theater and supported the other three in her extended family in good style. Tonight was her debut on the Paris stage. She was said to be blonde, petite, and utterly charming. Returning to her country, according to the Paris gossip sheets, she had insisted that she would honor the occasion by performing only comedy, preferably Molière.

Across town, the sixteen-year-old French actress Mademoiselle George had opened the night before last in Racine's *Phèdre*. Charmaine refused to compete with the more famous French girl who was turning heads with her talent. Charmaine was a scintillating twenty-three—and unlike most actresses, she was said to be a virgin. Many a man was said to be intrigued by that.

Ram, in no mood for comedy or anything else tonight, was here out of duty. He was intrigued that he would see the daughter of the man whose house he had rented in Saint-Germain-des-Prés. He thought it a curious tangle that the vicomte had bought the house for one of his mistresses. Ram wondered if the woman so honored was the one Charmaine Massey had fled with to England.

In all, it did not matter to Ram. He was here at Ashley's request. Molière did not thrill him, either. Really, why not give the crowd a right, good, bloody *Macbeth* or *Julius Caesar*? He savored the idea these days of proud men brought low by betrayal.

After giving his name at reception, he swung off his greatcoat and wended his way with the throng toward the wide marble stairs up to the boxes.

He rounded a chattering group and halted. Amber stood alone in the far corner. Cast in the glow of a chandelier ablaze with a dozen candles, she sparkled in a violet gown trimmed in gold lamé ribbons at her bodice and sleeves. A choker of gold and amethysts surrounded her slim throat. Her winter coat trimmed in white fox hung on her arm. She scanned those who passed before her, but when she found him, she locked her gaze on his.

Resistance was impossible. He strode toward her and, for the benefit of the gossips, smiled with the pretense of a former lover, now indifferent to her charms.

"Bon soir, madame." He took her hand. Her skin was gossamer silk. What hell this was to see her.

"Bon soir, monsieur. How are you this evening?"

How do you think I am? He glared at her and bent to her hand. "Surprised."

"Of course." Her voice sounded choked, nervous. But her lashes fluttered with raw desire as he rose to absorb her beauty. Had she not slept lately? Could he hope that was because she missed him? "Shall we go up?"

"You join the Ashleys?" He was surprised at that. She could sit with anyone in Paris. Even Vaillancourt. Did the jealous deputy chief of police allow her out with others?

She stared into Ram's eyes, and something there begged for a truce. "I asked if I might."

"Do you like Molière?"

"No." She took his arm, digging her nails into his sleeve. *Hell.* She presented such a nonchalant attitude toward the swarms around them that he wondered if it were she who might be the star in the play tonight.

Fury ate up his good intentions to present a friendly façade for this farce. They climbed the stairs to the boxes in silence.

How are you? he wanted to ask like a good actor—and a smitten fool. Instead, he put his hand atop her cold one and patted it like a good swain. *Is Vaillancourt not keeping you warm?*

"I miss you," she whispered blithely, gutting him as surely as if she'd done it with her little stiletto.

He fought for breath.

Her arm through his, she smiled and nodded to others as they reached the landing and made their way round the circle.

He spotted an alcove where no one stood—and he paused them both there, his back to the crowd. "Why are you here?"

"I must talk to you."

"There is nothing—"

"Please."

"No."

"Come home with me tonight."

He questioned her anxiety—and decided his own needed tending. "No."

"I know no other way. I must... Ah, *bon soir! Madame et Monsieur Dubonnet.* How lovely to see you here. Might I introduce you to my friend, Lord Ramsey? Here on diplomatic duty. *Oui.*"

Ram had no choice but to grit his teeth and contribute to her charade. When the couple departed, his shock at her proposal had died at the hand of the obscene desire to accept her offer. To be alone with her—here, at her house, anywhere in the damn world—was not his wisest decision, but it would bring him more relief than he'd ever hoped for, at least for one night. "Do Gus and Whit know why?"

"No, monsieur. Please smile and pretend we are friends. I need you," she said as if they were discussing the delights of being here for the entertainment.

"You have news?"

"Of many things."

THE GROUP IN the theater box was subdued. Amber attributed it to the news that the relationship between Bonaparte and the British ambassador lately had grown chilly. When the Corsican frowned, many among the Parisian *beau monde* shivered. The fact that so many British appeared tonight was expected. For months, British in droves had taken the opportunity to come to Paris. It was indicative of their curiosity to taste the Parisian high and low life, but also to see what the French had become since the Terror. Certainly, the English aristocrats in their box this evening crowed over the fashion and the manners of those around them.

Kane, who expressed regrets for the absence of Gus tonight because of her delicate condition, occupied himself with introducing their newest countryman, Tate Cantrell, Lord Appleby, to society. Appleby appeared a jovial fellow. Or he had, until he froze once Charmaine Massey appeared on stage.

"Do you know her?" Amber asked, leaning toward him. She knew the actress as the sister of the young woman, Diane Massey, who had died so brutally at the hands of guards in Carmes Prison.

"Very well." His broad, angular face had gone to stone at the sight of the petite blonde who commanded the stage. "Too well."

Amber asked no more because her memories of Diane's death were so dark. Over the years, she had heard of the Massey family's troubles, fleeing the Terror with what they could wear and what they could pile into their pockets.

When Amber and Ram had lived in the house in Saint-Germain-des-Prés, he had told her it had once been owned by the family of Neufchateau. But she had pushed horrid memories of Diane's death from her mind.

Meanwhile, Appleby was definitely interested in Charmaine as he leaned forward to examine the actress. Lost to anyone's conversation, the man focused on the blonde beauty. He was mesmerized.

Amber was pleased at that. Seated to the left of Appleby, she was positioned closer to Ram. She could devote herself to getting him to talk to her.

That was difficult, but she had expected no less. He sat beside her, cool, composed, one long, muscular leg crossed away from her. His program in his hand, he pursed his mouth in a such a way that she saw etched there his desire to avoid her.

"Lord Appleby knows the actress," she tried. "Have you heard of her before tonight?"

Ram did not even deign to look at her, but nodded. "I have seen her in a few comedies in London, yes. She is accomplished."

"Word is that she supported her father's mistress and her sister with her earnings in the theater."

"So I have heard." He did look at her then.

What she saw written on his features was a melting of his ice to the warmer fires of his regard for her.

"She is lovely," she said, because her mind clouded with her desire and she could do nothing else but gaze at him.

As his pale blue eyes traced her hair and brows and lips, he met her regard, wordlessly telling her torrid tales of his longing. "Is she?"

It was no question, but a compliment to her.

Her racing heart picked up.

The performance was long. But the hours found him whispering now and then about the play. If he did so because he wished to appear congenial for the other guests, Amber took what she could get.

She'd make a better play to get him to agree to talk at length with her.

His desire had always been her leverage. Now, however, she would not use it and be unfair to him. Tonight, she wished to aid both their causes. Only that.

THE PARTY DISPERSED into the night air. The Chilterns and Manning thanked Kane for the evening and called for their own carriages. Appleby also excused himself, with regards to Kane for the evening. He said he would find his own way home but hurried off for the theater's backstage to find Charmaine, who had so enthralled him. Kane, who called for his own large town carriage, offered Amber and Ram to ride with him.

Amber spoke first as she gathered the white fox collar of her opera cloak to her throat. It was now or never if she was to persuade Ram to come home with her. "I hope you'll excuse me, Kane. I wish to hail a carriage myself."

"You cannot go alone," Kane objected.

She gave him a look that said otherwise. "I often have."

"I'll go with her, Whit." Ram stared at his friend.

Kane, surprise written in his narrowed eyes, checked the expressions of each of them. "I return home alone, then."

"Give Gus my best wishes," Amber told him.

"Mine as well, Whit. Good night." Ram took her arm. "Come," he said to her with the first smile of the night. "We'll have a better chance of getting a good carriage if we leave the crowd and stand down there."

Minutes later, Ram hailed a cab and gave the groom Amber's address. The two of them climbed into a well-appointed fiacre that smelled fresh and clean.

Ram sat opposite her.

The horse took to the streets with a regular clip-clop that punctured her composure—and left her planned speech full of holes.

In the flickering shadows of night, Amber watched him remove his hat and run two hands through his hair. He wore it longer these days, a pirate's appearance that suited his endearing swagger.

She had to shut her eyes to his allure. She was not here to seduce him.

"Now then," he said as he cocked a long black brow at her, "what is it you want to tell me?"

Chapter Nineteen

"NOT HERE."

"Why not?" Impatient, he raised a hand. "We're alone."

She lifted her chin. The defiance poked at his awareness of the way her cloak fell half open and how the moonlight gleamed on the perfection of her décolletage. She clutched her fingers together. She could not hide a bad case of nerves.

He gave in.

Silent, he counted the minutes as they traveled across the city to her house. She glanced up and down the street as their carriage slowed. The road appeared empty. Somewhere a cat howled. A few houses away, another carriage jangled to a stop. From inside, voices rang out as a man and woman argued loudly.

Ram felt in his greatcoat pocket for his pistol. He was wary of them. Of anyone. Across from him sat his darling, and while she was in his presence, she was his to protect. He wouldn't put it beyond Vaillancourt to watch her house—or to plant a ruse such as a couple arguing. The deputy chief of police had a fascination for Amber that bordered on the obsessive. How and why she had been able to avoid becoming his mistress was a subject Ram wished to ask her about, but never would. She did as she wished. He was now only her friend. Her friend who loved her still.

A footman emerged from her foyer and jogged to the street to pull open their door. Ram left first as he surveyed the street. Beyond them, the carriage that had stopped swayed with what appeared to be a tussle. No sound came forth. Did they pose, feigning a battle so they could report to Vaillancourt that the lovely Madame St. Antoine welcomed a man to her home tonight? Alone?

Let them. He defied them and spun to offer his hand to her. "Come, madame, the night is cold."

She grasped his fingers and swept past him to lead the way inside.

Nodding to her friendly *majordom*, Ram gave over his coat, hat, and gloves and followed her to her small private salon on the second floor.

"Brandy?" she asked him as he prowled toward the window that faced her back garden.

"No." He faced her in a slow and careful manner and watched her pour a generous draught for herself. "Why not just tell this news to Kane or Gus?"

She took a long drink, studying him. Looking sad and rather chilled, she shook back long tendrils escaping from her coiffure— and turned valiant. "I have many reasons. The first is that I wanted you to know first. I want to prove to you that what I did… The reason I left you was not without good cause."

"You owe me nothing."

She bit her lower lip.

Hell. You are an ungracious bastard. She's trying to be helpful. He ground his teeth. "You don't, Amber."

"I have news about the muskets."

What had he hoped she'd say? *I love you? I want you? I wish to leave this life?* He suppressed his sorrow and waited.

She smiled at him, triumph in her large brown eyes. "New shipments of muskets are being sent to Strasbourg."

That *was* news. "Shall I ask how you learned this?"

She shook her head once.

No, then. Very well. "You believe the source?"

"Of course."

A document? And you won't tell me what it is. Wise. But the danger she had put herself in to acquire such information spiked his fear for her…and his anger at himself that he had no means to protect her.

She sauntered toward him, he unmoving as he stood before her roaring fire, burning up with the need to put his hands on her and kiss her into tomorrow. Her glass dangling in her hand, she stood so close he could smell her cologne. *Peonies and spring grass?* God, she drove him mad.

She sipped her brandy, her gaze a smoldering invitation to drink her in and never let her go. She waved her glass, careless, perhaps even a little spiteful, as she said, "In addition, new muskets manufactured at St. Etienne in the south may go to Strasbourg."

He did not even breathe. That city stood on the Rhine, across the river from the territory of Baden. That nobleman, now a duke, had been cozying up to Bonaparte since last spring. He was not alone. A few other German potentates did too. Many German princes had lost homes and land to those who attempted to align with the hungry French first consul and gain more land from other, less agreeable German princes.

Last month, Vienna had agreed to let certain imperial cities and small principalities leave the Holy Roman Empire. Whit had often heard of this possibility from his cousin and colleague, Dirk Fournier, who had gone to there in late May. Dirk believed Bonaparte wanted alliances with the south German nobles so he could march across the territories freely.

"This is vital to us," Ram said.

"To us all." She took another sip.

"Have you any idea when they are being sent?"

She held his gaze, sure and steady. "No. But I will."

Ram frowned. To be certain of that, she had to count on her source. Its reliability and her ability to learn more about it. All of it was dangerous to discover. Dangerous to transfer the information, too. For that, she could be taken to *la Force* and shot for treason. His heart turned over. What in hell was she doing sacrificing her life for such news?

Ah. But he knew the answer to that. Now she was not only protecting her friends from the likes of Vaillancourt, but also transferring information about military supplies.

And he could not dissuade her. He'd never been able to. Instead, he tried to make her add relevance to current news. "Bonaparte and the British ambassador are not getting on well."

"Too many issues remain unsettled." She watched him, her dark eyes pleading for something softer, kinder. "They fight over who owns Malta. Bonaparte wants to sell land to the Americans."

Ram knew about both. "What worries me is not who occupies an island in the Mediterranean, but what Bonaparte will do with all that money from the sale of Louisiana."

"Fifteen million American dollars." She stepped up next to him with her brandy in hand—and held it out to him. "He will finance war. But I've learned more, and I need you. I need you for...for everything, Ram."

The warmth of her, her fragrance and her nearness, undid him. He took the glass from her and put it on the mantel. Anger died. Desire undid him. He reached for her...and she came like a river to the sea. Like his one and only love.

His lips in her silken hair, his hands to the satin skin of her spine, he inhaled her.

His arms had been empty for too long, his mind a red rage that he had emptied and filled now with her essence, her strength, her dedication.

She kissed his jaw, blessed the hollow behind his ear, and put her lips to his cheek.

Lured, he turned and found her mouth. This was what he'd craved—her soft surrender, her vibrant demand of his lips, his tongue.

She broke away with a start. Her dark eyes wide with want,

she grabbed his hand and led him to the door, to the hall, the stairs, and up, up, up to her rooms, and privacy.

He went like a man in a trance. She needed him, and he was hers to have.

In her sitting room, she spun and closed the door.

Inside her bedroom, he turned and locked the door.

She led him on. Her fingers were busy on his cravat, his frock coat, pulling his shirt from his breeches.

He spun her around, his fingers nimble, her gown gone, all else whisked from her and thrown to the floor.

He walked her backward to the bed, where she promptly sat and admired him as he dispensed with his breeches.

She reached out to cup him with one hand and stroke his length with the other.

He sucked in air and told his conscience to go hide. Her mouth was on him. Her body, his wine. Her pleasure, his only heaven.

For tonight, she was his.

THE FEEL OF him, the smell, the sounds of pleasure that stirred in his throat blended together and poured into her soul. For months, she had more than missed him. She had pined for his care, his affections, and his love.

He did love her. He didn't have to tell her. She'd known for months.

Perhaps from the very start.

His reverence as he kissed the hollow of her throat and that between her breasts spoke of his sorrows. His ardor as he blessed her nipples with sweet kisses told of his passion for her. But as he wended his way down her ribs to her hips, then urged her to open wide, his tenderness expressed his sole desire to make this moment the expression of all that she was to him—and all they would never realize beyond this night.

The torment of that knowledge had her sinking her fingers into his long hair and winding her arms down around his shoulders to hold him close.

Even that was not enough of him.

His mouth on her, she writhed in the ecstasy to be possessed by him once more. He rose, hovered above her, and kissed her. The taste of herself on his lips had her lifting her legs and twining them around him.

He sank into her, and a sob left her throat. This love would be the last she'd know from him. This would be her memory to carry her onward.

He slid more deeply inside her and held. With one hand he brushed her long hair from her cheeks to fan upon the pillows. As if he painted a portrait of her, he paused and smiled with a benevolence that defied the reality that they were parting. This was the last time he would make love to her.

She broke into sobs, gasping for breath.

He brushed her tears from her cheeks with flicks of his fingers. "Don't," he whispered—and began the rhythm that would make her his.

She arched, taking him, wanting more.

He gave it with a quickening cadence that told the story of their love upon her body in fierce, pounding thrusts.

She came in a rush, her cry as loud as his.

Then they were silent, still, replete.

And there was no more.

No more of him for her to have ever again.

THEY WERE DONE. Too fast. Too well. Too finally.

Ram eased himself up on his elbows and spread tiny kisses over her eyes and cheeks and chin. She regarded him with sweetness dwelling in her heart. This was all he had ever wanted in a woman.

He had known it soon after they met.

He angled away and took her to him. Memory had to serve him for years to come, and so he traced his fingers over her brows and the elegant contours of her pretty face. With his open palm, he caressed her throat and her torso, the rise of her hip and the sleek line of her thigh. With the encouragement of a smile from her, he lifted her leg at the knee and hooked it over his hip. He tickled the bottom of her foot and made her squirm. He loved her.

And he had to leave her.

⊱⊰

AMBER SAT UP and watched him dress. He took his time, a tribute, she took, to her. He did not want to go.

She tried to smile at him as he strode toward her and caught her around her shoulders, brought her up to him, and kissed her like a pagan.

She swallowed an objection as he made for the door.

"I will have more news soon of those shipments." Not exactly true. But she had to see him as she perused these next leads. The lists. Her friends and his who might die. She would tell him her memorized lists.

His strength always infused her with the vigor to go on.

Concern darkened his brow. He narrowed his eyes on her. She could see that what she did to get more information was not anything he wished to know. It would drive him to distraction.

"Meet me." She sat up. Naked in the faint rays of moon from the far windows, she held him in place. What she proposed could be her nightmare and his.

"When?"

She swallowed hard. "Once a week will be sufficient."

He winced, but he did not thwart her. "Where?"

"The cemetery of St. Pierre in Montmartre."

"At the butte of Montmartre? The church?"

"Yes."

"I know of it."

"It is secluded. The trees, the shrubs. Come at noon. Wait for me."

"How will you cover your actions?"

"I will. Never fear."

He nodded.

He did not need to tell her to be careful. She was an expert. He did not need to warn her not to meet him if she feared discovery. Nor did he need to tell her that none of this was worth losing her life over. She knew it all so well.

But that she would see him, meet him each week, meant he had more of her than he had had in the past miserable months.

A spark of hope lit, that he might yet wrest her from this life she'd created for herself.

He told himself he was a fool to allow the spark to turn to flame. Yet it did.

But he let it burn. He loved her, and there was nothing—*nothing*—he would not do for her as long as he had breath. Indeed, she was more than he'd ever asked for in a woman. More independent, more stubborn, more dedicated. More honorable. He would adore her and no other until the moment of his death.

She took a step toward him. "Ashley, Gus, and you are on a list of Vaillancourt's. Also two friends of mine." She listed them. "Tell Ashley. Be careful."

This was what she'd worked for. This was what she could die for.

He could not touch her again or he'd carry her out of here, no matter what she said or did.

She moved to embrace him.

He raised a palm to ward her off.

"I am yours," she said as if she read his mind and knew he'd run away with her if he could. "Not as other women were or will ever be. But I belong to you, Ram. You saved me. Helped me. Never deserted me. I am here doing my work because of you. For that, but more because you loved me, I am yours."

Her admission stunned him. Her understanding that he loved her had him reeling. Whatever it was that inspired her to say the words was the prize he would take with him.

He whirled away for the door. He could bear no more.

"Ram?" she called to him, and in her voice, he heard tones he had never before perceived whenever she called his name. Curiosity burned away his plan to leave her without a second glance.

She held a sheet to her naked body, the linen falling from her clutch of the fabric to her breastbone. Moonlight gilded her gracious curves. Her gaze grew torrid, sweet, then sad. "I love you, Godfrey DuClare. Remember always that I love you."

As comfort, her declaration filled him for a wild minute in obscene ecstasy.

As a benediction, it tasted bitter in his mouth. It should have made him wish for death.

But on second thought, he saw her plan for what it was. A way to end Vaillancourt's vainglorious career...if, for Amber's efforts, the heathen did not kill her first.

Chapter Twenty

T HE CEMETERY OF St. Pierre in Montmartre sat atop the majestic butte that overlooked the thousands living in Paris. Nestled in the corner of a churchyard, it was small and intimate. With few souls buried in the earth, the tiny resting place offered a bench for those who came to mourn and reflect.

In the unsettled spring snow, rain, and sleet, Ram and Amber met each week to walk among the stones that marked the lives of those who had hungered, loved, hated, and fought for the life they wished. In mid-March Ram heard from Kane that at the Tuileries, Bonaparte and Ambassador Whitworth openly argued. It was the worst of the two men's recent encounters.

Ram told Amber how relations grew worse. She knew. She heard the same in her own circles.

Under the spreading limbs of ancient trees, the bare branches would sway in the wind when first they met. As weeks went by, the buds sprouted and burst into the darker, larger greens of April. The flowering of Paris provided fragrant camouflage for their joyous reunions.

Each one had a rhythm.

She would throw her arms around him and kiss him on the cheek.

He would hold her to him for the space of one eternal minute.

Her heart would pulse with regret at what she had to do and pride at what they accomplished together.

"News?" he would ask her.

Occasionally, she would tell tales vital to Ram. An Englishman had fallen afoul of Vaillancourt and been imprisoned in the Temple. A Dutch merchant was arrested for failure to pay his export taxes. Two new cannon were being cast in Mauberge—and they were to go to Vauban's pretty fortress in Strasbourg. Sometimes she had no information.

Ram never asked what Amber did or who she saw, nor even what she sought. If he began to think that she had asked him to meet regularly so that she could enjoy his company, he was not entirely wrong. She needed his love for her, his belief, to bolster her. For the truth was, she grew tired of her task. Her ambition flagged with her energy. She knew not many days or nights she would have to go on to look for the list of her friends whom Rene would assemble and kill. She knew not how many nights she could continue to listen for the right conversations to get what information she needed.

She did not describe her life for Ram. Her days were so ordinary, they merited no description. Her nights amid the whirl of Bonaparte's Society required a library to hold all she learned from the gossip. Ram did not need to know it. He certainly did not wish to hear her trials and tribulations. He wanted her out of that life, and she knew it.

But then came one night at dinner at her Aunt Cecily's house. There, she overheard that a group of spies were soon to be rounded up and arrested. Vaillancourt had the orders and the plans.

Amber held her breath. Were Kane, Gus, and Ram to be arrested?

But no one she knew was jailed that night.

That was the most frightening night and day she'd experienced. But more days passed and no one was arrested. She told herself it was simply a pause in the terrors.

"DOES HE PRESS you to sleep with him?" Ram had ventured to ask her one day as a chilly rain fell upon them at the end of April. She had a large umbrella, but the poor thing was soaked in a few minutes.

They both huddled into their winter coats. The chill of their topic defied any protection.

"He tries to be a gentleman." She looked away toward the moss growing over the stone markers of those departed. Had they loved like she loved Ram? Had they wanted the one person in this world whom they had to reject, as she did? Had they sorrowed for it?

She hung her head. What was the use of such speculation?

She put her gloved hand to Ram's jaw. He bore a morning's growth of dark beard. His hair covered his ears, even longer lately. He'd become careless of his hair and beard. He worried about her nearness to Vaillancourt.

Ram's gaze, tortured and lost, examined hers. She sought an answer that would not increase his anxiety. "I lead him along on what strings I have. He is…enthralled. God knows why," she murmured.

"I know why," Ram whispered.

She raised a hand, denying him and herself the pleasure of his comfort. If he touched her, she would dissolve in a mist of misery. Her agony made her sensitive, teary eyed. Unable to bear the grief in her heart and in his eyes, she twirled away. "Until next week."

THE NEXT FEW days, the gossip sheets flooded the Paris streets.

Ram's servants brought them home to him. He could overhear them talking to each other with their speculations that the Treaty of Amiens drew to a close.

Ram visited with Kane more frequently and learned his friend had ordered his *majordom* Corsini to begin to close his house. "I tell you, Ram, get ready. Pack. Hide your passport. Have cash on hand. Your route of departure planned. The gendarmes will come for your servants, too."

Ram prepared his faithful staff for his disappearance. He also gave them sufficient funds to hide or leave Paris, whatever they wished.

For much of that, Ram had planned long ago. When he and Amber lived in the Neufchateau house in Saint-Germain-des-Prés, he had planned carriages, routes, changes, and even set aside great sums of cash. Now he checked his previous contacts, but not all were at his disposal. He would have to make new contacts. And, like that day months ago, he would not leave Paris without Amber.

She did not know that. He would not tell her. The argument she would give him would be outrageous.

But she would not win this time.

Chapter Twenty-One

May 2, 1803
380 rue Saint-Honoré
Paris

AMBER HAD NO callers. Ever. She never invited anyone, either—and she preferred it that way. With what she contemplated doing, becoming closer to Vaillancourt, she figured she was not fit company for anyone. Not these past few days, certainly. She would go to Vaillancourt to live in his house, be in his bed, rummage through his life, upset his order. She had to. She'd found nothing lately. Nothing.

Now she longed only for the company of Ram. Only for his embrace, his smile, his acceptance. She felt ill with the longing for him and her fright of Vaillancourt.

So it was a shock when she heard Gus at her front door, raising a ruckus and running past her *majordom* and up into her salon.

"What in hell are you doing here?" Amber shot to her feet. Dizzy at her rise, she was shocked to see her friend after so many months so heavily pregnant, and angry too. Had Ram perceived she was moving into Vaillancourt's house? Had he told Gus and Ashley? *No, please no.* "And in your condition, too?"

Gus blew out a breath. "Allow me your chaise longue, will

you, and do be quiet." She lumbered over to the large pink couch and plunked down with great relief.

She was very great with this child. Amber feared for her health. "Water? Tea?"

"Nothing, Amber." Gus was curt, feral almost. "I come to tell you we are leaving Paris."

Amber smiled. She had expected it. "I am thrilled. Good for you."

Gus peered at her, her lips thin with determination. "Come away with us."

Amber stiffened. She had not expected this. "You are heavy with child, and I see the stress has affected your mind, too."

Gus frowned. "Don't be flippant with me, my friend! To the matter. Come away."

"You know my answer."

"Why? What can you do now?"

"Continue."

"You will be arrested. Vaillancourt will not allow your operation to continue if France and Britain are at war. Be sensible."

"He does not know." *Nor do you. Thank heavens.*

Gus scoffed. "And I am ignorant? A troll beneath a bridge? Are you? What is *wrong* with you? Come away."

"Aunt Cecily does not go."

"Aunt Cecily *never* goes!" Gus spat. "Not under *any* threat. Why will *you* not go?"

"I do better work here."

"Unto your death."

Amber nodded. "So be it."

They stared at each other.

Gus struggled to her feet.

Amber swallowed back her regret, but did not rush to help her friend rise.

Gus took one last look at her. "You have a chance of love and laughter. A long and happy life."

Amber fought tears. *I see Ram now when I can, and I must be content with that.* "I do."

"You will not take it?"

"No."

"Oh, Amber. You did once. You loved Maurice and valued every day with him. Ramsey loves you, and I know you love him."

Gus was correct. But loving Ram did not protect him or anyone else Amber loved. *I know what I am about.* "I must do this alone. I must."

"You think you are invincible," Gus accused her.

"Like you?" Amber taunted her. "Did you not once tell me that? You were an island. A creature alone. No, Gus, I am not a creature alone. But I do what I can. Go. Leave me in peace."

Gus stood for a long minute, incredulous. Then, with her hands fisted, she gave a cry and fled the room and Amber's house.

Blinded with regret, Amber fumbled with the arm of her chair and sat down with a cry. Gus, gone, was one more tie to her past broken. Tomorrow morning she would move to Rene Vaillancourt's house in rue Saint-Martin. By that act, she would show the town she was now his creature. Not Aunt Cecily's niece. Not Maurice's widow. Not Society's leader. Nor the one who'd fled Paris. Or the one who'd had a scandalous affair with the British envoy Lord Ramsey.

But now Rene Vaillancourt's mistress.

She put a hand to her mouth, sick unto death at the prospect.

THE RAIN WAS hideous the next day. Amber's move to Vaillancourt's house went well. Yet she was pleased that the rain had posed a problem. She could avoid too much time with Vaillancourt by proclaiming that she needed to sort her clothes and effects after such a deluge.

She stared out the window of her boudoir in his house and

scoffed. Did the world cry with her because she was here?

God knew she was nauseated with the thought of the life before her. For days, she had loathed the very idea of being so near to her nemesis.

How she would hold herself up for today—for all the days to come—she knew not.

Chapter Twenty-Two

May 3, 1803
10 rue Saint-Martin
Paris

BY LUNCH, AMBER questioned why she had moved in with him this morning. She could not bear his presence. Oh, he was more than gallant. He practically oozed ardent attendance on her. His pandering disgusted her. She had the impulse to gather up her skirts and avoid the contamination of his touch. What a struggle it was to tolerate him.

But he persisted. Escorting her into the luncheon room with a kiss to her hand, seating her too close by his side, dropping a kiss to her shoulder, he was the perfect gentleman. "I am so delighted you are here, *ma chérie*. For us to be together leading Society is what I have wanted for so very long. I promise to make you deliriously happy."

You will never be capable.

She smiled, the actress in her in full bloom. "*Merci*, Rene."

But as the luncheon progressed, she noted he was preoccupied. He was a good actor, but not superb. At odd moments, he seemed to seethe.

What niggled at him? The quality of the entree? The sputtering candles? The service? Indeed, he watched the head footman serve the portions of soup and fish and dessert with an eagle's critical focus. Meanwhile, he did lead their conversation to tonight's dinner party, who would attend, how he was delighted she would be his hostess.

"At last, you are mine," he cooed in a tone that to most ears would have seduced a dedicated nun. His lips as he blessed the back of her hand between courses were a chilling horror.

She had all she could do to force her body to absolute stillness. She feigned a corpse. Dear heaven, she could not even dine next to him. How was she to tolerate this man all over her body, inside her, filling her with his venom?

She swallowed hard. The fish gurgled in her stomach. Or was it the mushroom soup?

The dessert came. A *galette de roi*, a pastry filled with crème and almond flour, a tasty concoction that resembled a light cheesecake. She usually loved it and asked for a decent portion.

Vaillancourt had none. "Not to my taste. Too rich," he explained.

Her enjoyment of the pastry was the highlight of the meal. She took her time, partly to relish it and partly to see if she could outlast him in the luncheon room—and give her time alone.

But Vaillancourt remained.

Stubborn but suppressing her frustration, she said, "I will have a cup of tea, then withdraw to see how the maid does with my belongings. I assume there is no need for me to discuss with your *majordom* the service for this evening's dinner party?"

"None, *ma chérie*. However, he has requested to meet with you."

"Oh, very well. I will ring for him when I am ready."

"No need. Your maid Marie is his daughter. Simply tell her when you wish him to appear. He is at your service."

"I will. *Merci beaucoup*."

Then an odd thing occurred. The footman who stood by a sideboard dallied so long pouring her tea that she turned toward him. He stood with his side near her and stirred the poured brew. Had he put something in there that needed to be blended? She'd not seen that occur but…still.

As he served her, she noted her tea seemed a natural color. She turned to Vaillancourt, who waved the footman away. "You do not like tea?"

"Too British for my taste," he said with a sly smile.

She'd seen him drink it before…but rarely. She lifted her cup and sipped. It tasted fine, and she finished it.

Minutes after Vaillancourt excused himself, Amber went to her rooms to survey the area.

The young maid, Marie, was at work unpacking Amber's trunks and putting her clothes into the two tall matching bureaus.

"Madame, are you well?" Her sweet blue eyes ran over Amber's features.

"I am." *I am not. I did not feel well this morning. Nerves ate me up. Worse, now I am imagining something silly.* Her upset stomach was due to her abject fear of what she was about to do in the house of the man she'd grown to hate.

Now that she was here, she admitted to herself, she was very afraid.

"Shall I fetch you some tea?" the girl asked.

God, no. The worst thing I could want. "A mix of apple juice and ginger, perhaps?"

"At once. Will you sit down and wait?"

She did. As the girl hurried off to the kitchens, Amber sat replaying in her mind's eye the scene of the footman and the tea.

Through her bedroom window, she watched the sun drift down to the edge of the earth and mourned all she had surrendered to come to the bedroom, this house, this terrible point in her life.

Today, she had missed her scheduled meeting with Ram in their little hidden cemetery in Montmartre. He would worry. He would wait. He would even investigate as much as he could. Which, really, was very limited. Vaillancourt let little slip from his house. Hell, that was why she was here. To steal from him. *Just as he and his nefarious colleagues stole our peace and our very lives from me, my friends, and those like Diane Massey.*

She shook off her doldrums.

Today was just one day she would miss her regular meeting with her charming Ram. She would go next week. Then she would share with him anything that she had learned here. Ram never asked how she had obtained it. He hated for her to ever describe it…and she would not. Nevertheless, dear man, he passed on again and again whatever information she learned.

She nestled into her plush chair and put up her feet on the cushions. Proud of what she and Ram did together, she could say she was pleased. She could never say she was happy. That was for another woman who loved another man, far from this terror. Far from this life she had created for herself. Here she would do as she must. For what she learned here would be so timely, so accurate, and so useful.

Scarlett in London would recognize it for its pristine value. After all, it came from the reliable source of Vaillancourt's whore.

THAT NIGHT, AMBER excused herself from Vaillancourt's dinner guests right after dessert and took the stairs to her rooms.

She had not seen the footman with the wine pour hers. He had his back to her, and her wine tasted…odd.

She had just stumbled past her sitting room toward the bed when Vaillancourt burst through the connecting door to his suite.

"What in hell are you doing? Trying to disgrace me in front of my guests?"

A hand to her forehead, she swayed before him. "Don't. I—"

She sagged.

He caught her up his arms and set her down on her bed. *"Ma chérie, you perspire."*

She stared up at him. His face swam before her eyes. His

features, so classic and elegant, could have marked a dashingly handsome man. But Rene Vaillancourt was no heroic figure. Enthralled by his own power, he had ruined so many over the years, including many she knew, imprisoning so many, abusing them. Innocent victims. *And I am just your obsession. Your symbol of revenge against Maurice…and Ram.* "I don't feel well. I could not go on, Rene…"

The anger drained from his face. He loved it when she addressed him by his given name, as if she truly cared for him. She smiled, a pitiful thing. Such a false illusion that was. He took crumbs. She hadn't meant to give them only to persuade him to leave her alone.

"What can I do, *ma belle femme?*"

"My maid. Get her." The girl was so solicitous. And for a reason Amber could not explain other than instinct, she trusted her. "I want to get these clothes off."

"I can—"

"No, no." She didn't want him touching her intimately in any way, not now, not ever. Certainly not when she felt so dreadful. "I cannot. I will be ill and ruin your clothes, Rene. Get me Marie, *s'il vous plaît.*"

He kissed her forehead, his lips cold and hard. A lizard's fond regard.

She shivered.

"You have caught a chill."

"I have. I have." *From you. Always from you.* She squeezed shut her eyes and squirmed in misery. "I hate a dank, dark place."

Visions of the weeks, alone and freezing, when she had hidden in the tunnels of Compiègne floated back to her. Endless hours without the sun or the wind in her hair before she emerged into the light and found the brilliant refreshment and comfort of the man she loved.

Tears filled her eyes. *Ram, Ram. I need you.* But she bit her lip. She must not utter his name to this man.

"*S'il vous plaît.* Marie," she beseeched Vaillancourt.

Off he went.

She was alone in her misery. "Ramsey, darling," she whispered to the shadows closing round her. "He knows I took the names from him. He knows."

Chapter Twenty-Three

THE FIRST AFTERNOON Amber had not appeared at St. Pierre had Ram waiting for two hours, then walking the rough, tangled terrain of the old cemetery. He passed elaborate crosses and majestic sculptures of those gone, those loved, those mourned. A few stones bore faded inscriptions, others whose names were obscured with flowers brought by grieving friends or relatives. Always he kept Amber and his bench in view.

Her absence that first day, he argued with himself, was nothing to alarm him. She had not been able to excuse herself from Vaillancourt. Or the deputy had required her at some surprise social chance meeting by an official. Kane kept Ram informed of any little thing he learned about the deputy. The latest news was that he had a new mistress who lived in his house.

Ram could do naught but accept what he could not change. He went home, poured himself a stiff brandy, and decided to attend a dinner party to which he'd been invited.

Later that night, he learned that the Americans had arrived to sign the treaty for the sale of land to the French. The territory along the Gulf of Mexico west to Spanish territory was to belong to the new United States government for the price of fifteen million American dollars. That money, beamed the gossips, would pay for Napoleon's ambitions. Ram knew those desires included funding French armies and building up supplies along the northern and eastern borders.

One week later, Amber again did not appear on their appointed day at the cemetery. Ram remained in place for only an hour past their usual time. Hiring a shabby public fiacre, he ordered the coachman twice around Vaillancourt's avenue. Ram got out to walk far down the street, but in the next four hours, he did not see Amber go or come.

Beside himself, he walked to a nearby florist's shop, bought an armful of roses, and hired the boy who worked there to knock on Vaillancourt's kitchen door and ask if the lady of the house would like any. He wished to sell them, the boy explained, or his master would be furious, he told the maid. But the boy returned to Ram, his arms full of the roses Ram had bought, and word that the lady of the house was indisposed.

For the next few days, Society in Paris convulsed with the schism of Bonaparte and the British ambassador. Kane and Gus left the city for London and home. Ram attended a few social gatherings only to get gossip.

Bonaparte was getting ready to officially end the peace with Britain, and those who had any sense in their heads were packing their trunks to head for the coast. The streets crawled with those frantic to leave Paris. Carriages stood before countless front doors. Horses whinnied and cried, wearied with the wait. Stray dogs wandered among the chaos, begging for scraps, searching for anything that looked like a treasure.

In the melee, servants lifted trunks into the rear hatches of coaches. Carts filled with odd goods, pots and pans, furniture, and cages with cats and dogs. All clogged the streets. Fearful women dabbed at their cheeks. Men shouted at their coachmen like lunatics. French creditors banged on doors, waving long sheets of invoices for goods and services rendered.

This morning at dawn, wild from a sleepless night, needing to escape the house and think how best to get Amber out of Vaillancourt's house, Ram had his horse saddled and went for a long ride along the Champs-Élysées and back.

When she did not appear again that afternoon in the ceme-tery, it was the third time. Ram considered everything, from barging into Vaillancourt's house demanding to see Amber to bribing the man's servants to let him in.

After a long breakfast and two stiff whiskies, he was deter-mined that bribery of Vaillancourt's *majordom* was his answer. First, he had to call upon a few people to help him in his next quest.

Then he would go appeal to Amber one last time.

AMBER STRUGGLED UP on an elbow and bent to the side of her bed. She shrank back at the foul odor of her own vomit in the pot on the floor. She had been ill all night. Often. Too often.

Get up. Get to the bellpull.

She pushed up and the room spun. In a whirl, she clamped shut her eyes and felt for her pillows. The urge to vomit hit her again.

Why did she do this? Why? The footman. He's the cause because he...

"Madame?" Marie called to her from so very far away. "Let me..."

Amber gazed at the pretty girl in the shadows of the morning. Whatever she said made no sense. "Marie..." She licked her lips. And her gorge rose again.

"Oh, Madame. Madame..." And on the girl chattered.

What's wrong with me?

Dizzy. Dry throat. Ugly vomiting.

"Marie, water. *S'il vous plaît.*"

"*Oui*, madame. But you do not keep it down." The girl put a glass to Amber's lips, but she could not open her lips. The water dribbled down her chin. "You must try, madame. Try."

Someone banged on the door.

The girl cast her attention to the sound. "Enter!"

Who comes? Not him. Do not let it be him. "Please, I do not want—"

A man's voice shouted.

A woman's cry rent the air.

Is that mine? Am I dying?

"Amber, *ma chérie!*" Aunt Cecily loomed above her. She looked haggard, her black hair in a haphazard style. Her green eyes were small and dark. "Darling girl. What is wrong with you?"

I am dying, Aunt. He gave me poison and I am going to die. Tears dribbled down Amber's cheeks.

Her aunt wiped her tears away and gave her a watery smile. "Sweet Amber. I heard you are unwell. People speak of it in court. Last night at my dinner table. How long have you been like this, sweetheart?"

I don't know, Aunt. Hug me. Stroke my forehead like you used to when I was small and sick.

"How long, Marie?" her aunt demanded of the maid, her gaze never leaving Amber's.

"When she arrived a few weeks ago, madame, she looked pale. But she is now quite ill and gives up everything."

"When did she last eat?"

The maid said she was not aware.

"Poison, Aunt," Amber murmured, but Cecily did not look at her. *The footman put something in my wine. In my tea. Vaillancourt is poisoning me.*

Her aunt winced and looked at Marie. "Take this chamber pot away and bring us a new one. Bring me tea and biscuits."

Ugh. No biscuits.

"A clear soup, too. A fresh nightgown and hot water, toweling! At once." Aunt Cecily plumped the pillows and straightened Amber's covers. Then she cupped her cheek. "Not to worry, dearest. I will get a physician. We will get you better. Marie, summon Monsieur Vaillancourt to me at once."

"But madame, he has a guest."

Aunt Cecily shot up and glared at the poor maid. "Tell him to come here now or I will make myself known to him *and* his guest. I guarantee your master will not like what I have to say to him either in front of his visitor or alone. But he will hear from me *now*. Go."

⇶⫷

JUST AFTER FOUR, Ram had concluded his withdrawals from his account, sent his Parisian banker on his way, and deposited his gold coins in his wall safe, when his *majordom* appeared once more at his study door.

"Monsieur, you have two callers." His butler, a Frenchman of wide experience and great discretion, looked flustered.

"Two?" Ram expected only one man, Kane's former *majordom*. He had much more to do to prepare his departure, and all this was wasting time. "Who are they?"

"The one you expected. Monsieur Umberto Corsini. I showed him to the green salon."

"Excellent." Kane's former *majordom* was a young Italian of many talents and numerous contacts in Paris. Kane had pensioned off his butler, but before he left for London, he had told Ram that Corsini remained available to all their colleagues in Paris. "Good. And the other person?"

"Madame le Comtesse Nugent calls."

Cecily?

Ram ran two hands through his ruffled hair and reached for his frock coat.

"I have taken her to the yellow salon, monsieur. I ordered tea."

"Make that brandy." For Cecily to come here to him, she either had news about Amber—or the lady was here to condemn him to hell.

Either merited a good, stiff drink.

Chapter Twenty-Four

FOR DECADES, CECILY Ann Struthers-Sumner, Countess Nugent, had made a reputation for doing the outrageous, the unpredictable. At age seventeen she'd become the mistress of the Prince of Wales. But the enchantment did not last. Within months, she had been ordered by him to marry Earl Nugent, a sickly, simple-minded creature. Soon after the wedding, Cecily disappeared from court. Many speculated as to the cause.

But eleven months later, and suddenly a rich widow, she appeared in Paris. She became the talk of the town, a friend of Madame du Barry. Soon, Cecily was the mistress of the infamous Duc d'Orleans. That man, though a Bourbon close to the throne, increasingly voiced liberal causes. Later dubbed Philippe Égalité for his sentiments, he nonetheless was carted off to the guillotine. Because of her association with him, Cecily was sent to Carmes Prison along with her young charge, an English girl Cecily had brought into her home. The orphan was Amber.

But Cecily's friendship with Josephine Beauharnais saved her. The young wife of a successful military man, Josephine took Cecily into her home and the new Parisian Society.

Cecily had long been heralded as a beauty. But she was also wily enough to befriend dutifully those in power. She burnished her earlier reputation by never openly consorting with any other men—and saving the fortunes her two famous lovers had generously bestowed upon her.

Cecily had never called on Ram. She had always been reserved with him, polite, never warming. But then, she had no reason to do otherwise. To her, he was an English envoy, a friend of Lord Ashley's, and therefore most likely another agent of the Crown. Her friendship with Josephine, more than any other characteristic, kept Cecily from regarding Ram in any other way than she had. Indifferent and aloof. For her to come here now that he and Amber were publicly estranged was surprising. Unless the lady knew that he and Amber met regularly and that, for some reason, Amber had stopped.

Ram opened the salon doors and closed them firmly behind him. Whatever the woman had to say to him was most likely a tirade, but God only knew about what. In any case, his household did not need to hear it.

She paced before the elaborate alabaster mantel. Dressed formally for calling upon others, she wore a sedate mix of embroidered amethyst silk with fuchsia trim. The colors should have complemented her complexion and made her vibrant. Instead, she was drained of every color, her pallor ghastly. She'd been in such a hurry or in such distress this morning that her attire might be superbly fitted and exotically rich in fabric, but the rest of her was untidy, to say the kindest. Tendrils of her black hair escaped her coiffure. Her gold-rimmed green eyes were swollen, the whites red. She walked stiffly, her fingers working a tall, thick ivory-tipped walking stick.

She appeared aged, much older than her forty-some-odd years. Her full lips were pressed tightly to a thin line, and her greeting to him held no smile. Why she would call upon him, he hoped, she would quickly reveal. He had better things to do than be upbraided for his love of her adopted daughter. Her lovely child who now mysteriously could not meet him. Might the lady know why? She usually knew everything in this city.

"Madam," he said as he strode toward her, "since you have

never regraded me with any approval, I doubt you come to me now with a change of heart. Will you sit?" His gaze dropped to her ivory stick. "Or will you run me through?"

Her green eyes flashed, and in that moment, he thought he saw the same look of another woman, Gus.

But Ram shook the thought away as the lady mashed her lips together, unhappy with him. "No assassination, Ramsey."

"So then…" He offered the nearest chair.

She dug her hefty stick into his Aubusson carpet. "We've no time for that."

"Very well." He put his arms behind him and clasped his wrists. If he did not hold himself together, he would fly about the room in helpless rage. "I've much to do to leave Paris. Whatever you want, both you and I are in a hurry."

"I have been to see Amber."

That struck him. Whatever means she'd used, he might use too. "Vaillancourt let you in?"

"No. I have friends on his staff," she bit off.

"How good for you," he said with venom.

Cecily narrowed her eyes upon him. "You have not seen her lately, have you?"

"I, unlike you, am not welcome at Monsieur Vaillancourt's house."

Canny woman, she eyed him as if she speculated whether he told her the whole truth. "I went this morning, Ramsey."

"Good of you."

Once more, she used her stick on his carpet. The poor rug would have a hole if she kept that up. "Amber is ill."

His heart stopped. It took him a moment to process that odd news. Amber, who had lived in a cold, dank tunnel under Cecily's house in Compiègne. Amber, who had walked the streets of Reims and Varennes in the chilly nights. Amber, who had cold hands…unless they clasped his. She was ill?

He took care not to show how his mind reeled. "What's the matter with her?"

"She is weak, cannot eat, tries to drink but loses anything she puts in her stomach. She is pale. Her skin…" Cecily touched her own cheek. "Her skin is drawn. She has lost weight."

With each of her words, she drove her nails into her skin.

He felt his stomach turn. "What does she say?"

"Little. She is hoarse from all her vomiting. Her eyes are clouded. She is so weak, she is not cognizant of all around her. She recognized me only after I forced her eyes open and demanded she tell me who I am."

His head swam with a torrent of disaster. Amber ill. Amber barely conscious. Amber unable to recognize her aunt who had saved her and loved her. *Like I did. Like I do.*

He strode to the window overlooking the boulevard. Outside, the sun shone. Carriages clogged the streets. Pedestrians hurried past. The British were leaving and in a mad rush. Life and tragedy converged in the streets…and his beloved was ill.

"What did she tell you? What is the problem?"

"She lolled her head upon her pillows. I doubt she understands. She is so weak. She needs tea, broth. Water."

He grimaced. "Did you speak with Vaillancourt?"

"I did. I asked him how long she has been like this."

It's been three weeks. Three since she has not met me in the cemetery in Montmartre.

Cecily came to stand behind him. "He says she has grown worse this past week."

Ram squeezed shut his eyes. The last time when they walked together, Amber had seemed distracted. He worried she was losing her focus—and her love for him. But she had been pale and thin then.

Had she been ill that day? Yes, most likely that was the beginning, and he had not noticed. *Fool. Fool.*

Cecily grabbed his arm. "I know what she did."

He blinked. If she meant his and Amber's collaboration… "You know nothing." She could not know the facts that Amber had fed to him. If Cecily did, it was only because Amber had, in her delirium, recited them to her. Could his darling be so ill that she would share such information?

Whatever Cecily knew or thought she did, no one should know but him. And Kane. If Amber had murmured any hint of what she did to anyone, the news was her death warrant.

Had Amber told Vaillancourt what she did?

Did Vaillancourt know Amber had searched his desk and found lists of those he would jail? Was he angry, desperate that she had betrayed him?

All was nothing, however, to the news that Amber was weak, unable to digest or keep food down.

He turned toward Cecily.

"Ramsey, Amber says Vaillancourt poisons her."

Ram grabbed the back of a chair to keep from reeling.

Dear God. The man had no boundaries. *And if he knows that Amber used him, he would rather kill her himself than have Fouché or Bonaparte learn he has failed them.*

Vaillancourt had told Amber he craved her. But love? No.

He does not love you, my darling.

Ram clasped his hands together. He could not stop them from shaking.

"Ramsey," Cecily said, calling him from his reverie, "you must take Amber from him."

"I have planned it myself, coincidentally today."

He examined Cecily. For the first time in more than a year, he saw beyond the picture of her created by the dossier of her past that he had read in London. He gazed past his personal interactions with her. The social events that denoted her as a leader of the court, a confidante of those most high. Now, he saw her as the surrogate mother to two accomplished young charges. The undaunted young woman who had saved both girls, encouraged them, fed and clothed them, then educated them in the ways of the French *bon ton*, in the manner of survival in a land of snakes.

So had she also by precept or example taught them more?

Taught them to love freedom? How to prevaricate and subdue? How to…spy? No, surely not.

"Who met you at Vaillancourt's door?" he asked. Amber had told him Vaillancourt's butler was a fine fellow of like mind, once associated with a man on her aunt's staff.

Cecily gave him the half-smile that said she was pleased at his turn of mind. "The *majordom*. An old friend of my own man."

"Who else is in the house?"

"Two footmen and Vaillancourt's valet. I know neither."

Of no help, then.

"But in addition, there is the maid, young Marie. She adores Amber. I know because I saw it today. She is"—Cecily sent Ram an evil smile—"the daughter of Vaillancourt's *majordom*."

"Useful?"

"I know she is. Her father, too. They receive, shall we say, a stipend from me?"

Ram cocked a brow. "After this day of helping you and me, they may need more from you than that."

She inhaled. "I am ready."

He needed only one more thing from her.

"And the location of Amber's bedroom?"

CORSINI TOOK MORE than an hour to find a Berline he could rent.

Ram met the Italian and the coach best used for traveling at the corner, lest anyone watch his house. He'd noticed no one. He expected no one, either. After Amber had decided to part from him last year, no one bothered to watch his house nor track his comings and goings.

He climbed into the shabby cab and thumped on the roof to signal the coachman to drive on. He had instructed Corsini to tell the man to go to Amber's address and find the servants' door.

It was mid-May, so dusk came half after nine at night. Ram had set ten for the time of his arrival. Corsini had learned that

Vaillancourt gave a dinner party this evening. Ram could not care. He had his pistol and a knife. Not that either would be to hand with his arms full of his darling, but he would nonetheless be prepared. Still, he hoped he'd need neither.

He climbed down from the cab and pulled out the extended seat concealed in the opposite bench. It added three inches at most, but it was better than nothing. Amber could lie down, even if the jostling of the coach would hurt her back.

He took a deep breath and rapped on the kitchen door.

"Your *majordom, s'il vous plaît*," he said to the young girl servant. Ram hoped he'd enter with help, but if the man balked, he still had Cecily's map of the house.

The maid scurried off, leaving him in the cramped scullery.

Minutes later, the *majordom* appeared.

"I am the friend of Comtesse Nugent, monsieur. I ask for your help finding Madame St. Antoine's bedroom."

The man lifted a hand as if to listen for voices and movement, then he crooked a finger.

Ram followed.

At the servants' stairs, they paused. The butler raised a staying hand. Off he went, and in a moment he returned with a young girl. "My daughter, Marie."

The girl nodded at Ram and tipped her head toward the stairs.

She opened the door, and Ram noted the width of the staircase. It was so narrow, he'd never get down this with Amber in his arms. He'd need to take the main staircase. Being discovered by the deputy and his illustrious guests would work in Ram's favor. What man would admit to giving a party with his paramour ill unto death upstairs? Ram would walk out of that house with Amber, so help him God.

"I'm sorry," he whispered to Marie. "Continue, please."

Up the steps they raced. At the second turn, Marie stopped and, with a finger to her lips, slowly opened the servants' door to the hall. She stepped out and surveyed it, and with another tilt of her head, Ram followed.

Down the hall they went with careful footfalls.

Ram noted that Marie led him past the landing of the center stairs. Rising from below were the sounds of many voices, mostly male, conversing and laughing. Good. They were well occupied.

At the second door, Marie stopped. Again with a finger to her lips, she opened the door and stepped inside a moment, only to turn back and urge him to enter.

Rushing around her, Ram came to a pause when he realized that this was a sitting room and sat at the rear of the building. He whirled. At either side was a doorway. This meant the rooms were built *enfilade*—one after another. He raised his arms in question.

"This way," she said, and spun toward her left.

At the threshold, he had to stop. The sight of Amber on the bed weakened his knees.

She lay on her side facing him, her mouth open, her eyes closed, one hand tucked under her chin. Her child's pose was one of pain and abandonment.

But you are no longer alone.

He charged forward. Bent down. Went to his knees beside her. Alarmed at how slowly her eyes opened, he groaned.

She looked drugged, hazy, dreamy. "Godfrey DuClare." She did not so much speak his name as mouth it. Then she gave him a smile. Weak. Tortured.

He put his palm to her cheek. He felt the bone beneath. She was thin, cold.

"A blanket," he said to Marie.

He lifted her bed covers back from Amber's torso. She huddled into the mattress.

"I'll keep you warm," he told her, and shook out the folded blanket. "Come away with me now, my darling. Put your arms around me. Can you?"

Amber gazed at him. "I dreamed you here." She smiled to herself.

"Here, sweetheart." He tugged her toward him. She was a dead weight. But she was lighter than she'd ever been.

She shook her head. "Hurts."

"I'm sorry." He pulled her toward him more securely.

"He's bad, Ram."

"I know."

She clutched his cravat. "He poisons my tea."

Ram stared at her. *No, no.* "He will no longer, sweetheart." Then he lifted her and stood. "The door, Marie."

The maid hurried around him.

"Ramsey," Amber whispered, her voice rough. "Are you here?"

"I am, darling. I am."

Into the hall, he trod slowly with her, Marie in the lead.

Below, men debated some issue.

There was nothing for it. He'd have to walk down the main stairs and out the front door.

"Marie," Ram called to her, "get my carriage to come round the front."

"But monsieur," she whispered, "that is not wise."

"But necessary, Marie. Do it."

And away she went, down the servants' stairs.

Downstairs, the *majordom* conversed with a man whose voice became louder, angrier. Two men continued to argue.

All at once, footsteps were on the circular stairs below.

Ram heard people charge upward.

Merde.

Marie's father, Vaillancourt's butler, ran behind Vaillancourt as the two of them reached the first landing.

"Monsieur le Vicomte Ramsey," said the deputy, coming to a halt steps below Ram. "Where in hell do you think you are going?"

"Away from you, Vaillancourt."

"You cannot have her."

"But I do." Ram gave him a sardonic smile and took the steps down to face the man. "Out of my way."

"No. She is ill."

One well-dressed man appeared on the steps below. A visitor, Ram assumed.

Good, an audience. He would nail Vaillancourt to his own cross. "And what have you done to nurse her back to health, eh?"

"She is sickly. I have had a physician." He glared up at Ram. "Given her medicine."

"Really? And you have also fed her poison?"

"Never!" Vaillancourt darted in front of him. "She will not go!"

Ram scoffed. "But she does. Step aside, Vaillancourt!"

Their voices had risen, and a commotion below resulted in three more men appearing at the landing of the first floor.

One of them was an assistant to Talleyrand. At sight of Ram, the man, whose name was Didier, circled the others and looked up at Ram. He knew the Frenchman well, having met him at court when he, Kane, and Fournier first arrived more than a year ago.

Vaillancourt saw his guests assembled and stiffened in his bravado. "She is mine."

"Monsieur, she never was." Ram meant to walk around him. "Move."

Didier mounted the stairs, his expression a mix of shock and anger.

"*Bon soir*, Monsieur Didier," Ram bade the diplomat. "I take Madame St. Antoine from Vaillancourt, who treats her badly."

"Poison," Amber announced to him loud enough that Didier heard—and blanched.

Ram rejoiced that Amber could tell her own tale.

"He put poison in my tea," she moaned. "In my wine."

"I did no such thing!" the fellow objected, indignant.

Five people regarded Vaillancourt with curled lips. With the wall to one side, Ram took the rest of the stairs down, balanced with his hip at the railing. Step by step, he descended to the foyer.

In his arms, Amber kept repeating a breathless "Poison."

If Ram had ever thought he might smote another where he stood, he'd have killed Vaillancourt in that moment.

But as he gained the foyer, and the various guests joined Vaillancourt, Ram had the impression that Didier would do much of that work for him. Spreading the word that Vaillancourt was accused of poisoning his mistress—the illustrious niece of the honored Countess Nugent—would do much to hamper the influence of the young deputy of police. Didier's superior, Charles-Maurice de Talleyrand, had a fine opinion of Cecily. Plus, Didier would tell Vaillancourt's superior, the vainglorious chief of police Joseph Fouché. That man was a bastard to anyone he remotely suspected of any crime. But in private, the minister of police was a devoted family man. Fouché believed one loved dearly. And one did not treat loved ones so basely as to try to kill them.

In Ram's arms, Amber trained wide brown eyes on the deputy. She appeared now for the first time this evening to be aware of what was happening.

"Monsieur," Ram addressed the *majordom*, "the door, please."

Ram stepped out onto the wide front step just as his carriage rounded the corner.

He strode down the remaining steps. If Vaillancourt were to try to stop him, it would have to be now.

The coachman halted the carriage and climbed down from his perch to yank open the passenger door.

Ram placed Amber inside as best he could and stepped in carefully beside her.

"Go quickly," he told the coachman before he shut the door against the evil before them.

In the flickering flames from the lamps on the porch, Ram watched Vaillancourt glare at the departing coach. Around the deputy stood Didier and his four other well-tailored guests. None was happy. Least of all the deputy chief of police.

THE NEXT MORNING, Ram surveyed the traffic in the convergence of streets from the bedroom window of his and Amber's former house in Saint-Germain-des-Prés. Intent on secrecy, he had gone to Gaspard before he went to Vaillancourt's house. Ram was overjoyed to learn from their former *majordom* that the house was empty, and paid a handsome sum for the letting of it for an extended period.

He turned to watch Amber. She slept peacefully in the bed near him. He had tended her all night. Her retching had lessened in frequency. She breathed more easily. Slept less fitfully. And she drank—sipped, really—everything he offered.

Outside, everyone scurried to and fro, like wild animals caged. They had good reason. Gaspard came in at dusk with a handful of gossip sheets. News came from London late yesterday that Parliament had declared war on France. He and Amber were therefore illegals. Caught, they could be sent to prison. Fouché and Vaillancourt were already at it. Rounding up British of any ilk, French gendarmes could arrest and detain anyone with papers of passport or without.

This house was the best place to bring Amber. It was on the left bank—out of Society. He had always liked the house, small, comfortable, close to a main road to the south, but far enough away from the abodes of the highest Parisian Society that few of any import would note that these particular chimneys belched smoke again.

CORSINI CAME TO check on them every night at ten.

The first night, Ram said, "See if you can find a vintner among those in the Halle by the name of Bechard. Luc Bechard."

"I know him."

"You do? How?" Ram asked.

Corsini grinned. "He came a few times to meet Monsieur le Comte Ashley."

Amber trusted Bechard and so did Kane. That meant the man worked for both? Intriguing. Ram shook his head.

"Monsieur, may I suggest that you go south to leave the city? The Paris streets north are at impasse. The roads northwest to Rouen and barges along the Seine, too. None of it is safe. The gendarmes, monsieur, are out in force to capture any British, young or old."

"*Merci beaucoup*, but I have my own plan, Corsini." Ram would not share it in total with anyone, however. "I'll need a coat and hat for madame. Something modest, old, and worn."

"And you, sir?"

"*Merci*, Corsini. I have my own disguise to go *incognito*. As for madame, I also need many clean, old blankets for her comfort. She is weak and cold. Get me good brandy."

"A few *petits four* as well?"

"That might entice her as little else." Ram wanted to smile amid his fear for her. "She will appreciate that you thought of her so dearly."

RAM KNEW NOT how long it would take Corsini to find Luc, nor how long for Bechard to make the right connections to get them out of Paris. Still, Ram saw by Amber's improvement the third morning after their departure from Vaillancourt's that his decision to come here, where she could feel comfortable, was right.

"I dare not bring her to your house," Ram had told Cecily that day she visited him and drew him a diagram of Vaillancourt's floor plan.

"Never. But he will come looking for her there and everywhere."

"We will leave Paris, madame, and I will not tell you how or where. I will simply go as far as I can as fast as I can."

Cecily had nodded once. "I want to know only when you both are safe. Whenever that is, find a way to get word to me. She is my darling. One of my two children who came to me by choice and circumstance. I am proud of each. Mad with sorrow to lose them. But I know Augustine went with a good man who loved her. I take comfort that Amber also leaves with another good man who adores her."

He took Cecily's hand and kissed the back.

"I leave her to your care," she had said, choking back tears, then dug from her reticule a leather folio. "For Amber's eyes only."

Ram turned to view Amber now, tucked up securely in a mountain of bedclothes and pillows. She slept, pale, her chapped lips open as she breathed in a steady pattern. He checked his pocket watch. For more than four hours, she had not awakened to cough or vomit. A good sign.

He took the chair beside her and sighed with the first small relief of many days. Weeks, really. He had her with him. Finally. Even if, now, her health was ravaged by that bastard. He prayed that Amber was wrong and that Vaillancourt had told the truth and not poisoned her, but had ordered a medication to add to her tea and wine.

Ram ran a shaking hand through his hair. The apothecary he had called here to examine her the day they arrived told him he could not determine if she had been poisoned. True, she was weak and vomiting, but she had no signs of delirium in her eyes or her pulse. Aside from that, the chemist could not predict what would happen.

"Keep her warm. Give her liquids. Tea. Honey. Broth. Anything she keeps down. Fresh water every ten minutes."

Ram had not known whether to hug him or kiss him.

Amber stirred, her large brown eyes drowsy but clear.

"Ram?" She slid her hand across the bed covers. "You are here."

"I am." He bent to place a kiss into her palm and reached for the crystal glass filled with fresh water. "Have a sip of this."

She drank and sank back to the pillows. Her beautiful eyes on him, she whispered so low he barely heard.

But his heart did.

"I love you, Godfrey DuClare. I love you."

"I know you do, my darling. Now sleep."

"You will be here?"

"Always."

A WEEK LATER, Corsini told Ram the story of how he had found Luc Bechard leaving Cecily's house on Île Saint-Louis. Corsini quickly took Luc to a café and presented his proposal. Luc was eager to help Ram escape and asked for his address. Corsini declined to share it. "The fewer who know, the better."

Luc had secured a small house in Amboise on the shores of the Loire, southwest of Paris. He wrote a note for Corsini to give to Ram that included the location and description of the house. *It will be ready for them by next Sunday.*

Two days later, when Corsini came to the house to check on them, Ram gave him two hundred old Louis to arrange a carriage.

"I will do it," Corsini told him. "The man will ask for you. But who shall I say he must ask for, monsieur?"

Ram sniffed. "Monsieur Debray." The name of a man buried in the old St. Pierre churchyard was the only one that popped into his mind. Amber would smile at that. "Wait for me with the coachman and help me settle madame inside for our journey."

"I will tell the coachman you go far and to prepare," Corsini told him.

Ram smiled and dropped a hand to the Italian's shoulder. "I will tell you how very grateful I am for your help."

"No words, monsieur, are necessary."

They hugged instead.

Ram saw the man out, locked up the house tightly, and went upstairs to sit with his patient. She slept soundly. He picked up the book he'd been trying to read these past few days.

But tonight he would not turn many pages.

He loved her. He had grown up with love all around him. The acceptance of all that he was, the affections for whatever he did, had allowed him to flourish. If it also made him a gadabout, a man-child carefree and careless of his future, that had changed when he saw what happened to countless Frenchmen and women in the Terror.

He vowed such atrocities would never happen in his own country.

For that, he had applied his talents, doltish as they were in the beginning, to Scarlett Hawthorne's spy ring. A stolen document, a bribed criminal, a government MP blackmailed and thereby retired for his abuse of army funds—all were child's play compared to this dire business he did in France. But he had risen to the occasion.

Or rather, he had done all he possibly could to protect Amber, even from herself.

Woe unto him that he had fallen in love with her.

Now he had truly saved her from the vices of Vaillancourt. Taken her from that man's house, his arms, his ability to determine her life or death.

Now, Ram faced a new challenge. He could improve her health. He could sweep her away to England.

But would that please her? Would that be enough to fill her life? Or would she wish to leave him?

He recoiled at the possibility and put down his book.

If she returned to France, took up her role again, she would by necessity operate very differently. She would have to work in anonymity, away from Paris and all she had known. Could she? Would she have the contacts, old or new, to make that worth her while and useful to the downfall of Bonaparte and his minions?

He shook his head.

He doubted it all.

And he could not, would not argue the issue with her. She had to see it for herself. She was not a person who took well to others' analyses of her life or her decisions.

For now, she was here, his to care for and his to love.

That was his goal. All else would come in some far-off tomorrow that he could not color with his own desires for a future with her as his darling, his beloved wife.

SECURE IN THE safety of Corsini and Luc Bechard's plan, Ram was even surer of Amber's ability to endure the trip south. She had improved greatly, eating and drinking sparingly, but often. She felt well enough to endure the jostling of a coach. For the journey, Ram had Corsini rent a comfortable travel coach, and off he and Amber went. Seven hours after departure, they crossed the river at the fortified palace town of Amboise. Climbing more than one hundred feet above the river, the ramparts of the old palace of the medieval and Renaissance kings of France rose like giant arms to protect those who came.

The town spread along the southern banks of the Loire and around the castle walls. Their house Ram discovered by asking for "a blue cottage with white door facing the huge brown-pink stone palace walls."

"The iron key," he told Amber as he read from the instructions, "is beneath the *decrottoir*."

"The boot-scraper?" She laughed. "You may have to lift the stone beneath it to find it."

He did. When Ram opened the front door, he was pleased at the sight of a large room filled with upholstered chairs and sofas. Even the bedroom and boudoir were well appointed. The house was the sort courtiers would have loved to rent so they might with ease attend the court of the kings and queens of France in the lavish Renaissance palace of Amboise.

The two of them stayed for three days, just enough time for Ram to find his friend and colleague, Yves Pelletier, and plan to head west. Yves, once an émigré to Britain, now worked for Scarlett Hawthorne, just as Ram did.

Pelletier ran his own nest of French spies, all of whom worked for the benefit of Britain. He kept it that way. Few in number, rabid in dedication, one agent knowing few others. In many ways, Pelletier had copied his operation on the workings of Scarlett's. His base of operations was in Amboise, and he worked the Loire River from to the Atlantic coast.

Yves met Ram beneath the old town clock that spanned the street to the town center. They went to the local patisserie to drink coffee and eat pastry.

"You will have to start in Tours to sail to Nantes. I could not get any fisherman with a boat big enough who was willing to go from here all the way to Nantes. The town of Tours, west of here, holds many friends of mine who will, for a good sum, do much. The man I have for you is totally trustworthy, and you will be well cared for. My one piece of advice is to have Madame St. Antoine do much of your talking. Her French is undoubtedly better than yours, and your English accent will not be one any will love."

The next morning, Ram and Amber closed up their small, comfortable house and boarded a coach headed for Tours. The medieval town of half-timbered houses and shops was filled with friendly people who offered Amber directions to Pelletier's fisherman. The fellow, happy to see them, suggested the two of them stay in an auberge across from the cathedral of Tours. They left the next morning on Jean Pierre's small fishing boat. Two days later, they docked in Nantes.

A disturbance at the docks had Jean Pierre leaving Ram and Amber to learn the cause. When he returned, he suggested the best way to get transport to the coast of Southern England was to go by carriage to a small village south of St. Nazaire. He said he would accompany them to find a certain fellow whom he was hopeful would take gold coin to take them around the points of Normandy and northwest to England.

"But we have a challenge," he told them. "This area is home to many who still sympathize with those who revolted against the consulate and those before it. They are with the revolutionaries of the *Vendée*. A nasty bunch, cut your throat for a bite of bread. I will negotiate for you. It's best."

Ram was not happy about that until Jean Pierre returned with news that the man he'd hired to take them to England was a known smuggler. "He'll be taking you to Plymouth or Weymouth."

"He does not know which port?" Amber asked.

"It's all how the wind blows, madame. And how the British fleet and the revenuers work that day."

"You mean," Ram asked, "we could be attacked?"

Jean Pierre nodded. "None of this is guaranteed. But he is a good sailor. Best I know."

For ten days, that last was little compensation for the rough seas that finally took them to a small fishing town near Weymouth.

When the two put feet to dry land, Ram wanted to kiss the ground. He had sickened the first day. Amazingly, Amber did better than he. In fact, she tended to bloom in the sea air.

When they landed, it was Amber who had voice to ask for a local inn where she and Ram could spend a day recovering.

"One aspect of this journey works for us," Ram told her as they planned to leave the next day. "My estate is not far. A few hours' journey north."

Chapter Twenty-Five

DuClare House
Near Salisbury, England
Mid-June, 1803

JUNE IN LONDON was the season for gaiety. Amber's new maid Jane told her so. But going into that Society was not Amber's desire. Nor, thank heavens, was it Ram's. He wanted her to recover her health. She needed it too, scared as she had been that her days were numbered. But now that the second physician whom Ram had invited to the house yesterday had consulted with her, Amber was delighted at the man's diagnosis and thrilled to know she had so much to look forward to in her life.

Her new residence at Ram's gracious country house was the first of many recent pleasures. His home was two centuries old, filled with every imaginable delight, from portraits of his ancestors to books in every language imaginable and rooms filled with tapestries and furnishings fit for a king. She teased Ram that he had not told her of his wealth and position. He replied he had not thought it important.

And he was right. What he was to her was never any of this magnificence. More to the point of his uniqueness was that this magnificence was nothing to the purity of his character. All that he was and ever would be was his ethical nature, dedicated to her and all in which he believed. She marveled daily at her new life with the humorous, gallant man who had carried her from Vaillancourt and into a world filled with sunshine, soft breezes, fresh air...and the most endearing affection beaming from his blue eyes.

They had arrived to his country home near Salisbury four days ago. His mother and grandmother welcomed her with open arms. Cheerful and kind, the two ladies were polite yet so careful of Amber's health and alarmed by her recent illness. They insisted on immediately summoning the local apothecary and physician. The apothecary who came three days ago had found no evidence of poisoning. His friend the physician arrived the next day. He had declared poisoning impossible. But she wanted another physician's opinion, and Ram had called for another man to come from Salisbury to examine her. It was that man's visit yesterday who had set Amber's heart aflame with hope and new ideas for her future. How to divulge them to Ram was what Amber had pondered since the physician left her, alternately frowning or smiling to herself.

Apart from those three men's visits, Amber's days were filled with calls from the local modiste and cobbler. All were a respite from the difficult journey and her illness. She did indeed feel recovered. Still tired in the mornings and a bit queasy, she was careful what she ate and drank. But she had gained back some of her weight, and when she looked in her dressing table mirror, she looked pink and healthy.

She was kept that way by Ram's attentions on her—and by those of his mother and grandmother. Both ladies were sweet, kind, and asked few questions. What she shared of her background was minimal. Perhaps soon she would tell them more, but at the moment, she was frankly too tired to speak of her past. In truth, she was still assessing what had happened to her and how Ram had saved her. That the two ladies were without foibles, open and accepting, was helpful, even if they made eyes at her, gleefully expecting she would soon be the lady of the house.

As she sat in the sun on the breakfast veranda the fourth day, she eyed the morning delivery of yesterday's London newspapers. She had refused to read them prior but told herself she should start soon. Ram gave her the news that many British still fled France. Ram worried about many, including his friend Lord Appleby. Amber remembered meeting him the night they had attended the Théâtre de la Gaîté, and he had disappeared afterward to seek out Charmaine Massey. Appleby, to Ram's knowledge, had not returned home to England. Neither had his other friend Dirk, Lord Fournier, about whom he had often spoken. Fournier had gone to Baden last year and not returned to Paris.

Ram worried about the missing. News, he said, of those who had been trapped when the declaration of war occurred was that they were marched off to prison. Many were forced into many days' march from Paris to Verdun.

Amber quivered at the thought of being waylaid in such a place. Huge, forbidding, the Verdun prison looked like so many others. Damp and cold. The food terrible. The comforts nonexistent. She remembered what it was like to live in the squalor and degradation of Carmes. Never would she wish such an existence on anyone.

"Good morning, sweetheart." Ram appeared in the open doors and came to drop a kiss to her cheek.

"You are up late this morning," she said with a smile of welcome.

"You are early," he said. "While I have been catching up on my rest." Poor man—he had worked so diligently to bring her here at risk to his life and limb.

"And I have had my fill of rest." She raised her face to the sun. "I do love it here."

"I'm glad," he told her as he pulled out a chair and sat beside her. On the table, he placed a brown leather portfolio.

He did not usually bring work to the dining table.

"The modiste comes again today." The local woman was sewing an entire wardrobe for her. Much needed, the clothes would thrill Amber. She'd been living in whatever Ram could buy in the town markets of French villages. She needed the day gowns and evening dinner attire. His mother and grandmother kept to formal dressing for their luncheon and evening meals. And Amber needed pelisses and nightgowns, a robe, shoes, stockings. So much. So much. She worried that Ram would be buying it, because she had no money to pay for any of it. The idea did not sit well. She was not his responsibility. Not in that way. And she hated to be a burden or to appear presumptuous, allowing him to think she approved of such dependence.

"Before she comes this morning, I urge you to look at this," he said in a solemn voice. "It is yours."

She glanced at it on the table between them. She had never seen it before.

"I carried it with me from Paris."

Amber tipped her head in question.

"Your Aunt Cecily gave it to me the day she came to see me. The same day I came and took you from him." Between them, they never mentioned the man's name. Such a pact of silence between them appealed to her. Greatly. "Your aunt told me it was for you alone. I honored that. And have not opened it. But it is yours. From her." He stood. "I leave you to it."

She caught his hand. "Don't go."

"I think what is in there is best received in the solemnity of one's heart, alone."

He worried. Poor man, he worried a lot these days. Amber saw it as they sat in his marvelous library, reading, delighting in the peace. Yet occasionally she would look up and find his gaze on her. Worried about her health, he also feared what she would choose for her future. Even before she knew of this folio, she knew what she would tell him today.

"I can share it with you," she told him.

"Later you can." He stood, gave her half a smile, and headed down the stone steps to the garden, alive with his mother and grandmother's roses waving in the breeze.

She gathered her thoughts and pushed her expectations far away. Whatever she had wanted for her life, even as recently as a month ago, was now very different. After she looked at the contents of this portfolio, she would tell Ram what she hoped and what she wanted. No matter what was in this folder.

Unwinding the leather ties, she admired the fine leather and reached inside. Out came a stack of letters. Documents of different sizes and on different quality vellum and paper. On top was an open letter in her aunt's handwriting.

My dearest darling Amber,

Since you were nine years old, you have been a constant light in my life. I have tried and often not succeeded too well to show you how I value who you are and the wise and witty woman you have become. As you leave all here in France, I hope to give you the courage and the means to live in the land of your true heritage with the inheritance that will ensure your survival.

You and I have not spoken often of your parents. But I want you to avail yourself now of the opportunity to travel to Bath and satisfy your natural curiosity about them.

Your mother, as you know from my own words about her, was a childhood friend of mine. Annette Timmons de Vray comes from an old family who lived in West Yorkshire, descended from a Norman family in an area called Vray. She had bright-red hair, like you, and large, expressive brown eyes. With great humor and a jolly approach to life, she and I took French lessons together from a tutor my father and hers hired for us. Annette was my dearest friend, consoling me when I first became acquainted with the prince regent and later, when I had to marry Earl Nugent. She supported me when I decided to move to Paris, and we wrote often. When she became pregnant, she was overjoyed. Hoping for a son, as did her husband James, she wished to pass to her boy the gift of land and money her mother had set aside for her.

Your father, a very upright man, James Notting Gaynor, I liked very much. Tall and impressive with deep-blue eyes and brown hair shot with red, he was a dashing creature and loved your mother from the moment he first saw her.

I know not much of his family origins. Perhaps now you may investigate it for yourself. I know only that he came from a merchant family who lived and traded in Brighton. As James would tell the tale, living there in that town, he became acquainted with the prince regent and his younger brother, the Duke of Kent, by happy accident on the shore one day. James soon went into service for the duke, and in time, the regent knighted him for his loyalty.

Of your father's devotion to your mother, I will say I never heard the equal. He was more than courteous and honorable. He was kind, chivalrous, and a husband all others should emulate. His passing soon after your mother died was a tragedy.

I learned of it from the prince regent himself and hurried to England to bring you home with me. I dare to hope that when I meet my God, He will judge me at least half as wise and tender as your mother and father were to each other and to all who were fortunate to be their friends. I loved you, my dear Amber, as if you were my own—and what I taught you by word or example about love of country and your fellow man and woman I hope can buoy you throughout your life.

The enclosed documents will be useful to you as you begin your life in Britain. You will find each useful, a spur to greater understanding of those who bore you and those who nurtured you.

I urge you to use them each to your benefit and your joy. For wealth and land are comforting. Knowledge of one's ancestors is enriching. Using all to build a satisfying existence for oneself and one's loved ones is the finest gift to yourself and all who know you.

I press this page to my heart and send you all the love and courage I have to help you meet your new challenges. I urge you to consider the enormous love Godfrey DuClare bears you, for he gave all of himself to deliver you from evil.

Honor and keep him. One loves once totally. Twice, rarely. But when love comes upon one, it is vital to nourish and protect it.

I wish you well, my darling girl.

Accept all within this portfolio as your honest and legal due.

With my love,
Your aunt.

⭲⭲⭲❯❮❮❮❮

MINUTES LATER, AMBER rose from her chair and made her way toward Ram. The roses greeted her with a perfume that intoxicated her. *Would that it also inspires me to say the right words to him.*

He had wandered far to the other side of the orangery. She found him sitting on a bench, which surprisingly reminded her of the one she had often sat upon waiting for her superior in the Saint-Germain-des-Prés Abbey gardens. A duty now done. A duty well done—and one she took pride in, but left now happily to others.

She had other prospects before her. Other duties. To herself and to the man she loved.

She sat down beside him and took one of his hands in hers. "I love this garden."

He smiled. But his heart was not in it. And he did not look at her, but stared off into the distance.

"I always wanted to grow roses."

"I remember."

She cleared her throat. "I am an heiress."

He frowned. "What?" he asked, as if he did not comprehend.

"My mother bequeathed me five thousand acres in Yorkshire. I also have a bank account with Child's in London. Aunt Cecily knows not how much is there. When she came to take me with her when I was nine, the total in the account was more than eight thousand pounds."

"Dear God," he murmured, his expression going from shock to delight. All for her.

"That is in addition to a good sum of money that Aunt Cecily grants me from her own investments. I have shares also in an American shipping company out of Baltimore, Maryland, in the new United States."

Ram stared at her. At once he blinked and reached to enfold her in his arms. "That's extraordinary!"

She giggled. "It is, rather, isn't it?" She gave a little shake of delight.

"Not many can say such a thing. You will be unique, and all in London will rush to call upon you."

"Oh? Are we going to London? I thought you said it was best if we stayed here because the Season is so hectic."

"It is mayhem. But now that you have all this to take care of, you should go. Did Cecily tell you the name of a solicitor to administer all that?"

"She did." Amber waved a hand. "I forget his name. I'll find it, and then you must tell me if he's any good."

Ram snorted. "I doubt the Countess Nugent entrusts her financial dealings or yours to a hack."

"But I want you to come with me. Tell me if he meets your standards."

Ram got to his feet. "Sweetheart, the man most likely walks on water."

She gave a laugh and let her head fall back to view how handsome her beloved was. She had missed him in her bed these many months. They had not made love since that fateful night in February when they reunited at the theater and later in her bed. "I have missed you, my darling."

It was as if she had poured ice water over him. He stiffened—and spun on his heel to stride away.

She shot up to catch him. But like that night in Charleville, he marched onward, focused on nothing but getting away from her.

"Wait! Wait, Ram!"

He jammed his hands in his trouser pockets and went on.

She ran in front of him, her hand out. "Stop! You are angry because I tell you I want you?"

"Yes."

"Don't be."

"Not easy, my girl." He made to go around her.

She planted her feet. "Do. Not. Leave. Me."

He halted and slowly turned his head to gaze down at her. "You are unkind."

"How?" she breathed.

"You come sit beside me and list all the ways in which you will become your own woman, your own person, wealthy, landed, respected, and you expect me to be happy."

"I know you are," she said, ready to cry that he was so forlorn.

"Fantasy."

She wanted to scream at him, but tried something more logical. "It is fantasy. That you are mine."

"No."

Oh, he is stubborn! "Deny all you like. You love me! You would not love me half as much if I were not already my own woman—money, land, or not."

He did not move. He did not speak.

"You love me," she repeated in a saner tone. "You have never said the words. But I know you do. Each time your eyes hold me or your arms take me. Each time you have saved me from others, from myself. Whereas I have told you often that I love you. I burst with it, Godfrey DuClare. I belong to you and you do to me."

"It's not enough, Amber."

"I agree. So don't you think it wise that you marry me? I mean, I know now where my birth is registered, and I understand one must know such things to be married in England in the eyes of church and state. I love you, Ram, and I am asking you to marry me, sir. I am a widow with land and money in both England and France. The French wealth may not be claimed, sadly, while a few ogres are in power, but here in England, I am rather, so say the documents in Aunt Cecily's packet, a good catch."

His smile, which had dawned when she first asked him to marry her, was now a broad grin and about to be a chuckle. "A good catch?"

She nodded eagerly. "Quite so. I mean, you have all this here"—she extended a hand to sweep over the beautifully appointed landscape—"but we could administer more, don't you think? You and I are wise and—"

He snatched her up in his arms. "You tease!"

"Do I?"

He allowed her to slide down his form, held fast within his embrace. "I accept your proposal, Madame St. Antoine."

She beamed at him. "*Merci beaucoup,* Monsieur le Vicomte."

He cupped her nape, while his eyes adored her. "What say you to a wedding next week?"

"So soon? Can we?"

"I will see to it." He kissed her cheek.

"I need a new wedding ring. One to go with mine from Charleville."

"You still have it?" he asked as if nothing in the world pleased him more.

"It was a part of you from which I could never part."

He pressed her closer to him. "Never part from me again."

She shook her head and grinned at him. "Never a moment without you."

He kissed her, a ravenous claiming of his fine lips. Then he stroked her cheeks with his thumbs. "We'll go to London. We must for a special license."

"Only for the wedding. Not to stay," she said. "I do not want to deal with the *ton.* Not just yet."

"You won't have to. We'll take Mama and Nana with us for the ceremony. And we'll invite Kane and Gus."

"Oh, yes, I'd like that!"

"Then we'll go on a honeymoon."

"Wonderful! Where does an English couple go for that?"

"For us, it will be Brighton."

"Fitting," she said, and squeezed him. But then she grew quite serious and pulled away from him. "However, I think I... I cannot do it. I cannot marry you."

"What? No?" His whole body stiffened. "Why not?"

"You have not said you love me." She planted her feet and pouted. "How can I marry a man who cannot admit he loves me? It is a—"

"Nightmare. A problem. An insult. How could he not?"

She beat one fist into his chest and pushed at him.

He hauled her back and held her flush against him. "He can say it."

"When?"

"Every day. Every hour. You will grow weary of it."

"Weary me now, sir."

He picked her up to swing her around in his arms. Then he stopped, and all the angels of heaven could have heard his deep and darling voice. "I love you, Amber St. Antoine. From the moment I saw you. From the second I held you. Each time you smiled at me. Each time you argued or aided or walked away from me. Yes, I loved you. I was caught. Honored. Enraptured. You were my beginning and my end. My breath. My salvation. And yes, so often, too often, you were my ruin. I loved you then. I love you now. I will love you till the end of time."

Her knees failed her. "Ramsey, you are my everything."

He grinned and gave her a smacking kiss. "Soon to be your husband."

"And the father of our child."

Chapter Twenty-Six

20 Portman Square
London

THE FOLLOWING FRIDAY in London at his townhouse, Ram stood in the salon awaiting the appearance of his bride-to-be. For the unexpected occasion of his wedding, he'd summoned his tailor for a special suit of clothes. He felt new, different, at ease. Most of all, he wished to appear as he was—content.

The woman he could not live without was about to marry him. Live with him. Love him for decades to come in all the wedded bliss they would shower upon each other.

Furthermore, his bride was well. Very much so. As the second physician that saw Amber had declared—and she repeated to Ram after her announcement—Amber St. Antoine had suffered a severe case of nausea and discomfort with the onset of her pregnancy.

"Some women do suffer in the extreme," the man told Ram the day after Amber revealed the news to him. Ram had to call the fellow back to the house just to hear the assurances from his lips. Plus he had to ask about the effects, if any, of what she had endured upon the babe. Assured of her health and the child's, Ram asked about traces of poisoning.

"I find none," the physician replied.

Ram, who had stood dumbfounded at Amber's spectacular declaration, recovered only after he kissed Amber and swept her to the lawn chaise and his lap. He had to sit, of course, because the joy of her announcement had doubled his delight that his lady had just agreed to marry him.

"I would like to help your mother and grandmother tend their roses," Amber had said with a nonchalance that had him clamping her close and kissing her breathless. "Then, too, I must win back some of my gambling losses to your grandmama."

"That will take some time, I fear, my love," Ram told her.

"I know it! The woman counts her cards better than Aunt Cecily. I must learn how she does it!"

His nana, however, was showing no signs of allowing her soon-to-be granddaughter-in-law win anything except the bounteous approval of her marriage to her grandson…and her love. Ram's mother, overjoyed as well at the news of a grand-child, announced she would not play cards with Amber. "Discourteous, but I know not how I win at cards. Honestly, I cannot teach you. I simply…intuit!"

At the moment, both women stood talking with Scarlett Hawthorne. Ram and Amber had agreed the lady should be a guest at their wedding. It was she who, in a way, was responsible for their happiness. Plus a friendship between Scarlett and Amber now seemed assured. Scarlett had come to luncheon last week, and, during the purely social call, the two women who had got on famously. They had also speculated that when they were children they had met briefly when their parents socialized together in Paris.

At the end, Scarlett had indicated that she had need of both Ram and Amber for work in London. She asked if they would consider it—and they took only a second before agreeing. Ram had asked Amber, after Scarlett's departure, if indeed she would do that.

"Why not?" she asked. "You and I have, as you once said to

me, a certain knowledge of life in Bonaparte's midst. We should use it to defeat him. Besides, I would wager good coin we join Kane and Gus in the effort. That will make the mission more successful, don't you agree?"

Ram did.

He glanced at the man before him. Today, Scarlett had been accompanied by her chief clerk, Todd Carlton. Her watchdog, Carlton resembled a large jungle cat. Muscular, with ink-black hair and a white streak across his brow, the man wore a black eye patch. Carlton had been hired by Scarlett's father years ago to protect her. He took his job very seriously. If he ever smiled, Ram had never seen it.

"I am to tell you," he said to Ram as they stood there drinking bubbling white wine from Reims, "that we have heard from Dirk Fournier."

"The best news I've heard in a while," Ram said. "We worried about him. For months."

"He never sent word to Paris of his activities because he feared any message would be intercepted. But he regularly sent word north to Amsterdam and onward to us at the office. He fears for his family, his friends…and works to get them out."

"He'll remain, then?"

"We hope," Carlton said, and shook his head, "not for long."

"And what of Lord Appleby?" Ram asked. "Before I left Paris, just as war was declared, I had not heard from him in days."

Carlton winced. "We fear he was caught up by gendarmes. We have agents attempting to find him. One, we think, is close."

"I don't suppose you will reveal who that is?" Ram asked.

Carlton slowly smiled, giving his rough appearance a handsome veneer. "A lady who does very well for us."

"I wish her well." Ram nodded, then glanced at the door. His butler was showing in Kane and Gus. "Excuse me a minute, Carlton, as I welcome Kane and Augustine."

The Ashleys had come earlier in the week to greet Ram and Amber. Because Gus had recently given birth to her and Kane's first child, the two stayed for only a few minutes. But all four had time to exclaim over their escapes from France, and their relief at being in Britain now that hostilities were upon them. Gus and Amber had renewed with great affections their sisterly relationship. All delighted in the news of Amber's condition and in the birth of the heir to the Ashley earldom.

Ram now kissed Gus on her cheek and shook Kane's hand when Amber appeared on the threshold. She wore a dress of cambric muslin atop a mint-green muslin lining. With pearls entwined in her upswept red hair, she glowed as she came forward to put her hand in his.

Ram took her to one side for a private moment. "My darling, as ever, you are lovelier today than yesterday."

Her brown eyes danced. "And I hope less trouble to you today than any before."

"All that you are, I wish to have beside me forevermore. What came between us in the past is no more." He lifted her hand and kissed it.

"I love you, Ram. I told you that months ago. It was the true then. It is now. It will be from this day forward. Only love will I give you until the day I die."

THE CHALLENGES CONTINUE...

Travels with Cerise

What others do affects us—sometimes—greatly. I cannot deny that life has gotten in the way of some of my own objectives. A few times with disastrous consequences I could not alter.

And while in romance we like to solve all our heroes' and heroines' problems, occasionally we cannot. In LORD RAMSEY'S RED-HEADED RUIN, Ram's love for Amber could not alter her devotion to saving her friends and family from René Vaillancourt's machinations. She could not allow others to die because she had found love.

Ultimately, Ram's love and that of her Aunt Cecily do save her—and she must accept with grace that living is far better than dying at her nemesis's hands.

What is historically accurate in RUIN includes a few delicious facts. There are tunnels under the city of Compiègne. Under Paris as well. In fact, you can visit them and view the skulls of thousands whose bodies were buried there for decades. Also, on the butte of Montmartre sits the lovely little cemetery of St. Pierre. You can go there and, on days when the proprietor opens it, may too sit on the bench where Ram and Amber met.

Reims Cathedral, where all French kings were crowned, was closed during many of the first years of the Revolution. During the consulate, government lawyers did take up residence inside. Only later, when Bonaparte allowed Catholics to worship once more, did the cathedral return to its original purpose.

The famous Charleville guns were indeed the ones France shipped to the American colonists, and it is those weapons credited with winning the American Revolution.

The small towns of the northeast—Sedan, Varennes, and Verdun—were increasingly fortified during the consulate. Many weapons factories were located in the north, and similar modern facilities still exist there today. The method of learning how many weapons were delivered to each fortified town by sending aides-de-camp who knew not precisely what they were doing, or why, is true. Many of them grumbled over what they thought were useless missions far from Paris.

Famous salonnières like Julie Recamier appear in this story and in the next. Recamier was aiding her husband, who was a banker, in befriending Bonaparte. The first consul who did not care for bankers or their profession. But he did tolerate Monsieur Racamier and allowed the man to fund his rearmament.

Meanwhile, Josephe Fouché built a tight network of police and spies. Talleyrand courted everyone, though he failed to influence Bonaparte to keep the peace of Amiens.

I included the day-to-day collapse and tensions of the peace of Amiens. The increasing antagonism between Bonaparte and his British ambassador, Charles Whitworth, was based on their personal dislike of each other. But, of course, worse were the political issues neither man could solve.

Throughout the winter and early spring of 1803, Bonaparte increased his arms production and fortifications on the boundaries of France. He purposely increased the territory of a minor German margrave, Karl of Baden, whose land sat on the Rhine. That man increased taxes on his citizens and began a conscription of soldiers from his citizenry. My great-great-grandfather was one of them. In the coming years, he fought in many battles as a German for the French emperor. He lived to tell the tale.

Bonaparte diminished the power of the Austrian empire and befriended other German states. Thus he made secure France's borders to the east. He became more popular with the French public, improving the economy and ensuring greater safety among the populace. Among his colleagues, he accumulated power—and focused on increasing his own status as emperor. He knew Britain would not allow it.

As Bonaparte closes the doors of the Continent to the British,

Ram secretly carries Amber out of France. They live to fight against him another day, another way.

I hope you join me for LORD APPLEBY'S GORGEOUS IMPOSTER, where Tate Cantrell, Lord Appleby, remains in France past the peace and risks his life to help the woman he loves exact revenge on those who destroyed her family.

Happy Reading,
Cerise

About the Author

Cerise DeLand loves to write about dashing heroes and the sassy women they adore. Whether she's penning historical romances or contemporaries, she has received praise for her poetic elegance and accuracy of detail.

An award-winning author of more than 50 novels, she's been published since 1991 by Pocket Books, St. Martin's Press, Kensington and independent presses. Her books have been monthly selections of the Doubleday Book Club and the Mystery Guild. Plus she's won nominations and awards for Best Historical of the Year, Best Regency and scores of rave reviews from *Romantic Times, Affair de Coeur, Publisher's Weekly* and more.

To research, she's dived into the oldest texts and dustiest library shelves. She's also traveled abroad, trusty notebook and pen in hand, to visit the chateaux and country homes she loves to people with her own imaginary characters.

And at home every day? She loves to cook, hates to dust, goes swimming at least once a week and tries (desperately) to grow vegetables in her arid backyard in south Texas!